LIU ZHENYUN

CELL PHONE

A Novel

LIU ZHENYUN

CELL PHONE

A Novel

Translated by Howard Goldblatt

MerwinAsia
Portland, Maine

MERWIN

A S I A

www.merwinasia.com

Distributed by the University of Hawaii Press

ISBN 978-0-9836599-2-1 (paperback)

ISBN 978-0-9836599-3-8 (hardcover)

Printed in the United States of America
The paper used in this publication meets the minimum requirements of the
American National Standard for Information Services—Permanence of Paper
for Printed Library Materials, ANSI/NISO Z39/48-1992

Translation of cell phone message on the cover:

'I gave you a hickey in the car, so don't take off your undershirt
when you go to bed."

Contents

LIU ZHENYUN

CELL PHONE

A Novel

Prologue

A careless mistake led to Yan Shouyi's divorce. Light breezes and gentle waves had accompanied him as he left home in the morning; an exploding land mine greeted him when he returned that night.

"Wow, that was fast!"

From this initial reaction to the explosion Yan Shouyi learned that the mind of an accident victim is characterized by extreme clarity just before death claims him, leaving him just enough time to utter a few last words. Urgency forces him to snatch the opportunity, and whether those last words fit the situation or not is anyone's guess. There is always the possibility that they are complete and utter nonsense. Yan Shouyi sensed that the affairs of the world are like rubber bands: you stretch them as far as you can, then let go, and they snap right back. What really scared him was his wife, who'd never been much of a talker, and who always smiled before she said a word, no matter who she was with. Now, in the presence of an exploding land mine, she'd ratcheted up the speed, starting with the affair and not stopping until she was talking divorce. Rat-a-tat-tat, a machine gun raking the area. But her expression did not change—still smiling, like that twentieth-century soldier Dong Cunrui, who grinned as he set off a satchel charge—blowing himself to bits meant nothing so long as he took the enemy pillbox with him. Yan Shouyi, on the other hand, lost his composure in the face of the detonation. As a TV host, he was a master of cheerful banter, but now his brow creased with a frown and he could think of nothing to say.

Yu Wenjuan, it turned out, was barren. When they emerged from the district office, having completed the divorce formalities, she seemed somewhat unsteady as Yan stared at her back, and he was tempted to catch up to say something. But try as he might, he couldn't come up with a thing. That changed when she turned and asked for the apartment key.

"Take care," he said.

The words were barely out of his mouth when he realized it was probably the stupidest thing he could have said.

The grounds for divorce were simplicity itself. On the eleventh of February, thanks to Shouyi's cell phone, Wenjuan discovered that he had another woman. At first he assumed she'd divorced him solely because of that other woman, but would later learn that it was not the only reason.

Chapter 1

Lü Guihua

—Another speaker heard from

1

Old Niu, who was in charge of the township's telephone, had sold onions with Yan Shouyi's father back in 1968.

Before that, Yan's father hardly ever spoke. During the long, hot village days he'd never utter more than ten comments, six of which were unavoidable, and those never exceeded a word or two, whether it was something major, like building a house, or as trivial as buying a bedpan. If he was in favor of something, he said, "Do it," and if not, he said, "Hell no." The remaining comments tended to be emotional outbursts over things that made him happy or made him mad: "I'll be fucked!" But that changed once he began selling onions. Half a year into the business, he could tell a story from start to finish. Shouyi recalled that back then his father had two favorite stories: one was about eating fried mung bean balls; the other was about eating glutinous rice cakes:

Once there was a man who, at year's end, went to market to sell door talismans alongside a peddler of fried mung bean balls. He bought four catties of the fried balls from the man, who, since they were on friendly terms, gave him a little extra. The man ate them, one after the other, until they were all gone. He stood up and, *thump*, crumpled to the ground. The first story.

Once there was a man who, during the fall harvest, lost the family ox and couldn't find it after searching for two days. Hungry, he went back to his village, where he met a seller of glutinous rice cakes, someone he knew. "Give me five catties of those on credit, Elder Brother." After finishing them off, he went home. "I'm thirsty, Mother," he said, and then, *thump*, he crumpled to

5

the floor. The second story.

Yan Shouyi didn't think either story was very funny at the time, but now, forty years later, he laughed whenever he was reminded of them. At first, he thought his father had learned to talk from all the people he'd met when he was out selling onions. Eventually, he discovered that the one and only person who had taught him to talk was Old Niu. At night, when the family was hunkered down around the stove eating dinner, his father would chuckle to himself, shake his head, and say:

"Boy, that Old Niu."

Shouyi knew that though his father was physically there, eating dinner, his mind was off with Old Niu, selling onions. At the time, he believed that the single most interesting activity in the world had to be selling onions.

On the day of the Winter Solstice, 1968, Old Niu and Shouyi's father were returning home from selling onions at the Changzhi Coal Mines, some two hundred li distant, when they passed through Yan Family Village and Old Niu stopped in at Yan's house. Up till then, Shouyi had imagined Old Niu to be a big man with a large mouth and a booming voice. But when he saw him in person, the man's head barely cleared the top of the table, and though his mouth was big, he had a womanish voice. He'd heard so much about Old Niu he should have been too tongue-tied to even try to talk to him, but to his amazement, the man actually gave eleven-year-old Shouyi a bashful smile, took off his fur cap, and wiped his steamy head with the earflaps. Shouyi's father invited Old Niu inside for some water. Shouyi followed him in, but his father jammed his foot into his belly.

"Get out of here, you stink!"

The two men sat there drinking water, and Shouyi didn't hear Old Niu say much, only an occasional comment on the food at places where they'd stopped on the way home. Or how much they'd fed their donkeys. Other than that, the only sound was *glug-glug-glug* when they drank. After Old Niu left with his donkey, Yan's father announced to the family:

"He really can talk, just didn't feel like it today."

A week before year's end, on the twenty-third, Yan Shouyi's father took a hog's leg over to Niu Family Village for Old Niu. While he was there, they calculated how much they'd made selling onions. That morning he'd left home all smiles but returned at dusk, seething. He hunkered down in the doorway and puffed loudly on his pipe. When Orion settled in the west, he stood up and rapped the bowl of his pipe against his head.

"Damned if I'll ever sell onions again!"

The next day, Shouyi's granny (his mother had died when he was just a boy, in 1960—starved to death) told him that his father and Old Niu had quarreled while they were divvying up the onion profits. From that day on, his father had nothing more to do with onions or with Old Niu, and reverted back to his sullen, silent ways.

Shouyi had an uncle, Old Huang, who owned a dye-works in Huang Family Village. In the spring, he came to recruit Shouyi's father to travel from village to village gathering fabric to be dyed. Yan shook his head.

"I can gather the fabric, but I can't manage the sales pitch."

"All you have to say is: I'm from the Huang Family Village Dye-works!"

Yan shook his head and refused to do it.

In the spring of 1989, Shouyi's father suffered an incapacitating stroke, paralyzing the left side of his body. But unlike other people who suffer strokes and lose the ability to speak, he was actually able to string sentences together, albeit with a stammer; and while other people who have strokes usually suffer a loss of memory, he was able to recall everything that had happened in his life more clearly than ever. At the end of the year, Shouyi traveled from Beijing to his family home in Shanxi to celebrate New Year's. As they sat around a brazier, his partially paralyzed father facing west, Shouyi facing north, they started talking about Old Niu, of when the two men had sold onions back in 1968, and how they'd stopped being friends after divvying up the profits. Raising his good right arm, Yan Shouyi's father waved his hand in the air and, with difficulty, related what had happened:

"He padded the accounts!"

"There were gaps everywhere, money fell through the cracks!"

"It's a bad idea for friends to go into business together," his son said.

"I could live with the padded accounts. It was the twenty-third, and we spent the whole day working on the accounts. Just before sunset, I picked up my share of the profits and walked out the door. But then I realized I should ask where we ought to sell onions the next year. As I walked back into the yard, I heard Old Niu say to his wife, Yan's an idiot."

"It wasn't the money, it's what he said."

He continued with tears in his eyes:

"I never had many people to talk to, only him, and he called me an idiot!"

He pointed to his chest.

"That's been bothering your dad all his life, right here."

In the summer of 1995, Yan Shouyi's father suffered another stroke. His mouth twisted to the left and he started to drool. He died without saying another word.

After Shouyi's father had left on that day many years earlier, Old Niu never again sold onions. In 1969, when the township's first crank telephone was installed, he went to the post office to check it out, one of a couple of dozen men. The postmaster, a man named Shang Xuewen, who parted his hair down the middle, called them together:

"Whoever's in charge of the telephone has to have a good, loud voice. Let's hear each of you give a shout."

One after the other, they shouted for the postmaster. Old Niu was the loudest. Even with his womanish voice, he cracked the window in the department store across the street. And not just loud—he drew his shout out longer than anyone, from the time Shang Xuewen lit a cigarette until he stubbed out the butt. Shang told him to stop.

"That'll do. Not even a donkey can bray that long!"

In 1996, Yan Shouyi was hired as the host of the TV talk show "Straight Talk." His becoming a small-screen celebrity made perfect sense to people throughout the country, except for those in Yan Family Village:

"I'll be fucked! His father never spoke more than ten sentences a day, and this one talks for a living."

2

In 1968, Zhang Xiaozhu was Yan Shouyi's best friend. Shouyi, born in the year of the rooster, was eleven; Xiaozhu, born in the year of the monkey, was twelve. Xiaozhu's head was shaped like a lopsided pumpkin, his skinny arms and legs looked like horse-cart shafts; his head was so heavy it bore down on his shoulders like a millstone. His right eye was glassy, and he had to rub the left one before he could see a thing. His mother was not the brightest woman in the village, and his father worked in the Changzhi Coal Mines, some two hundred li away; so Xiaozhu lived with his maternal grandmother in Yan Family Village. Shouyi had no mother, Xiaozhu had one, but she wasn't very bright. The two of them often walked to school together, schoolbags on their backs. In 1968, Xiaozhu's father came home from the Changzhi Number Three Coal Mine and gave his son a discarded miner's lamp. At night, with the aid of a discarded battery, the boy turned on the lamp, which could be seen for a couple of li. The sky above the village was black as coal, blacker than ink, and the boys often went to the hill behind the village to write words on the sky blackboard with the lamp. Xiaozhu usually wrote:

You're not stupid, Mom.

Shouyi usually wrote:

Where are you, Mom?

The two lines of writing would linger on the black screen of the sky for up to five minutes.

The Yan Family Village school was located in a building that had once held cattle. The teacher's name was Meng Qingrui. On the fifteenth day of the eighth lunar month, Meng locked the children inside the schoolhouse before heading off to the market, instructing them to memorize their lessons while he was gone. Yan Shouyi, Zhang Xiaozhu, Lu Guoqing, Jiang Changgen, and Du Tiehuan climbed out through a hole in the rear wall that had been used to remove the manure. They took off their shoes, tucked them into their waistbands, and waded across the stream on their way to the rear slope to steal watermelons. The man guarding the watermelons was the slightly deaf Old Liu. Concentrating at first on the theft of the watermelons, Yan Shouyi and his pals made it to a spot behind the shed where Old Liu slept and saw him dump an armload of *jiaozi* into a pot of boiling water. They decided they'd rather steal *jiaozi* than watermelons. So Shouyi and Changgen went into the field, pretending to steal watermelons, and as soon as Old Liu ran out to chase them away, Zhang Xiaozhu, Lu Guoqing, and Du Tiehuan scooped the *jiaozi* out of the pot and let the water drain through the scoop. Stuffing them into their pockets, they ran back to the rear slope to wait for Shouyi and Changgen, to divvy up the loot. Old Liu did not catch Changgen, but he did catch Shouyi, who was the only one who never got his share. That afternoon, Meng Qingrui investigated the incident, but before he had a chance to cane the palms of the culprit's hands, Shouyi snitched on his friends. As dusk fell, the students were free to go home, except for Shouyi and his friends, who were told to stand against the back wall of the cattle pen. On that fifteenth day of the eighth lunar month, as a full moon climbed into the sky, Meng Qingrui nibbled on a moon cake he'd bought earlier at the market and said:

"Since you ate all those *jiaozi*, you ought to have enough energy to stand there till the sun's up tomorrow, when we'll hold class again."

After that, Yan Shouyi could no longer hold his head up at school. Not because of the theft of *jiaozi*, but because he'd snitched on his friends. Zhang Xiaozhu hated him worst of all:

"Ratting on *them* is no big deal, but I was his best friend. How could he do that to me?"

They stopped speaking.

Half a year later, Zhang Xiaozhu's father came to take him to the Changzhi Number Three Coal Mine. That was because he'd brought Xiaozhu's not so bright mother out to the mine and wanted Xiaozhu there to look after her. On the night before he left, Xiaozhu went to see Shouyi and gave him the discarded miner's lamp, the one they'd used to write on the sky. First thing the next morning, Shouyi went to see his friend off. Xiaozhu was sprawled in his grandmother's doorway weeping when he got there. His grandmother was crying too. Xiaozhu's father was standing off to the side with his son's things. Finally, Xiaozhu's grandmother pried his hands loose from the threshold so he could get on the road.

Three months later, Shouyi received the first letter of his life. It was from Xiaozhu. The postman made three trips around the village without finding anyone named "Yan Shouyi." Finally, it was Old Liu, guardian of the watermelon field, who spat on the ground and said:

"It's White Stone, the little prick who stole my watermelons!"

The return address on the envelope, all in red, said "Changzhi Number Three Mine." So did the letterhead. The letter itself was short, in fact, only a single question: Did the lamp he'd given

Shouyi still work?

Shouyi wrote an answer to Zhang Xiaozhu. When the letter was ready, he asked his father for an eight-fen stamp. His father, who had just had the falling out with Old Niu and was still angry, reached out and slapped his son.

"Why does it cost money just to talk. I'll be fucked!"

The letter was never sent.

3

In 1969, twenty-year-old Lü Guihua came to Yan Family Village as a bride. Yan Shouyi could tell at once that her body smelled different from other people's. She had the same aroma as other brides, but there was something else. Sort of like an over-ripe apricot, cloying and sweet, and just being near her made his eyes sticky and turned him languid. In 1969, thanks to the arrival of Lü Guihua, his sense of smell developed in a hurry.

In 1969, the name Lü Guihua was well known within a radius of dozens of li. That was because, before getting married, she'd slept with Xiao Zheng, who ran the township's broadcast station, and who already had a wife. In 1969, every family in the village rose at six in the morning to the public address playing of "The East Is Red," followed by a selection of sayings by Chairman Mao. Xiao Zheng, who was in charge of the township's PA system, slept at the station. He was also an accomplished Peking Opera singer, and it was this latter talent that drew Lü Guihua to his room. One morning at six, he carelessly flipped the wrong switch, and instead of "The East Is Red" and the sayings of Chairman Mao, the people heard the pants and screams of a man and woman going at it. Though it was more enthusiastically received than the regular fare, the following day the man in charge of broadcasts was Xiao Yue, not Xiao Zheng. Once again the loudspeakers spewed "The East Is Red" and the sayings of Chairman Mao. As for those two—

Lü Guihua and Xiao Zheng—they never saw each other again.

Three months later, Lü Guihua married Niu Sanjin, or Three-Catty Niu, in Yan Family Village. Niu worked nearly two hundred li away as a miner in the Changzhi Number Three Coal Mine, alongside Zhang Xiaozhu's father. Word had it that while she was a willing bride, the villagers opposed the marriage. Even Yan Shouyi's taciturn father got red-in-the-face angry, and spat a gooey gob of phlegm past the door threshold.

"I'll be fucked, she's used goods!"

But one look at Lü Guihua, and Niu Sanjin was bound and determined to marry her. He said to his father:

"She's still new goods. Like a bicycle somebody borrows for a while and then returns."

Yan Shouyi did not see Lü Guihua on her wedding day, since he had gone into town with his father to sell a pig. First thing the next morning, on his way to school, he spotted Niu Sanjin at the village entrance heading to town on his bicycle, with Lü Guihua on the back, to buy a lampshade. From a distance, dressed in a corduroy coat, she was nothing special, but when he drew up near her he smelled that special odor. Next he noticed that she had eyes like nobody else: narrow, like those of a lamb, partially obscured by lazy eyelids. But then she opened them wide and her gaze fell by chance on Yan Shouyi, snatching the poor twelve-year-old boy's soul right out of his body. Twenty years later, he would meet a woman on Lushan with eyes just like those, and he realized that the attraction of women with those eyes was not restricted to the eyes alone; in the daytime, maybe, but not at night. The full impact of the term "allure" hit him at that moment. Such women were one in a million. What puzzled him was how an alluring beauty like that could wind up in a remote mountain village in southern Shanxi.

Ten days after the wedding, Niu Sanjin traveled the two hundred li to the Changzhi Number Three Mine to dig coal. That night, Yan Shouyi, Lu Guoqing, Jiang Changgen, and Du Tiehuan went over to

Lü Guihua's new house to make mischief. The game of pretending to sell onions on the threshing floor now seemed as stale as last night's leftovers. At first they sprawled atop the wall in Niu Sanjin's yard and glued their eyes to the lighted window, whose paper shone brighter than other people's because of the special shade over the kerosene lamp. Then, in front of a reed pond behind the house they formed two human ladders, with the boys on top licking the window paper to get a look inside. Lü Guihua was turning around in the lamplight singing opera the way the one-time station manager had done. Her favorite was *White-Haired Girl*. On this evening, she stopped singing long enough to pick up an enamel mug and take a drink of water. The boys thought she'd swallowed it, but she spun around and sprayed the window with water. Both human ladders fell back into the reed pond. The boys jumped to their feet, clambered over the wall, and ran into the house, where they pinned Lü Guihua down on the bed. With her legs up in the air, she nearly burst from laughing. Strangers no more. But Shouyi discovered a pair of scratches on his face from the reeds. Ever since ratting on his friends over the theft of the *jiaozi*, he'd been unable to look them in the eye, and so when they'd formed their human ladder, Lu Guoqing had perched on his shoulders.

"Hey, you're bleeding!"

Lü Guihua took the wounded Yan Shouyi in her arms and held him close to the light while she dabbed some disinfectant on his scratches. He nearly passed out from the rising and falling of her bosom and the smell of her body. The way he looked—sort of woozy—did not please his friends. Lu Guoqing spat on the ground.

"Sissy!"

Lü Guihua had been married on the twenty-sixth day of the ninth lunar month; Niu Sanjin returned to Number Three Mine on the sixth day of the tenth month. On the seventh day of the eleventh month, Lü Guihua had a sudden urge to call him on the phone. By then the township phone had been in operation for a month, and Yan Shouyi and the others were friendly enough with Lü Guihua to be in the same room and see her in a brassiere. As shadows danced in the lamplit room, she asked them:

"Have any of you ever made a phone call? I want someone to go with me to the post office in town."

They all jumped to their feet.

"I'll go! I'll go!"

Lu Guoqing stopped them.

"I'll go, since I'm the only one who's ever made a phone call."

Lü Guihua, who was washing her face at the time, looked up from the basin; water dripping on the floor:

"How would you do it?"

Lu Guoqing took off one of his shoes and held it to his ear.

"Is this elder brother Sanjin? It's Lu Guoqing. Have you eaten yet? Rice or noodles?"

They all laughed. Jiang Changgen was not impressed.

"Anyone can talk on the phone, but do you know how to turn the crank?"

Lu Guoqing made a circular motion with his hand, like turning a winch.

"Like that, same as turning a waterwheel, harder and harder."

At that critical moment, Yan Shouyi stepped up. The time before, when Lü Guihua had tended to his scratches, his stock had climbed a bit in the eyes of his friends, not enough to clean the slate after ratting on them over the theft of the *jiaozi*, but enough to allow him to raise his head from time to time. This was one of those times.

"Lu Guoqing's never made a phone call. Yesterday he asked me what a telephone looked like."

Lu Guoqing hit him over the head with his shoe.

"So I've never made a phone call. Have you?"

Yan Shouyi was seeing stars, but that didn't stop him from pinning Guoqing against the doorframe.

"No, but I know Old Niu, who's in charge of the telephone."

As he wiped a trickle of blood from the corner of his mouth, Lu Guoqing looked at Yan Shouyi as if seeing him for the first time.

"So you know Old Niu, big deal!"

"I don't know how to turn the crank, but Old Niu can do it for me."

Du Tiehuan walked over next to Lu Guoqing and pointed at Yan Shouyi.

"You're not a good enough talker! What if your call doesn't go through and you screw it up?"

Yan Shouyi took off his cap and flung it at Du Tiehuan.

"If I can't get through, I'll personally go to Number Three Mine!"

He raised his fists to fight Du Tiehuan. But by then Lü Guihua had finished washing her face and was braiding her hair. She looked over all the boys, finally stopping at Yan Shouyi.

"Tomorrow morning, White Stone, OK?"

Thanks to Lü Guihua, in 1969 Yan Shouyi made his first phone call. Thirty years later, he reflected that, if not for her, his first phone call on this earth would have had to wait another ten years at least. For a nation to start using telephones ten years early or ten years late has quite a powerful impact on its economic development.

4

In 1969, Yan Shouyi's voice began to change, going from the squeak of a bantam rooster to a raspy quality that made him sound old. He put that to good use in winning the chance to make a phone call. But, in a repeat of that earlier time, when he'd ratted on his pals, he offended them again, this time with an added wrinkle: Lu Guoqing and the others assumed that he wanted to take Lü Guihua to town just to be alone with her, which wasn't entirely true. Two months earlier, he'd received that letter from Zhang Xiaozhu and didn't have the money to send a return letter; maybe when Lü Guihua made her call to Niu Sanjin, he could relay a message to Xiaozhu that the discarded lamp he'd left behind no longer worked, that the battery was dead, which meant he couldn't write on the sky, and he wanted to ask Xiaozhu if he could scrounge up another battery and send it along with Niu Sanjin the next time he came home. This he could not reveal to Lü Guihua or Lu Guoqing and the others. If getting a chance to make the phone call was bad in the eyes of his friends, this added opportunity would have been enough to drive them nuts.

But all that was easy compared to what would happen if Shouyi's father found out. That time before, when he'd wanted a stamp to send a letter to Xiaozhu, all he'd gotten was a slap across the face. Now, if he asked Niu Sanjin to bring a message from Xiaozhu, it would be like dredging up that old matter all over again. At the same time, though Lu Guoqing and the others knew he was going to the post office to make a phone call, that too had to be kept from his father, since the parties to the call were Lü Guihua and Niu Sanjin, two of his father's mortal enemies. If any one of the three concerns or any one of the three people was revealed, Yan Shouyi was sure to be smacked again.

Thank God for seeing to it that his father was laid up with typhoid fever, wracked with chills and the shakes. He'd freeze under three blankets one minute and then drench all three blankets in sweat the next. When he returned home from Lü Guihua's place, Shouyi stood by his father's bed frowning and looking helpless before saying in his raspy voice:

"Are you cold, Dad? Want me to heat a brick for you?"

"Are you hot, Dad? Want me to get you some cool water?"

Just hearing his own words turned him emotional:

"I miss Mom."

He turned to his granny.

"We can't let my dad lie there and do nothing about it."

His father and his granny looked up at him.

"I'll go into town tomorrow and get some medicine for Dad!"

His father's eyelids fluttered before he closed them; he said nothing.

"Our little Stone has grown up," Granny said.

That had taken some doing.

5

Old Niu, the man in charge of the town's telephone, and Old Niu, the onion peddler, were two different people. Yan Shouyi recalled how genial Old Niu had been as an onion peddler, but now he was full of himself. Back in 1968, he'd talked like a little old lady; in 1969, he was "the man." Changing jobs sometimes requires a change of voice.

The distance from Yan Family Village to the town of Five-Li was nearly forty li, and they'd gone about halfway when snowflakes began to fall. The chain kept coming off of his bike, and it was stop-and-go the rest of the way. It was a major market day. Finally, Shouyi, carrying his bicycle over his shoulder, and Lü Guihua, clutching a bag to her chest, threaded their way through the crowd up to the post office, where Shouyi discovered he'd lost a shoe somewhere along the way. Now that the snowfall had stopped, he went back and found his errant shoe in a mud puddle, returning to the post office just in time for Old Niu to close up for the morning.

"Quitting time. Come back this afternoon."

Two bundles of alkaline batteries hung from the wall of the telephone room. Old Niu was putting the crank phone into a wooden box, which he secured with a padlock. Since it was market day, the office was packed with people waiting to make a phone call. Yan Shouyi, his face beaded with sweat, squeezed through the crowd up to Old Niu.

"Master Niu, we've come forty li by bicycle."

"You'd have to wait till this afternoon if you came four hundred. Even if I don't need the rest, the telephone does. It's worn out."

"Master Niu, my father is Old Yan of Yan Family Village; he used to peddle onions with you."

Old Niu looked hard at him, so Shouyi said in his raspy voice:

"Last year you had some water at our house over the winter solstice."

Without taking his eyes off of Shouyi, Old Niu took the key out of his back pocket and was about to open the telephone box, when he stopped abruptly.

"Nope, can't do it. I have my orders from Chief Shang. When it's time to knock off for lunch, not even my own father can make a phone call."

Lü Guihua threaded her way up front, clutching her bundle to her chest.

"What time this afternoon, Master Niu?"

Old Niu looked hard at Lü Guihua for a long moment and smiled.

"I'll go home for steamed bread and some soup, and be back in the time it takes to smoke a pipe."

Lü Guihua's question ruined Yan Shouyi's plans for that eighth day of the eleventh lunar month of 1969. Either making the phone call right then or waiting for Old Niu to come back after a long, leisurely lunch would have worked fine, since both options would have given him time to race to the pharmacy and pick up medicine for his father. Lü Guihua had come to town for one thing only, while Yan Shouyi had three reasons for being there. But since Old Niu said he'd be back in the time it took to smoke a pipe, no more, no less, leaving now was out of the question. Shouyi had been troubled on his way over, wondering whether he should tell Lü Guihua that he planned to pick up some medicine for his father while he was in town. If he did, then the trip would have a two-fold purpose, which might destroy the aura surrounding the two of them going to town to make a phone call. So he didn't tell her, and they carried out their unspoken agreement that she would ride on the rear rack of the bicycle with her arms around his waist; if he sprang it on her now that he needed to run off to buy some medicine and leave her to wait to make the phone call—each of them off on individual errands—it would no longer be a case of killing two birds with one stone and would, instead, become one of having a hidden agenda. *So, you've been lying all along, I see. Public salt has now become your private stash.* And so, Shouyi could only hope that Old Niu would follow through on his promise to eat a quick meal and be back at his post in about the time it takes to smoke a pipe. By waiting to buy the medicine until after the phone call went through, he could make it appear to be something he decided on the spur of the moment and, at the same time, earn some points with Lü Guihua. "You should have said something!" she'd remark.

Yan Shouyi and Lü Guihua each ate two flatbreads while they waited in the post office doorway, an activity that used up about half the time it takes to smoke a pipe. Old Niu, it appeared, was taking a bit longer than usual to finish his meal, and he didn't shuffle up to the post office until the sun was well on its way west. "A guest dropped by," he announced with a yawn.

Then he unlocked the phone box, and the crowd surged forward. Yan Shouyi, risking bodily injury, elbowed his way up to the head of the line, the twenty-cent bill Lü Guihua had given him clutched in his hand. He handed the money to Old Niu, who took it from him.

"Where do you want to call?"

"Changzhi Number Three Mine, I want to call Number Three Mine!"

A bulb in Old Niu's head apparently lit up his dim brain. He flung the money back.

"Number Three Mine? Out of the question!"

"Why?"

"Too far. Over two hundred li, not enough telephone lines! You can barely hear someone over at the County Headquarters, a few dozen li, and you want to call Number Three Mine!"

Yan Shouyi was nearly in tears.

"Grandpa Niu, I've been waiting all day. I haven't moved from here!"

"Then go to the end of the line and let me make the local calls first."

"We'll just have to wait," Lü Guihua said to Shouyi. "I'll be happy as long as we make the call today."

Shouyi would have cried if he'd had the tears. The more time that passed, the harder it would be to bring up the medicine purchase. He was feeling sorry for his father, who was home in bed suffering from alternating chills and fever. Finally, when the sun was about to set behind the mountains, the room was occupied only by the three of them—Old Niu, Yan Shouyi, and Lü Guihua.

"I'm telling you two that this is not going to be an easy call to make," Old Niu said. "I give you no more than a twenty-percent chance of getting through."

No longer caring whether the call went through or not, Yan Shouyi handed Old Niu the money.

"Go on, give it a try, Grandpa Niu, whether it goes through or not."

Old Niu pulled a long face as he cranked the phone.

"Number Three Mine," he shouted into the mouthpiece. "Connect me with Number Three Mine!"

The only response he got was a few short rings before the connection was lost. With a wave of his hand, he said:

"See, I told you it wouldn't go through, but you didn't believe me!

"I've been in charge of this phone for more than a month," he went on, "and I've never once gotten through to Number Three

21

Mine!"

Yan Shouyi looked at Lü Guihua.

"Since we can't get through, Sister-in-law, shouldn't we head back?"

Lü Guihua walked up to Old Niu.

"Elder Master," she said, "try it one more time. It's important."

Old Niu looked at Lü Guihua.

"Lots of people manage important business without making phone calls. I'm telling you, I'll try once more, and that's it."

He tried again, cranking the phone with force.

"Number Three Mine, I want Number Three mine!"

This time, against all odds, someone was on the other end.

"Where? Who do you want?"

"Not you, that's for sure. I want Number Three Mine!"

"That's what you got, Number Three Mine. I'm at Number Three Mine."

Old Niu reacted with a bit of panic and considerable doubt.

"How can that be? I've never gotten through to you before. Who are you, who am I talking to?"

"I'm Old Ma, at Number Three Mine, Old Ma, in charge of the telephone. Who are you? Who am I talking to?"

Old Niu was gleefully surprised.

"Hey, it's really Number Three Mine. I'm Old Niu, calling from Five-Li, Old Niu, in charge of the phone here. It's market day, Old Ma. I peddled onions at your place last winter, that's who I am. Remember me?"

Old Ma hesitated.

"Old Niu, which Old Niu would that be? Lots of people peddle onions here at Number Three Mine."

"Two days before the winter solstice, I had on a train engineer's cap, and my donkey stumbled while it was pulling my onion cart over the train tracks. Came up lame."

Old Ma didn't say anything for a long moment, probably

scrolling through his memory. Finally he muttered:

"Oh, sure, I remember you now."

"Old Ma, it's turning dark here. Have you had your dinner?"

"Not yet. My replacement hasn't shown up."

"Will you be eating porridge there at the mine tonight, or noodles?

"We had porridge last night, so tonight we'll probably have noodles."

Lü Guihua nudged Yan Shouyi with her elbow. He went up to Old Niu.

"Grandpa Niu, how about letting her speak to them?"

Only then reminded that he'd made the call for Yan Shouyi and Lü Guihua, he grudgingly handed her the phone.

"Go ahead, but be quick about it, and keep it short!"

Lü Guihua's hand trembled as she held the receiver; so did her lips.

"Is this Number Three Mine? I want to talk to Niu Sanjin."

On the other end, Old Ma said:

"Niu Sanjin? Who's that?"

"One of your miners."

"There are thousands of miners here, and one telephone. How am I supposed to find the one you're looking for? Tell me what you want to say, and I'll pass it on to him later."

Lü Guihua handed the receiver to Yan Shouyi and said softly:

"Can't find him. It's somebody else. You talk to him."

Shouyi took the phone with a trembling hand and stood there without saying anything. On the other end, Old Ma said impatiently:

"Say something, or I'm hanging up!"

In a hoarse voice, caused by panic, Yan Shouyi said:

"Elder Master, I'm Yan Shouyi, White Stone is my nickname. The woman is Lü Guihua, and she wants to know when Niu Sanjin is coming home."

"That's it? That's what you called for?"

"Bam!" The other phone was slammed down, the sound jogging Shouyi's memory that there was something else he wanted to say, which was for Niu Sanjin to pass a message to Zhang Xiaozhu to send him used batteries. But Old Niu had snatched the phone out of his hand and was already putting the lock back on the phone box.

Yan Shouyi rushed from the post office on his bike, with Lü Guihua behind him, racing for the pharmacy. It was closed, and stayed closed even after he nearly broke down the door. An old peddler of specialty flatbreads told him the pharmacist had closed up shop only a few minutes earlier and had left to treat a sick pig at the Ma family farm five miles away. Back in 1969, the town had one pharmacist, who treated both people and animals. The old peddler said that if they'd been there a little earlier, say half the time it takes to smoke a pipe, the pharmacy would still have been open.

6

After returning home from making the phone call, Yan Shouyi was beaten black and blue by his father, who used the well rope as a strap. A wet strap. The beating did not result from not buying the medicine; that had actually turned out right, because not long after Shouyi rode into town, his father's symptoms had abated. The alternating chills and shakes had run their course in five days. His father had climbed out of bed and, steadying himself by touching the wall, walked out of the bedroom and continued on outside, still somewhat lightheaded. Swirling snowflakes gave an unreal quality to people out on the street, where he ran into Shouyi's cousin, Black Brick, who was fourteen that year, a couple of years older than Shouyi. Two years before, on the eighth day of the twelfth lunar month, the boys had gotten into a fight over a lamb hoof that was cooking for the family dinner. Shouyi had thrown a bowl at

Black Brick, opening a gash on his forehead; they'd been enemies ever since, no longer on speaking terms. Seeing an opportunity for revenge, Black Brick reported in detail why Shouyi had really gone into town, thus accomplishing what Lu Guoqing, Jiang Changgen, and Du Tiehuan had failed at.

Shouyi stopped talking altogether for ten days following the beating, and he stopped going over to Lü Guihua's. As he saw it, his days on this earth had come to an end. Then, on the eleventh day, Niu Sanjin came home from the mine. On the twelfth day, Jiang Changgen told Shouyi at school that they'd gone over to Lü Guihua's place the night before, where Niu Sanjin told them how Shouyi and Lü Guihua had phoned the mine a dozen or so days earlier. There was only one phone at the mine, he said, and all incoming calls were broadcast over the loudspeaker by Old Ma, who was in charge of the phone. The mine was ringed by mountains that were themselves surrounded by more mountains. Old Ma broadcast the message Yan Shouyi had given him over the phone:

"This announcement is for one of the men: Niu Sanjin, looking for Niu Sanjin. Your wife, Lü Guihua, wants to know if you'll be coming home soon . . ."

Niu Sanjin told them that they were in the midst of a shift change at the time, and thousands of miners, with lanterned helmets on their heads and coal-dust-blackened faces, were emerging from mine openings, while others were on their way below ground. It was snowing, and Old Ma's voice bounced off of mountaintops, reproducing itself over and over amid swirling snowflakes, until there were thousands of Old Mas. With snow accumulating on their heads, the miners smiled at the broadcast, exposing bright white teeth. Over the next couple of weeks, the incident was put to song. At each meal, the men would bang their rice bowls and sing:

Niu Sanjin, Niu Sanjin
Lü Guihua is your wife's name

And Lü Guihua wants to know

If you'll be coming home soon

Yan Shouyi wept.

7

Thirty years later, noted TV host Yan Shouyi created a segment of his breezy TV show "Straight Talk" entitled "Making a Phone Call," which not only sent the program's ratings higher than ever, but popularized the ditty "Niu Sanjin and Lü Guihua." Thanks to this segment, at the year-end variety program awards show, Yan Shouyi was voted by viewers winner of the "Golden Mouth Award." A year later, Lü Guihua's daughter, Niu Caiyun came to take the entrance exam for the Acting Department at Beijing's Academy of Dramatic Arts. She stayed at the home of Yan Shouyi. The minute he laid eyes on her, he exclaimed:

"The spitting image of your mother. I never saw her again after she moved to the mining town."

Without a trace of bashfulness, Caiyun replied in a heavy Shanxi accent:

"Mother laughed out loud every time she saw you on TV. She watched the segment 'Making a Phone Call,' but according to her, it wasn't you who went with her into town to make the call, since you didn't know how to ride a bike then."

Surprised to hear that, Yan Shouyi asked:

"If it wasn't me, who was it?"

"Mother thought about that all night long, and the next morning told us it was no one, that she didn't go into town to make a phone call that year at all."

"I'll be fucked!"

The words, straight from the year 1969, leaped out of Yan Shouyi's mouth.

Chapter 2

Yu Wenjuan, Shen Xue, and Wu Yue

1

Yan Shouyi had a friend named Fei Mo. Throughout his twenties and thirties, Yan had had lots of friends, people he'd hung out with just about every day. Their get-togethers were as lively as a steamy, boiling hot-pot. But now that his fortieth birthday had passed, he was down to this one male friend, sort of like a hotel lobby at two in the morning, where a lone guest sits bent low over a cup of coffee. Yan Shouyi was struck by the thought that back when his days were packed with excitement, his friends were always talking, though his brain had since been purged of every word they'd ever said; now he had one friend, and he couldn't say what the two of them talked about

Fei Mo had been born in 1954, the year of the horse, which made him three years older than Yan Shouyi. He was fat, short and fat. A university professor born and raised in Beijing, he wore thick glasses and an unlined Chinese jacket the year round, adding a muffler in the winter. His speech was a mixture of classical and colloquial, reminding Yan Shouyi of an old-school intellectual from the 1920s and 1930s. Fei Mo and a maternal uncle of Yan Shouyi's wife, Yu Wenjuan, had been university classmates. Yan had met him six years earlier, during the "hundred-day" celebration of this uncle's infant son, where the guests were treated to a hot-pot meal. At this first meeting, Yan assumed that Fei wasn't much of a talker, since he didn't say a word as he focused on the task of dipping the shaved meat into the boiling water and then in the spicy sauce, until his fat face was beaded with sweat. No one at the table paid him any attention, as their conversation ranged from political

Liu Zhenyun

jokes to dirty jokes and eventually to hot-pots themselves, starting with Beijing hot-pots, moving from there to Chongqing hot-pots, and then to Sichuan hot-pots; Yan Shouyi concluded that the origin of the hot-pot had to be Sichuan, since the province itself was a basin, just like the pots. At that point, Fei Mo removed his glasses and wiped his sweaty face before launching into a leisurely exposition, during which he kept his eyes fixed on the ceiling, not on the faces of the other guests. He did not deal with the origin of the hot-pot right away, but started out talking about barbarian tribes, citing the classics. From there he moved to Genghis Khan, and from there to the Qin dynasty and the hot-pot helmets the soldiers wore. A hot-pot was involved in the Qin dynasty's annihilation of the Six Dynasties, he claimed. The others assumed that would bring things to a close, but Fei Mo skipped through the centuries down to the Qing . . . and then he began talking about ceramics in primitive societies. From ceramics he moved on to the discovery of iron, and from there to the emergence of bronze implements. A simple leap from bronze implements back to hot-pots brought that discussion to a close so he could move on to the difference between nomadic and farming peoples, and how the Manchus united the two . . .

"Don't forget to eat while you're listening," Yu Wenjuan's uncle called out.

To everyone's surprise, this simple comment sent Fei Mo back to the meat in front of him and brought his monologue to an end, leaving the Manchus in limbo and hot-pots up in the air; it was as if, except for Fei Mo, everyone else at the table was only interested in gobbling up the food. The same thing happened often after that. Whether at a meeting or a dinner party, the conversation could be about flora or dinnerware, and Fei Mo could lead the discussion into new areas. And then someone would say something that offended him, and that would bring his exposition to a screeching halt. Taking note of the man's eclecticism and the pleasure he took in lecturing, Yan offered him a job as an idea man for "Straight Talk,"

30

since that was just what was needed for a TV talk show dealing with daily life. With so much to talk about, Yan was not worried that Fei Mo might be out of his element. Where a time commitment was concerned, he wouldn't have to give up his university professorship, and needed only go to the station with suggestions and pointers when he wasn't in class. For a minimum of conversation he would be paid a handsome monthly salary. But to Yan's surprise, Fei Mo turned down the first two invitations to join the show.

"I'm not much of a talker."

By this time, they had become friends.

"If *you're* not much of a talker, then the rest of China's population might as well give up breathing."

Fei Mo glared at Yan Shouyi.

"That's not what I meant by 'not much of a talker.' "

Yan Shouyi realized that he was referring to willingness, not ability.

"How come?"

"Talking has its own values. For me it's not a meal ticket."

"You hold lectures at the university. Doesn't that make it your meal ticket?"

Again Fei Mo glared at Shouyi.

"They're different—education and entertainment. With one you impart knowledge, while the other is self-mocking; one is Confucius, the other is an actor. Got it?"

That cleared things up for Yan Shouyi, who let it drop for the moment. But two months later, he was back with another offer. During that period, he'd thought often about Fei Mo, and had laughed every time, just as his father had laughed back in 1968 when he thought of Old Niu while they were out peddling onions. And that—thinking about someone other than himself—was a new experience for Yan Shouyi:

"Old Fei, this is my 'third call at the thatched cottage,' if you know what I mean. I realize you consider us beneath you and would find it impossible to have an intelligent discussion with us. But you ought to consider the matter of influence. I'm not asking you for myself."

That surprised Fei Mo.

"For whom then?"

"For the common people of this world. You cannot continue to allow the rest of us to live in ignorance. You would be selfish if you spread knowledge only within the confines of the university."

Fei Mo giggled like a child. He pointed at Yan Shouyi.

"Since the day we met, this is the first funny thing you've said."

But, he went on:

"That doesn't mean I'm willing to sully my reputation just because you uttered one sensible comment."

"I asked you to join us not merely to get you to help me on the show."

This too surprised Fei Mo.

"Why then?"

"The show is unimportant, I'm just using that as an excuse. What I really want is to spend more time with you."

Fei Mo stared at Yan Shouyi. Then he sighed.

"I always thought you only knew how to fawn over people. Who'd have thought you could be so conscientious? I figured you were interested only in fame and fortune, and I'm surprised that you have at least a vague idea of what friendship means."

And so Yan Shouyi managed to talk Fei Mo into joining the "Straight Talk" team. At first he put no pressure on him, letting him show up when he felt like it; and there was always a generous remuneration waiting for him at the end of the month. After a while, Fei Mo grew uncomfortable with the situation and came on his own with ideas for the program.

"Go home and rest, Old Fei. We can take care of things around here."

"I thought you were a decent, honest man, not a schemer," Fei

Mo replied. "A man is not rewarded for nothing. Even that little bit of money makes me uncomfortable. Yan Shouyi, it's not fair to kill someone with a dull knife."

Once Fei Mo joined the program's brain trust, "Straight Talk" underwent a change. As they say, once an academic, always an academic. At first, Yan was concerned that Fei Mo could not abandon his professorial ways and that the relationship between the university and the TV station would be, as Fei Mo had predicted, a contrast between highbrow and popular culture, that there would be two distinct ways of saying the same thing. But he'd underestimated Fei Mo, who was, as they say, at home both in the kitchen and in the hallway, capable of moving from the profound to the mundane as easily as flicking a switch. He spoke and acted with slow deliberation, and Yan Shouyi never tried to speed him up. Over the years, Fei Mo gave birth to several shows, all winners. One, "A Letter from Confucius," dealt with roadside propaganda posters, ignoring the mistakes in grammar and concentrating on an analysis of the contents, most of which were as empty as the look in a moron's gaping eyes. Another was called "Clinton in Grade School." Clinton was still U.S. president at the time, and news of the the Lewinsky affair had just broken. Refusing to come clean, Clinton explained how, back in grade school, he had not done well in English, and as a result could not see how putting a particular noun and verb together conveyed the meaning that he and the women had had a sexual relationship. Yet another series was called "The Craze in Studying Languages," and dealt with Chinese trying to learn "crazy English." The English went crazy long before the people did. There were other, more emotional, themes. For instance, during a conversation with Yan Shouyi the year before, the show "Making a Phone Call" had been born. In it, the time in 1969 when Yan Shouyi had accompanied Lü Guihua into town to make a phone call was cited. A simple phone call to check up on someone two hundred li away, just to show she was thinking about him, wound up as an expression of concern for great numbers of people, above ground and down in the mines. "Loneliness, that's what it was all about," Fei Mo said. At the beginning and end of the program, the show's musical group played a rock version of "Niu Sanjin and Lü Guihua," the lines that had been broadcast over the PA system at Number Three Mine all those years before. Each of these was a big hit with the viewers, and the ratings for "Straight Talk" took off. At one of the cast meetings, Yan Shouyi said:

"It's the cultural component that sets 'Straight Talk' apart from other shows. Know why our ratings go up each year, while those for other shows decline? It's because Old Fei looks at the world and has things to say, while the others say things merely to cover up their ignorance.

"I say that from now on, instead of calling him Old Fei we use the more respectful Fei Lao."

Fei Mo looked out the window and sighed.

"Those who know me say I'm melancholy, those who don't wonder what it is I seek."

The others at the meeting felt like laughing at this classical allusion, but held back.

As time passed, Yan discovered that Fei Mo shared some of the petty traits of otherwise cultured people. At meetings or in restaurants, as a TV host with a recognizable face, Yan always drew a crowd of people wanting to say hello or take a picture with him or get an autograph; they ignored Fei Mo. Who cared if the man had a bellyful of wisdom and allusions? Dinner conversations always excluded Fei Mo when Yan Shouyi was around, and much of the time it was nearly impossible for him to get a word in edgewise. Yan always tried his best to shoehorn Fei Mo into the conversation:

"This is Professor Fei, head of the 'Straight Talk' brain trust. He's behind every show and every idea. I'm just his mouthpiece."

A bit surprised by this information, the people would turn to Fei Mo. "How nice to meet you," they'd say. But once the "nice to meet you"s were dispensed with, they returned to the mouthpiece like moths drawn to a lamp, turning their backs on the fount of ideas. They were unable to discern the source of the light, something that invariably plunged Fei Mo into a funk for the rest of the evening. Once the meeting had ended or the meal was over and they were back in the car, Yan Shouyi at the wheel with Fei Mo sitting sullenly beside him, the funk would settle around both men.

"Fei Lao," Yan Shouyi explained to him once, "don't let it get you down. You're Confucius, I'm just an actor.

"I was going to ask you to give them some hints on living until I realized they didn't care. Like it or not, that's the cultural level of our people. Since even the great Lu Xun threw up his hands in despair over such people, don't waste your time on them."

Fei Mo stared silently out the window.

On one occasion, Fei Mo dreamed up a program called "Notebooks." His thesis was that individual jottings paint a more reliable picture of the past than official histories or newspaper articles, and the plan was to have members of the audience from each generation read from their notebooks during tapings of the show. Here is how he put it in the original script: *You might be in Hell, you might also be in Heaven. No one can lift you out of Hell and into Heaven. You can, however, let your Heaven become a living Hell.* But the "Straight Talk" producer decided to ignore the script, elaborating instead on the idea by introducing notebook computers, thanks to the promised support of a computer company to the tune of half a million RMB. A link between the two concepts was impossible to find, which made things somewhat awkward. But the notebook computers were displayed, and the topic suffered no observable bruising, except that Fei Mo wordlessly shook his head the whole time. After the meeting, the computer company CEO invited Yan Shouyi to dinner; Yan asked Fei Mo to come along, since the original idea had been his. The meal went off without a hitch. The CEO was a fan of *Dream of the Red Chamber*, and even though Fei Mo was a professor of sociology, he was a worthy authority on the classical novel. Though the two men approached *Dream* from different angles, they quickly settled on something to talk about: She Yue takes a bath. Does the hero of the novel, Jia Baoyu, join her in her bath, and if so, how far does that "joining" go? The two men wrangled till they were red in the face. Yan Shouyi stayed out of the debate. Fei Mo's face glowed throughout the meal. But when they were about to leave, a problem arose as the CEO handed Yan Shouyi a notebook computer.

"Mr. Yan," he said, "this is for you."

He then took pains to point out the programs. Completely forgotten was Fei Mo, who stood off to the side, silently smoking a cigarette and staring at a mural entitled "The Qin Emperor on an Outing." Yan was amazed by the CEO's insensitivity. *You don't give a gift to one person when you've invited two to dinner. Besides, what difference can a few thousand make to someone who's invested half a million?* Not that a few thousand would have made a difference to Fei Mo, Yan Shouyi assumed, but slighting him like that was an obvious affront to his dignity. *Chairman Mao proclaimed that* Dream of the Red Chamber *is an encyclopedia, and you haven't understood a word of it.* And yet, since it had been given to Yan as a gift, it would have been unwise to hand it over to Fei Mo. After dinner, the CEO invited them—this time Fei Mo was included—to tour the company offices.

"Let's all go have a look. I've got a painting of 'Qin Keqing Sleeping in the Spring' hanging in my office."

Fei Mo turned away from the restaurant mural and stubbed out his cigarette in the ashtray.

"You two go ahead, I have things to do."

Yan Shouyi sensed that a tour would likely have been even

more awkward for Fei Mo, but what he said then actually made things worse:

"Sure, I'll do all the running around, so Fei Lao can go back to the station and work out program details."

Fei Mo abruptly turned hostile, shouting.

"There's nothing to work out. There'll be no program!"

A shock ran through the restaurant. Yan Shouyi was as surprised as anyone.

"Why not?" he stammered.

Fei Mo's face showed his anger.

"Too commercial, overblown. Not in the spirit of 'Straight Talk.'"

He stood up, retrieved his coat from the coat rack, wrapped a muffler around his neck, and walked out. This time, in Yan Shouyi's opinion, Fei Mo had gone too far, and should not be disregarding the general good over a personal slight. He'd overlooked the big picture. If they dropped the planned program, they could watch half a million go down the drain. But in the end, Yan chose to honor his friend's decision. Since "Notebooks" had not yet been born, he let it die in the womb; it hadn't entered Heaven, so might as well consign it to Hell. But Daduan, or "Big Duan," the show's producer, complained:

"You indulge him too much! Day in and day out, it's Fei Lao this and Fei Lao that. You've put him on a pedestal, and now look where that's gotten us."

"That's part of what makes Fei Lao such a charmer. I used to find intellectuals insufferable for their lack of an independent spirit. But the way I see it now, the only person here worthy of emulation is Fei Lao. Go home and read your *Records of the Historian* and ask yourself why Liu Bang's adviser Xiao He went out at night to bring Han Xin back into the fold."

Yan Shouyi did not divulge to Big Duan what was really on his mind. The main reason he'd been so acquiescent was that in only a few short years he and Fei Mo had become close friends, men who kept no secrets from one another. Prior to reaching the age of forty, Yan had not grasped the importance of friendships, but after his fortieth birthday, he understood the pitfalls of having no one with whom to share ideas and grew to appreciate how important friends were. Fei Mo, who often put on airs, revealed his true character only when he was alone with Yan Shouyi. When they were drinking, he became a different man. If it was just the two of them, he did all the talking and Shouyi the listening. He wouldn't stop till he was nearly foaming at the mouth. But once, when they'd been drinking heavily, he abruptly shut up, as if a plug had been pulled. After a long pause, a new connection was made, and he turned sappy and sentimental. Pointing to his own mouth, he said:

"Blather."

He pointed a second time.

"Except for spewing blather, I don't know what else this thing's good for."

Yan Shouyi consoled him in a tone of voice he'd learned from Fei Mo himself:

"Don't say that, Fei Lao. It may seem like blather to you, but what you pick from between your teeth is enough for us to live on for a lifetime."

Ignoring Yan's comment, Fei Mo went on:

"A mouth that produces blather is a sign of a mind that's depressed."

His face was quickly soaked with tears, and Yan said nothing for a long while.

When he was feeling dejected, Yan looked forward to heart-to-heart talks with Fei Mo. Things he would not tell his wife, he'd tell Fei Mo, even things in his life he could not stop from doing. He would never, for instance, reveal anything about his sex life to anyone but Fei Mo.

Needless to say, Fei Mo had his happy moments, particularly when he was with members of the "Straight Talk" team. Everyone associated with the program, more than a dozen in all, from Yan Shouyi down to the young woman who answered the phone, treated Fei Mo with unalloyed respect. Society at large might not have recognized the man's importance, but these people did, and they learned to listen even to what went unsaid when he spoke. He could look beneath the surface and grasp the essence of things. It was as if the meaning of life was revealed only in the tiny corner of the world he occupied. As time passed, members of the team began to talk like him, including the way he drew out each word. A simple comment by him would travel in a circle, head east and then backtrack to the west, seeming to go one way but really going the other, or, as they say, pointing to dogs and screaming at chickens. When he was in a good mood, he was almost childlike. He'd walk into the office with his briefcase under his arm, and one of the new members of the production team, Xiao Ma, a recent college graduate, would look up from her computer and say teasingly:

"Tea."

Fei Mo would put down his briefcase and waddle over to steep a cup of tea for Xiao Ma, like a student might do for his teacher.

At first, he came to the office once a week. But that gradually increased to twice a week, then three times, as if it was the only place where he could escape the icy confines of society at large and find a bit of warmth.

On the morning of February eleventh, Yan Shouyi pulled up in front of Fei Mo's building to take him to a studio taping. Normally, when they were on their way to a meeting of the "Straight Talk" team, Fei Mo's jowly face would be all smiles, and Yan would be slavishly deferential, taking the briefcase and opening the car door for him, to the old man's immense satisfaction. But on this day, when he emerged from the building, he wore a pained look and ignored Yan's attempts to take his briefcase and open the car door for him. Yan could see that his friend had not spent a pleasant night. Fei Mo's wife, Li Yan, was a travel agent who was no more understanding of the world around her than most people. Not realizing the importance of her husband, she regularly put him in a foul mood with her argumentative nature. This knowledge led Yan Shouyi to another discovery: in addition to pettiness, so often encountered in cultured people, Fei Mo had a penchant for taking his anger out on others. The program had suffered, for instance, because of his anger over the computer company CEO's slight. So whenever he and his wife had a fight, others suffered. Seeing him sit there glowering, Yan Shouyi drove cautiously out of the compound. Then, once they'd left the area, he asked guardedly:

"Fei Lao, shall we take the sexy route, via Pingan Road, or the sensible route, on Fourth Ring?"

Fei Mo ignored him and stared out the window, and Yan was wise enough to hold his tongue and just drive. But once they were on the Fourth Ring highway, Fei Mo began to vent, as expected:

"Old Yan, I keep telling you to sit down and read a book when you're not working. A lack of knowledge is a sure path to screw-ups."

Yan Shouyi stared straight ahead, puzzled.

"What did I do now?"

"Did you watch last night's show?"

The previous night's "Straight Talk" had been called "Things We Didn't Invent," another of Fei Mo's ideas, focusing on the indolent, slothful nature of the Chinese, a civilization with five thousand years of history that was blessed with only one talent: in-fighting. Prior to the Song dynasty, they had invented gunpowder and the compass; but from the Song to the present day, they'd invented nothing, not the washing machine, not the refrigerator, not the automobile, and not the airplane, though they were shameless enough to use them all. Yan Shouyi had been at a restaurant the night before and missed the show. He looked at Fei Mo and shook his head.

"There was a real screw-up, are you aware of that? Instead of giving your best when you should, you save it for a time when it's not needed. I was watching last night, the one show I didn't keep a close eye on, and, sure enough, there was a problem. How could you say that Newton invented the steam engine?"

Yan Shouyi was stumped.

"He didn't? Then who did?"

"Watt. You've heard of him, haven't you?"

Yan Shouyi realized he'd made a mistake, but that didn't alter the fact that peace had not reigned at Fei Mo's place the night before. Watt or Newton—at any other time, Fei Mo would not have made such a big deal out of it, and he'd have said so. But today that was not somewhere he wanted to go. He acknowledged his mistake:

"It's my fault. I don't know either one of them."

"You think you can say mea culpa, and that's that? My name appears on the script. People in the know are well aware of your intellectual inadequacies. But everyone else must think it was something *I* made up."

At that moment, Yan Shouyi remembered something a lot more important than Watt or Newton. Ignoring Fei Mo, he flipped his right-turn blinker to get out of the traffic flow, then sped from the fast lane over to the curb, where he stopped in a temporary parking zone. Fei Mo stared at him.

"What was that all about?"

"I left my cell phone at home."

If anything, Fei Mo's mood worsened.

"So what! We have a show to tape, forget the phone. I have plans for this afternoon."

Yan Shouyi clutched the steering wheel with both hands.

"Yu Wenjuan's home today."

Now Fei Mo knew what this was all about. Yan was afraid his

wife would find his cell phone, and that could spell trouble.

Forgetting he was supposed to be in a bad mood, he pointed at Yan and said:

"I'm telling you that insulting Watt was no accident. Your mind's been elsewhere the past few days. Your conscience is bothering you. Maybe I shouldn't say this, but the way you're out catting around all the time is bound to get you in trouble sooner or later."

He stared at him again.

"What makes you think that the 'she-devil' will pick this day to call you?"

Yan Shouyi poked the steering wheel with his finger.

"I don't 'think' anything. I just want to be prepared."

Fei Mo took out his cell phone.

"Call her on my phone. That should take care of it. There's no need to go back home."

"I'd still rather have it with me. I might mess up while I'm in the middle of a taping."

As they made a U-turn on the overpass, Fei Mo displayed his annoyance:

"Those people you hang around with, I could put it nicely by calling them 'sweeties,' but the truth of the matter is they're tattered shoes—sluts."

"Trouble, nothing but trouble comes of messing with tattered shoes."

2

Yan Shouyi's wife, Yu Wenjuan, who worked in a real estate development office, had the day off. She was practicing *qigong* breathing exercises when he arrived home to retrieve his cell phone. A native of Nanjing, she was fond of salted duck, while Shouyi, a native of Shanxi, preferred knife-cut noodles. With the exception of such gastronomical conflicts, ten years of marriage had been smooth sailing. Twelve years earlier, before he became host of the show, Shouyi had been one of its producers. Social dancing was in vogue at the time, and he and his wife had met at one of the dances. Afterward, she told him she'd fallen for him because he was so much fun to listen to, so funny she couldn't stop laughing. For him it was the opposite; Wenjuan had appealed to him because she talked so little, was unhurried in her speech when she did, and always with a smile. Eventually they were married, as all their friends had hoped. The only glitch was that their active, unprotected nighttime activity failed to produce any offspring. So they went to a doctor, who told them that the problem lay with her, not him. She reacted by ingesting all sorts of Chinese herbal concoctions, and when that failed, she went to see a *qigong* master, who taught her a breathing regimen. Most people practice *qigong* to combat cancer or with a view to the next life; Yan Shouyi's wife practiced *qigong* to get pregnant in this life. Hard work and lots of sweat could not keep her from it, but her diligence struck Yan Shouyi as slightly comical.

"You're wasting your time," he said. "For fashionable youngsters these days it's DINK—double income, no kids."

Wenjuan smiled an embarrassed smile.

"I'm not doing this for you, I'm doing it for Granny."

By granny, she meant Yan Shouyi's grandmother. Ten years earlier, after their wedding, they'd gone to his hometown in Shanxi, where his grandmother had given Wenjuan a ring, a family heirloom. After that, whenever they made the trip, over lunar New Year's, the old woman would stare at Yu's belly.

"An old village woman, what does she know?"

"I gave her my word."

Later, Yan Shouyi would discover that Wenjuan wasn't really trying to get pregnant for the sake of the grandmother; no, she knew him too well. His head was easily turned, he was impulsive, and he drank too much. She was worried he might get drunk one night and go astray. But a child could keep him on a short leash. Back when he was an anonymous TV producer, this would not have been a problem. But then, suddenly, he was the host of a talk show whose ratings had gone through the roof, and he had become an instant celebrity; that's when he realized what was on her mind, and he had to laugh. Who does she think she can keep on a short leash with a child, anyway? People with children are always winding up in divorce court.

Later still, he discovered that keeping him on a short leash was not the only reason she wanted a child; she also needed someone to talk to. After ten years of marriage, they had run out of things to say to each other. Early in their marriage, it felt as if they could talk the night away. Now, when they were in bed, they still made love, but without a word between them, before, during, or after. From time to time, one of them would try to find something to talk about, but that only made things worse, since all they could come up with was news about other people, and not very interesting news at that. Like a machine that runs out of oil and freezes up, their conversation would come to a shuddering stop. Wenjuan once surprised herself by saying:

"The only time I hear you talk these days is when you're on TV."

That surprised him, too, and from then on, he tensed up over the thought of having a conversation with his wife. Fortunately, by then they'd grown used to the silence, and she had stopped trying to figure out what had gone wrong. Mealtimes were the worst, since the only sounds were the clicking of chopsticks on bowls and plates. Then one night, Shouyi discovered that his wife had found a conversation partner. He was having dinner at a restaurant, when he suddenly felt queasy and excused himself to go home. Wenjuan didn't hear him come in. Going straight to the bedroom to lie down, he stopped in the doorway when he saw his wife, her back to him as she sat on the bed, holding a toy puppy in her arms and talking to it. She was telling it how she'd seldom laughed as a little girl, but had cried a lot. Her father had worked in a radio factory in Nanjing, her mother had sold tea on the street. Whenever her mother was angry, she'd hit her daughter with the tongs she used to stoke the little stove. Wenjuan had an uncle, a fair-skinned, roly-poly man who'd had his eye on her, and when she was fifteen . . . she'd never revealed any of this to Shouyi, and now she was telling her story to a stuffed animal. But rather than sympathize with her, he was horrified by what he heard. He quietly backed out of the room and went outside, where he walked around for an hour before returning home. After that incident, he never again tried to stop her from getting pregnant.

Yan Shouyi was neither happy nor unhappy in his marriage; it made no difference to him one way or the other. Sort of like a steamed bun that sits in the cupboard. When you're hungry, it's better than nothing, but when you've already eaten, it's like chewing plastic. He felt guilty each time he cheated on his wife, but when he was home, they just sat there, looking at each other and saying nothing. In most families arguments are a common occurrence, but Yan Shouyi and his wife could go all year without exchanging a cross word. He even found himself envying couples who could have heated arguments in public, turning red in the face, neck tendons bulging, oblivious to everyone around them, as if they were the only two people on earth. Where did all that passion come from, with curses flying back and forth, all that numbing creativity?

But he had no desire to get a divorce. People are like dogs. As time passes, they grow accustomed to their surroundings and have no desire to be anywhere else. And eventually, he realized that his wife had plenty of attributes he'd miss if she weren't around. Sure, she was taciturn, but that didn't mean she was cold, and in fact there was warmth in her silence. In the winter of 1999, he was stricken with typhoid fever, just like his father thirty years earlier, but worse. In the mornings he'd feel as if the house were one gigantic freezer; then in the afternoons he'd feel like a crab that's been thrown into boiling water. At nights he'd fill the room with delirious chatter. In his semiconscious state, he went back thirty years in time. With darkness all around, he and his childhood friend Zhang Xiaozhu wrote on the sky with the discarded miner's lamp. Xiaozhu wrote:

You're not stupid, Mom.

Shouyi wrote:

Where are you, Mom?

Mother then descended on the wind, a village woman who had died in the famine of 1960; but now she came to him like a movie star, hair billowing, lips reddened by lipstick, dressed all in white as she took Shouyi's head to her bosom. Wrapping his arms around his lip-glossed mother, he wept. When he came to, he discovered that he was in the hospital, that it was noon on the day following his loss of consciousness, and that Yu Wenjuan, not his mother, was holding his head in her arms, the way she'd have held a newborn child. He realized that he wasn't weeping, she was, her tears and snivel dripping on his face. When she saw he'd regained consciousness, she tried to lay his head down on the pillow and let him drink some of the milk on the night stand, but he wrapped his arms around her.

"Don't move."

So Wenjuan brought his head back into her bosom and continued sitting there. They both went without eating that afternoon. Her body had the smell of new wheat, the same odor he'd detected on her more than a decade before. In his semiconscious state, he swore to himself that as long as he lived, he would not leave Yu Wenjuan.

Understandably, she had qualities he did not like. First off, she was too stiff, like one of those TV news anchorwomen, an example of inviting, but untouchable, cuisine. She looked good during the day, but was inedible at night, and the thought of seeing her pregnant did not make her more desirable. As time passed, it became increasingly easy to forget that she was a member of the opposite sex. Second, when they were in bed, she had a thing about falling asleep with his head in her arms, reminiscent of that time in the hospital back in 1999 during his bout with typhoid. At first he found it touching, but before long, it smacked of a sisterly affectation. Now that they were in their forties, it was one fad they needn't follow. Besides, after an hour or more of having your head in someone's arms, you feel as if you're about to suffocate and fall into a dark abyss. This was taking reticence a bit too far for his taste. Third, Wenjuan was obsessively clean. Every night before bed, she made Shouyi, a boy who had grown up in a southern Shanxi village where they bathed once a year—maybe—wash up, from head to toe. With her, somehow he always felt dirty. And since things tend to reverse course once they reach their extreme, he yearned to see exactly how dirty he could get. Fourth, Shouyi's father had died in 1996, but his mind had gone south long before he died, and he was well beyond speech. A month before he breathed his last, Shouyi and Wenjuan had traveled to Shanxi to see him. That was when the TV station was getting ready to tape the pilot for "Straight Talk." During their ten-day visit, the station phoned to set him up for a screen test as host. He rushed back to Beijing, leaving Wenjuan at home to take care of his father. Three weeks later, the old man died, and when Shouyi returned for the funeral, his cousin, Black Brick, told him in private that although this sister-in-law of his was always smiling, deep down she was a sinister woman. After you left, he told Shouyi, and not long before your father died, he tried to tell her something, but she just sat on the bed, caught up in her own thoughts, ignoring him. In the end, he left no last words. But now his father was dead, and Shouyi had a funeral to arrange, so he let the matter drop. Besides, he thought, what could a doddering old man leave behind that had any meaning? After the funeral, on the train ride back to Beijing, Wenjuan told him that his father had turned weird just before he died, that he'd grabbed her hand while she sat on the bed. After not getting angry over Black Brick's revelation that Wenjuan had ignored his father, he listened to her explain what had actually happened, and he blew up. Not because she'd felt the need to tell him, but because this reality forced him to come to grips with yet another reality: the reason his father had been so taciturn, someone who seldom spoke, was that after 1960, when Shouyi's mother had died of starvation, everyone in the family, including the adult Yan Shouyi, had neglected to try to find his father another woman. The family had let his father down, and he held himself responsible, at least in part. But none of these issues had ever been open to discussion in the calm seas of a decade of marriage.

Yan Shouyi told Fei Mo to wait in the car while he ran upstairs. When he reached his flat, he stopped, took a deep breath to calm himself, opened the door, and strolled in. He had left his cell phone on the shoe cupboard on his way out the door, but it wasn't there now. His heart skipped a beat. He walked into the living room, where Wenjuan was practicing *qigong* to music on the stereo. The sight returned his heartbeat to normal.

Her eyes closed, Yu Wenjuan asked:

"What are doing back so soon?"

"I forgot some papers."

He went over to the coffee table and riffled through some documents. Then, papers in hand, he checked his pockets and said, as if it were an afterthought:

"Oh, and I also forgot my cell phone."

He picked the phone up off the sofa near where Wenjuan was standing.

"You had three calls a while ago," she said. "One from the station to get you moving, since the audience was already filing in.

One from a reporter who wants to interview you. And one from a woman called Wu Yue."

"Got it," he said as he walked to the door.

Now her eyes were open. "Who is she? She hadn't expected me to pick up the phone. What's she to you to find it OK to talk like she did?"

Another skipped heartbeat, but Shouyi forced himself to answer calmly:

"Oh, her. She works for a publishing house. She's always badgering me to write my autobiography. She studied with Zhang Xiaoquan. She always talks like that."

Zhang Xiaoquan had been one of Yan Shouyi's college classmates. This sort of thing had happened before. Anytime he was involved with something or someone he had trouble explaining away, all he had to do was mention the name of a friend to bring an end to Wenjuan's questions. He opened the door and left the flat.

If only he'd known that this time things would be different.

3

Yan Shouyi had hosted "Straight Talk" for seven years. Hosting a talk show for seven long years was enough to talk anyone out. It was like being married to the same person for that long. The first few shows are the beginning of the relationship, a time of uncontrolled passion. Your knees knock and your voice quivers during your early days on stage, and you can be talking one minute when your brain suddenly freezes up and nothing comes out. A year later, you and your audience have gotten to know one another, and you handle things like old pros—no major highs and no disastrous lows, sort of like riding a horse on a vast grassy steppe. Now seven years have passed, the horse has aged and the people are older; the passion has been worn down by the grassy steppe. Letting the horse out to graze has become a job. You stand on the set, mike in hand, like an actor playing the role of the former you. Just like life itself. But this is not the key issue, for there is a difference between this role-playing and the daily life of a married couple. Playing oneself in real life is a waste of time, since your opposite number will know it's all an act. In front of the camera, you might be bored stiff, yet the national audience feels energized, sensing that you are actually quite passionate. There's a sense of mutual familiarity. People might happily welcome the sight of a familiar child on a train station platform and are happy with the child next door; but they have a built-in aversion to strangers. You might lack passion as you glide across the floor, but people happily praise your dancing skills; yet if you try to change, they will feel an initial reluctance. *Is that still him? How come the neighbor's child has suddenly turned weird? Why run around in circles in the wilderness? You can't find any gold there.* In the past, Yan Shouyi had reached a tacit agreement with his viewers: We'll chill out together, neither of us moving, like a bored, middle-aged couple. What angered him was not that China's masses took a pass on seeking improvement, but that he was incapable of setting a fire under them. This truth was captured in something people teased him with:

"Your mouth isn't yours alone, it belongs to all the people of China."

That was why he said as little as possible when he wasn't in front of the camera. It was also an unspoken reason why he and Wenjuan had so little to say to one another. The people of China had ruined things for Yan Shouyi. Day in and day out he played himself on TV, which is why he was unwilling to do the same off-camera.

Li Liang, a station VP, was the man who, seven years earlier, had discovered Yan Shouyi and made him host of the show. What had appealed to him was not Yan's face, which in profile was sort of flat, nor was it his mouth or his gift for gab. Rather, it was the look of innocence on his face when he spoke. For "Straight Talk" we'll let a paragon of innocence supply the chatter, he decided. At the time, the hosts of all the station's other shows looked like news anchormen. In hiring Yan Shouyi, Li Liang prevailed over the other decision makers. But six months later, he himself was arrested over the financing of a certain evening show. In the public eye, Li had been a man of inner strength, and he'd played the part to perfection. But once the handcuffs were on, the man behind the pose showed up, and there was an outpouring of confessions: he'd been in financial trouble for more than a decade, during which time he'd embezzled funds, to the tune of a couple of million; the next time he made the papers was when he was sent off to prison. This surprised no one more than Yan Shouyi. It was not that the man was an embezzler, or that the curtain had come down on his performance, but that anyone that smart could actually get caught with his hand in the till. Yan would have liked to pay the man a visit in prison, but the fact that his face was so well known made that too risky.

Having retrieved his cell phone, Shouyi rushed to the station. He and Fei Mo were already half-an-hour late, and the taping was to begin in front of an audience that was starting to become restless. One woman was trying to manage a child who was loudly demanding to go to the toilet while the studio orchestra played an easy-listening number to fill in for Yan's absence. Cameras were swinging from side to side in an attempt to locate the best angle. After a quick stop for makeup, Yan slipped into the checkered sportcoat that was his trademark and walked onto the set; the spotlights went up and he bowed deeply to the audience.

"Forgive me, folks, for being late today. Traffic, you know. But that's not the only reason. I ran into one of the other hosts. I won't give you her name, but she stopped me to have a heart-to-heart, and I let the time get away from me. I just wanted you to know my side of the story, so please don't go spreading rumors after today's taping."

Not a bad performance. The audience laughed, and peace returned to the set.

"I know that many of you are here for the first time, my friends, and I need to explain something to you before we begin taping. Obviously, it's still daytime out there, but I'll be talking about 'tonight,' since that's when the show is aired. All I ask is that you not laugh when I turn day into night."

More laughter from the audience, which swept the annoyance of a moment before out the door. The people relaxed, body and soul. This was Yan Shouyi's stock warm up, and he was sick of it. And yet, each time he warmed up an audience that was hearing it for the first time, they rewarded him with boisterous approval. This is where things got a bit awkward with his audience, but then the red camera lights came on, and it was time to start the show:

"Good evening, this is 'Straight Talk.' I'm Yan Shouyi. The topic for tonight's show is 'When Does an Itch Occur in a Marriage.' The program was created by Xiao Ma, a college graduate who has just joined our staff. She's not married, by the way."

More laughter. Yan Shouyi was sick of this tactic of drawing laughter at someone else's expense, but it always produced results.

"Before we begin, for all of you in the audience and at home in front of your TV sets, I want to own up to a misstatement of mine during the show 'Things We Didn't Invent.' I said that the steam engine was invented by Newton. Our idea man, Professor Fei Mo, is on closer terms with a Mr. Watt, and he tells me that Mr. Newton was not the inventor of the steam engine. Well, I phoned Newton, who told me that the steam engine was a pretty ordinary invention, certainly not in the same league as the discovery of gravity. But it does appear that I was wrong, and I want to express my profound apologies to all my viewers."

Yan bowed deeply to the camera. Applause and laughter followed.

All the time Yan was hosting the show, Fei Mo and the other members of the "Straight Talk" team were watching on a bank of monitors in the control room. When Yan Shouyi mentioned Fei Mo and said that he'd phoned Newton, they all laughed and turned to look at Fei Mo. He was frowning.

"He's stealing someone else's material instead of coming up with his own!"

"Whose material?" Little Ma, of the writing team, asked.

"Someone named Old Cui. Now *his* mouth is a national treasure. Thousands of TV personalities have patterned themselves after him, though they all come up short."

His anger was building:

"How come they're all content with surface similarities instead of trying to master one's essence?"

"When does an itch occur in a marriage," Yan Shouyi was saying. "How many years? Three? Five? The popular saying has it as the seven-year itch. I've been married ten years, which means I'm well past that, but I've been hosting this show for seven years. How many in the audience have been married more than seven years?"

A climactic moment, as several hands shot into the air. Yan took his audience head-on.

"Apparently, the survival rate is still pretty high."

The audience laughed. Again, Fei Mo frowned.

"He's distracted. His face may not show it, but there's something on his mind."

"Why can't I see that?" Little Ma asked.

Fei Mo patted her on the shoulder.

"Maybe because you're not married."

4

The incident involving Li Liang prompted the TV station to initiate training classes for hosts and show producers. At first, these sessions dealt only with politics, the law, and ethics, all under the supervision of Li Liang's replacement as VP for Administration, an overzealous new appointee who added performance to the list of subjects treated. An end-of-the-year assessment of all four areas was announced. There had already been three sessions on politics, the law, and ethics, and today's session was to be the first devoted to professional training. After hosting the show that morning, Yan Shouyi joined other hosts in the afternoon as they hurried over to the Academy of Dramatic Arts, like students for a class on "lines." The session was being held in a tiered lecture hall. Half the fold-down chairs were broken, and the tabletops were peeling, their surfaces covered with obscene graffiti. The walls were also peeling, like diseased, flaky skin. The ground-floor hall was in the shade all day long, which made it seem especially cold and dirty. The twenty-one personalities in attendance came from all types of shows. These were people who made their living by talking, or, more accurately, people who talked without saying a whole lot. Having them attend training sessions was a joke. Day in and day out they talked into a TV camera and, as a result, had become celebrities. But while a celebrity in a crowd is always a celebrity, like a camel amid a herd of goats, now that everyone was a camel, height and girth didn't matter. The sight of the shabby lecture hall carried them back decades to their college days, but that bit of nostalgia was quickly supplanted by grumblings against Li Liang, who had bungled the simple task of embezzlement; some called attention to Li's spinelessness, which had made it necessary for the innocent to share the punishment meted out to the guilty. Walking into that cold lecture hall was like entering prison.

A bell rang, and a twenty-something instructor strode up to the lectern. She had shoulder-length hair, large eyes, a high nose, and a wispy figure, an eye-popping specimen who immediately warmed up the cold lecture hall. But she wore a somber, no-nonsense look, and as she gazed out at her audience she might as well have been seeing an empty lecture hall. To Yan Shouyi, she looked like a news anchorwoman, devoid of emotion. But she appeared to have made an impression on Ma Yong, the "Passion 37" host, who was sitting next to Yan Shouyi. Ma had the face of a pig, with one unbroken brow and triangular eyes. He was so ugly his audience laughed at nearly everything he said. Ma poked Yan and pointed his fat finger at the lectern.

"An ice beauty, that's what she is. Don't see many of those these days."

"Mind your manners. That's our teacher."

But instead of diving into her lecture, the instructor took out an attendance booklet and, like a high school teacher, began calling out names:

"Du Ya'nan."

Du Ya'nan was the host of "Happiness Theater." In front of the camera, whether the show was funny or not, even when there wasn't a titter from the audience, she laughed. But not now.

"Here," she responded simply.

"Wu Daying."

Wu Daying, the host of "Husbands and Wives," was a big, fat fellow. No response.

"Wu Daying!" the instructor repeated emphatically.

A tiny voice responded playfully:

"Didn't make it."

"Who said he could skip class?"

Whoever it was spoke up for Wu again:

"Besides hosting 'Husbands and Wives,' he does comic performances all over town. He doesn't have time for stuff like this."

Obviously annoyed, the instructor started to say something, but thought better of it.

"Xia Danxin," she read on.

Xia anchored the news. Silence followed until someone spoke up: "He's interviewing one of the national leaders."

The others in the hall saw that the respondent was Zheng Baichuan, the host of a sports program known for such misstatements as: "Now that the mid-autumn festival is behind us, a belated happy New Year everyone." Or, "Those interesting tennis shorts the girls are wearing are custom made so they can fit several balls inside. Oh, I see they're short skirts." Laughing at him was a popular pastime among viewers. He was up to his old tricks again, but all the instructor could do was glare at him and read on:

"Ma Yong."

The pig-ugly Ma Yong craned his neck and, like a prankish high-school student, shouted:

"Right here!"

Laughter joined the shout as it reverberated around the hall. The instructor glared at Ma Yong before continuing:

"Li Ping."

Again, Zheng Baichuan responded:

"She doesn't have a taping today, so she should have come. What does that say about the host of an educational program who won't even educate herself?"

This time the instructor displayed no emotion.

"Yan Shouyi."

At that moment, Yan's cell phone began vibrating in his pocket. He'd switched the ringer to vibrate before entering the hall.

"I'm here," he replied anxiously as he took the phone out of his pocket.

The instructor looked up, spotted him, and went on:

"Cui Dapeng."

Old Cui was the host of a children's show, a forty-something woman who wore her hair in tufts behind her ears, like a little girl. In a childish voice, she squeaked:

"Here!"

As she put away the name list, the instructor looked out at the class:

"There were supposed to be twenty-one members of this class, but only eleven of you showed up. The others will be reported for cutting class."

This was greeted with gloating laughter. She glowered and moved on.

"My name is Shen Xue, the instructor for your performance training. Nearly half of your number failed to show up for the first day of class, which is a breach of discipline. But enough about that. I can see by the looks on your faces that you fail to appreciate why you need training. I've watched you people on TV, and it's not my business to critique the content of any of the shows you host. What I do want to say is that none of you are up to standard when you speak your lines. It's a matter of pronunciation and enunciation, the basics of speech. We here at the Academy demand of our actors that when they are on stage, their every word can be heard without a microphone by someone sitting in the last row. Anything less shows a lack of respect for the audience."

"Are you talking about the nineteenth century?" Ma Yong muttered.

Ignoring him, Shen Xue walked up to Yan Shouyi, who was staring at his cell phone. He'd received a text message and was in the midst of answering.

"Yan Shouyi, you know that cell phones are not allowed during class, don't you?"

Hearing someone say something right above his head startled him. Quickly closing his cell phone, he looked up, smiled, and said:

"I was just looking at it, Miss Shen, not using it."

Shen Xue's gaze swept the members of the class.

"I know that your mouths have made you all famous, and for that you've earned my respect. I wish you'd show me some of the same respect."

Yan Shouyi found it necessary to speak up:

"Miss Shen, no one here disrespects you. But shouldn't you get on with the class? It'll soon be time to leave."

Her earnest reaction to that comment surprised him.

"Just what do you mean by that?"

Stammering slightly, he replied:

"I, I didn't mean anything. But half the class time has been wasted by all their nonsense. I didn't say anything, so why pick on me?"

With that, he lowered his head and continued writing the instant message. Shen Xue surprised him by angrily reaching down, snatching the phone out of his hand, and flinging it out the window. Fortunately, it landed on soft grass.

"Now you people listen to me. This is an educational academy, not one of your TV stations!"

Yan Shouyi was floored and angered by what she'd done. He jumped to his feet and pointed a finger at the window.

"I'm a college graduate, Miss Shen, and I think you should go outside and retrieve my phone.

Everyone sucked in their breath. The standoff lasted only about a minute, before Shen Xue turned and walked outside. She returned a minute later with Yan Shouyi's cell phone, which she banged down on his desk. She pointed to the door.

"From now on, if you're in class, I'll walk out!"

Tears welled up in her eyes, and he realized that this had turned serious. The other hosts felt that he had gone a bit too far. Zheng Baiquan, Ma Yong, and Cui Dapeng tried to smooth things over.

"Don't be angry, Miss Shen. Being angry at Yan Shouyi is a waste of time."

"Our Little Yan here was born in the year of the dog and can't take a joke. He's got a short fuse."

Cui Dapeng pushed Yan up to the blackboard.

"Hurry up, write an apology."

Yan Shouyi knew he needed to ease Shen out of her predicament, or he'd be seen as incredibly petty. Besides, he was anxious to respond to the text message he'd received, which this morning's "she-devil" had sent. So he picked up a piece of chalk and wrote on the blackboard:

> *Miss Shen, I was wrong. When I left the house this morning, my mother said I could goof off with the other kids, but not with my teacher, or I might not pass the test. But I forgot her warning when I acted up.*

He made a point of writing in a sloppy hand, like a grade-schooler. That got a laugh. Even Shen Xue stopped sobbing and laughed.

"Yan Shouyi, you're a bad boy!"

5

A culvert runs alongside Fifth Ring Road. It in turn is bordered by a secluded stand of poplars fronting a little stream, from which steamy mist rises tenaciously into the air as darkness settles. Yan Shouyi's car lay nestled amid the trees, its outline blurred by the mist. Cars and trucks, their headlights on, were coming and going on nearby Fifth Ring Road, turning the expressway into a stream of a different sort.

Yan Shouyi was in his car, but he was not behaving himself; nor was the woman with him, Wu Yue. She was not a pretty woman, with her boyish haircut and several freckles to the left of her mouth, but she had a terrific figure: narrow waist, shapely backside, and breasts that had the feel of basketballs. Wu Yue favored short jackets in winter, and when she stretched, a line of fair skin peeked out from under the hem. But it was her slitted eyes that truly captivated men, hooded and mysterious, and on the rare occasion when she opened them wide, she ripped men's souls right out of their bodies. She reminded Yan of Lü Guihua, way back in 1969. And it was the fifth lunar month—*wuyue*—which sounded exactly like her name, a time back in Shanxi when apricots were in season.

Yan Shouyi and Wu Yue had met on Lushan the previous summer during the taping of a "Straight Talk" program called "Conferences." During China's twentieth century revolutionary period, including the Maoist era, more conferences had taken place on Lushan than anywhere else in the country. These gatherings had produced stirring revolutionary movements and presaged the glint of daggers and the flash of swords, which in turn made it a natural setting for the TV program. Wu Yue was an editor at Panda Publishers, which was holding its annual meeting on Lushan at the time, and since Editorial Director Big Duan of "Straight Talk" and the director of Panda Publishers, a man surnamed He, had been college classmates, the two groups took their meals together in the guesthouse. Given Shouyi's celebrity, publishing house employees sat down to chat or have their picture taken with him, turning the meals into occasions of lighthearted banter. Director He clicked his tongue and said:

"No one would believe us if we told them about tonight."

"Why's that?" Yan Shouyi asked.

"We're having dinner with Yan Shouyi!"

He sighed and continued:

"Who'd have thought that one of the country's great talkers could be so easy to talk to?"

Shouyi knew sarcasm when he heard it. But he'd been drinking heavily, so he just rubbed his head and said lightly:

"I'm just a common, ordinary man."

To his surprise, Wu Yue, who was sitting across from him, said coldly:

"What else could you be?"

She took a breath and went on:

"Yan Shouyi, I wonder if you're aware that your fame isn't worth as much as you think it is?"

That took everyone's breath away. They turned to gaze at Wu Yue, who stared at Yan Shouyi and explained herself:

"You owe your fame to the TV camera. When you're not in front of it, you're nobody!"

It was an awkward moment, and sobering to Yan Shouyi. Not once throughout the meal had he given a second look to Wu Yue, who in turn had made no attempt to chat or have her picture taken with him. But now he noticed her hooded eyes, and each time she opened them, it felt as if a sword had been buried in his chest. Her words had a sharp edge, and she clearly intended to shock him, but he had to admit there was truth in what she said. He raised his glass.

"Thanks for reminding me of that and for keeping me from getting a big head. Here's to you!"

Director He, sensing that the mood around the table had lightened, said:

"Mr. Yan isn't the only one who owes his fame to the TV camera. People today all know the identities of the party and national leaders. But back in the Qing dynasty, the emperor could have gone out in public and an onion peddler wouldn't have known who he was. Drink up!"

Yan Shouyi drank more than usual that night. After dinner, everyone went for a moonlight stroll around Lushan's Ruqin Lake. Water cascaded down from every moonlit cliff and crag. A slightly tipsy Wu Yue and Yan Shouyi fell behind the others; emboldened by their diminished sobriety, they held hands. Then she stretched, revealing a line of fair midriff skin, even paler than the moonlight.

That is where he laid his hand; she doubled over and giggled. Then she put her face up close to his and said:

"You'd like to have sex with me, wouldn't you?"

That sobered Yan up in a hurry. He had strayed before, but his affairs normally unfolded slowly, like gradually turning on a tap. This was the first time he'd experienced a flash flood. He quickly pulled his hand back. Having unsettled him like that, she doubled over and giggled again. But then, without warning, she touched his face.

"I'm in room 102."

With that, she left him and ran to catch up with the others.

After midnight that night, Yan came downstairs from the third floor and went into 102. My god, breasts the size of basketballs, and such moans of passion! They both reached orgasm. Then there was her body temperature: she felt at least two degrees warmer than other people and seemed to melt wherever and whenever he touched her. Something gossamer-like rose from her forehead, a sort of antenna to send and receive signals. For the first time in his life, Yan Shouyi knew how it felt to have his thirst absolutely quenched; that included his relations with Yu Wenjuan and every other woman he'd known. In an instant, past sex was relegated to a boring exercise. This time, his thirst was quenched when, from start to finish, she filled the room with a litany of filthy language, and inspired Shouyi to respond with a chaotic stream of dirty talk that, for the first time, emerged from a hidden spot inside him. They kept at it from two till six in the morning. Not just their bodies and not just their mouths. Obviously, the thirst of their bodies was quenched; at the same time, the dirty talk seemed to cleanse their innards. All that filth made them feel as if they had shed dirty attire and changed into fresh clothing that cleansed them. The darkness retreated and was replaced by the bright light of dawn. Now Yan Shouyi understood the function of dirty talk, that through it a man was capable of being reborn and having his soul purified. It was a disinfectant.

Later that morning, Shouyi was unsteady on his feet and spoke somewhat incoherently during the taping in the Meilu Guesthouse. Big Duan stopped the taping.

"Are you not feeling well?"

"I'm a little hung over, that's all. Let's put this off till the afternoon."

He wasn't himself for a couple of weeks after returning to Beijing, as if life held him in a chokehold. In bed with his wife one night, out came the dirty talk. Wenjuan stopped him and asked guardedly:

"Shouyi, since when did you start talking like that?"

That snapped him back to the real world, and he started over, this time in silence. That was when the fear over what had happened on Lushan finally set in. Not because of his relationship with his wife, but because he wasn't sure what to do about Wu Yue. Past affairs had shown him that climbing into bed was easy, getting out was hard. Not because the woman made it hard for him, but because he couldn't control himself. Vices and debauchery were too great a temptation; the more craven the vice and the more serious the debauchery, the greater the temptation. But Shouyi wanted to keep his affairs within bounds and not let them influence other aspects of his life, and he certainly didn't want them to lead to a divorce from Wenjuan. Reality and a momentary loss of moral equilibrium are separate things. You cannot ingest disinfectants on a daily basis. If you languish in the dark for a long time, and the light is late in coming, the blackness can swallow you up. In the past, when one of his affairs ended, he'd turn off his cell phone for a week out of concern that the woman would try to contact him. He'd been there before. A girl from the Broadcast Academy had once told him she was pregnant and threatened to kill herself, making it necessary for him to enlist the services of a college friend, Zhang Xiaoquan, to put the girl through a week of political indoctrination. He had been on pins and needles that week. But he'd misread Wu Yue. He turned his phone on after a week, and there had been no calls from her. A month passed, and he could barely contain himself, as he recalled that night on Lushan and was reminded of the thirst-quenching, disinfectant coupling. He phoned her. But she'd returned to the real world before him. Sounding puzzled, she asked:

"What is it? I'm busy."

"Oh, nothing, I just wanted to say hello."

"Well, you've done that. Anything else?"

Yan Shouyi blurted out the truth:

"I'd like to see you."

So they saw each other again, and again their thirst was quenched, as it had been on Lushan, but even more fully, if truth be told. After that, they needed no invitation to get together. And yet each meeting increased his fears: experience told him that after a month or so, the woman would come up with demands. Surprisingly, even after six months, Wu Yue had asked for nothing, and he breathed a sigh of relief. Yet even that generated feelings of exasperation. So in the afterglow of one coupling, he could not keep from sounding her out:

"What would you call what we're doing?"

She gave him a puzzled look.

"You eat when you're hungry and you drink when you're thirsty."

Yan studied the look on her face, and she didn't look like she was playing hard to get, so he let the matter drop. They went on as before.

Today, however, there was a difference. Wu Yue had phoned him the night before to say she'd been seeing another man and that they were planning to get married. She wanted to see Yan one last time before she tied the knot. The news hit him in the pit of his stomach.

"When did you meet this guy? How come I didn't know about it?"

"Since when do I need your permission to see someone? Who do you think you are?"

Embarrassed, he replied:

"That's not what I meant. What I'm saying is, why the rush to get married?"

He was jealous, and he knew it. But he couldn't let her know. He'd always been afraid that the affair would go public. That hadn't happened, and now he was actually feeling a sense of loss. So they'd agreed to meet that night. Then he'd left his cell phone at home and was forced to rush back anxiously to retrieve it. Who could have predicted that Wu Yue would choose that time to call, and that Yu Wenjuan would answer? Lucky for him, his quick wits came to his rescue. Once he was out of the house, he called Wu Yue, who told him not to come to her dorm room, where they usually met. Her mother, she said, had arrived that morning from Shenyang and was staying with her. She told him to think up another place. No problem, he said, but after trying all day, he still hadn't come up with a place. A hotel would have been the ideal spot for anyone but Yan Shouyi, with his recognizable face. Someone was sure to spot him.

During the afternoon speech class at the Drama Academy, it was Wu Yue who had sent the text message to ask where they were supposed to meet; not having come up with anything, he had racked his brain while writing out a response. Only to have his phone flung out the window by Miss Shen. Later that evening, after picking up Wu Yue, they still had nowhere to go. So he pulled his car off of Fifth Ring Road and parked beside the stream.

Embracing Wu Yue in the front seat of his car was certainly different from doing so on Lushan or in her dorm room. Shadows flickering against the windows and headlights weaving back and forth on the road had them both on edge. Their movements were restrained, the dirty talk muted. Apparently, concealment was important, but it didn't take Yan long to realize that that was not the biggest problem; no, the knowledge that she had a boyfriend and was going to marry him soon was the cause of the psychological barrier. He wondered what this boyfriend looked like.

While he could have taken her into the back seat, the minute he parked the car in the stand of trees, he took her in his arms and kissed her. One kiss led to another, and he started to get aroused. His kisses moved from her lips to her face and then to her ear, as his hand went under her blouse to cup one of her basketball breasts. When his lips reached the lobe of her ear, he abruptly jerked his head back.

"What's that? It's bitter!"

"It's perfume, silly."

She brought his head back and buried her tongue in his mouth, as a police car drove out from the stand of trees, lights flashing, trying to merge with the traffic on Fifth Ring Road. As it swerved toward the road, its headlights fell on the windshield of the parked car and lit up the faces of Yan Shouyi and Wu Yue. It didn't stop, but he began to squirm. He sat up straight and began tucking his shirt into his pants.

"I'm not in the mood. Let's make it another day."

He hadn't expected her to be so horny. She grabbed his hand, pulled it down between her legs, and, as always, laid her face against his back; taking hold of his collar, she started in with the dirty talk and bit him on the shoulder.

"You big baby, what are you afraid of? Look at me, I'm not afraid."

"Ouch!" he cried out in pain, and pushed her head back.

"Be a good girl, no chewing."

Wu Yue, in no mood to stop, was panting.

"OK, no chewing, just screwing."

Yan Shouyi's cell phone rang. He sneaked a look at the digital read-out. It was Yu Wenjuan. After getting Wu Yue to stop, he flipped open his phone.

"Where are you?" his wife asked. "Aren't you coming home for dinner?"

Yan's heart was pounding. Busy all day and with plans for the night, he'd forgotten to call home. As calmly as he could manage, he said:

"Not tonight. I spent the afternoon at the Drama Academy, so the planning session was moved to tonight."

He heard the hesitant note in Wenjuan's voice.

"Planning session? It sounds like you're outside. I can hear cars."

Yan Shouyi replied casually:

"Fei Mo and I are looking for a restaurant, and we have to be outside to do that, don't we?"

"Somebody's breathing hard."

"We didn't take a car. Fei Mo and I were having a footrace."

Yu Wenjuan hung up. Wu Yue pulled Shouyi back to her.

"We're doing it tonight, and that's that. You won't see me again after I'm married."

The comment hit Yan Shouyi where he lived. He started the engine.

"Let's go somewhere."

Following the tree-lined road, he drove to a little village in the suburbs. To the accompaniment of barking dogs, he and Wu Yue spent two rollicking hours in the back seat of the car.

Doing it in the car was more thirst-quenching, even more of a disinfectant than doing it in bed. And with no interruption, since, as a precaution against outside interference, he had turned off his cell phone before they started.

How could he have known that Wenjuan would find out about

his affair with Wu Yue precisely because he'd turned off his phone?
Trouble was on the way.

6

To be fair, turning off the phone was not the only cause of
the trouble. It all began with Black Brick, Shouyi's cousin back
home, who placed a phone call to the Yan home. Shouyi would
later learn that when Wenjuan called while he and Wu Yue were
parked alongside the stream and asked if he was coming home
for dinner, even though his voice sounded strange, she suspected
nothing, assuming that a winter chill was the cause, and that the
panting was a result of running to keep warm. She had planned a
meal with four dishes that night: Nanjing salted duck, stewed leg
of lamb, pork with bamboo shoots, and pan-fried bean sprouts,
two of his favorites and two of hers. When she learned that
Shouyi wouldn't be home for dinner, she decided against the
pork and the bean sprouts, and settled on a bowl of rice gruel
and some duck. When that didn't seem quite enough, she made
a shrimp and seaweed soup. After eating, she did some *qigong*
breathing exercises. Twice a day, once in the morning and once
in the evening, forty minutes a session. After the *qigong,* she
filled a basin with hot water and carried it over to the sofa to soak
her feet, another nightly ritual, twelve months a year, adding hot
water at least once each time. Her husband's favorite comment
when he saw her with her feet in the basin was:

"That's like pulling down your pants to pass wind. A shower
takes care of your feet along with everything else, doesn't it?"

"Washing them is one thing, soaking them is another. I like the
way it feels."

While she was soaking her feet, the telephone on the table
beside the sofa rang. She answered. It was a call from Yan Shouyi's
hometown, a man with a voice so loud it startled her.

"Who's this?" he demanded.

Yu Wenjuan had to laugh at the Shanxi habit of neither identifying oneself nor asking for anyone, opening instead with a demand to know who had picked up the phone.

"Who are you looking for?"

"I want to talk to Yan Shouyi. I'm his cousin. Who are you?"

Wenjuan had met this Black Brick fellow once in Yan Shouyi's home. A man with the appearance of a black pagoda, he had a fondness for drinking, boasting, and screwing things up, which included just about everything he put his hand to.

"Cousin Black Brick, I'm Yu Wenjuan."

Black Brick appeared surprised and delighted by the news.

"Well, hello, Cousin. I guess I dialed the right number. You're just the one I'm looking for. There's something I need to talk to you about."

"What would that be?"

"A fellow from our village everybody calls Cat Face, but whose real name is Lu Guoqing, opened a restaurant in town and bought a new cell phone. I bought the old one from him for three hundred yuan, and I want to know if you think I got a good deal."

Yu Wenjuan laughed out loud.

"That's it? You live in a farming village and spend your days cutting grass on the mountain. What do you need a cell phone for?"

"That's barely the cost of half a pig, and with it I can talk to you and my cousin."

By then Yu Wenjuan had figured it out. In addition to sticking his nose into other people's business, Black Brick was forever looking for small advantages. So not only did he think he'd gotten a bargain in buying a cell phone for three hundred yuan, but the phone now made it possible for him to stay in touch with Yan Shouyi. Prior to that, after the summer harvest had been taken in and it was time for the fall planting, time to buy seeds and fertilizer, he was forced to write a letter in which, while he wouldn't come right out and say it, he'd ask for money. But now he had a cell phone, and it was no longer necessary to write. Not quite prepared to lay this all out in the open, she said:

"Besides the cost of the phone, you have to pay for your calls. Doesn't that concern you?"

"Hah. The most one of those calls can cost is two yuan, but I'd need to lay out two hundred to come to Beijing to see you two. Besides, I'm not buying the phone for myself, I'm buying it for our grandmother. Just yesterday she was grumbling about how she missed her grandson off in Beijing. That really got to me. I'm here taking care of you day in and day out, I told her, but you hardly notice, because you're so busy thinking about that worthless crowd in Beijing. I ask you, Cousin, am I right or aren't I?"

Yu Wenjuan couldn't help noticing how slyly he'd flown Grandmother's flag to justify his purchase of a cell phone. But she laughed lightly and said:

"You're right. You're not the worthless one, Shouyi is."

"Call him to the phone so he can say hello to Granny. I told her I now have the means to speak to her grandson in Beijing, but she doesn't believe me."

"He's at a meeting. Call him on his cell phone."

After hanging up, Wenjuan added some hot water to the basin in which her feet were soaking. Not two minutes later, the phone rang. Black Brick again.

"His cell phone isn't working. What's going on?"

"It's working. I called him on it before dinner."

"Let's get moving. These phone calls will start costing real money before long."

Yu Wenjuan laughed again.

"You hang up. I'll have him call you."

"Do you have my number?"

By then Yu Wenjuan had unconsciously switched to the Shanxi dialect.

"It shows here on my telephone."

Yu Wenjuan hung up, then dialed Shouyi's number. At that moment, he and Wu Yue were enveloped in a chorus of barking dogs. His voice message said:

We're sorry, but the party at this number has turned his phone off.

Nothing unusual there, since he habitually turned off his phone in meetings. If this had been only about Black Brick, Wenjuan wouldn't have given it a second thought. But since Shouyi's cousin had said that his grandmother wanted to talk to him, she decided to try something else. This grandmother had made quite an impression on Wenjuan during her several trips to Shanxi. Though she was illiterate, she was a wise and principled woman. They had no sooner met than she'd asked:

"How does Shouyi treat you? If he ever mistreats you, you tell me."

Granted, she'd let her gaze fall to Wenjuan's belly to determine if she was pregnant, but that was common enough, nothing to get upset about. After putting down the phone, Wenjuan thought for a moment, then picked it up again and dialed Fei Mo's number, since Shouyi had told her that he and Fei Mo would be eating together and discussing topics for future shows. She got through to Fei Mo, and that 's when the trouble began. Later on, Fei Mo would say that when he answered his phone, he had just finished eating dinner and was walking the dog. Before going downstairs, he had argued with his wife, Li Yan, who was in the habit of logging on to the Net and striking up a conversation with a bunch of strangers. She would chat up a storm, her face all lit up. Strangers had become her family, her family had become strangers. Their son was off at college in Tianjin, leaving just the two of them at home. Fei Mo had once walked up behind her, wanting to see what she was chatting about, but she had quickly moved over so he couldn't see the screen. Nudging her out of the way, he'd discovered that she was in a chat room talking about romantic relationships.

"I can't believe what I'm seeing, and at your age!"

Upset, Li Yan said:

"You never talk to me. Are you telling me I can't talk to other people either? You're suffocating me!"

Fei Mo shook his head.

"Life is short, time is of the essence. How can you let yourself fall this low?"

On this particular evening, Li Yan logged on without even washing the dinner dishes. Seeing the sink filled with dirty dishes, Fei Mo said angrily:

"Are you so eager to talk to strangers that home means nothing to you anymore?"

With a frown, Li Yan said:

"I wash dishes after every meal. Don't you think you could do it just one night? Am I the only person who lives here?"

Fei Mo opened his mouth to say something, but knew that was a sure way to start an argument. So he swallowed his anger, grabbed his Pekinese dog, and went downstairs to take a walk. Outside, the dog disappointed him. When it spotted another male dog coming its way, it struggled to mount it. The dog's owner, a young woman in leather pants and bright red lipstick, frowned and tugged on her dog's leash.

"Disgusting!"

Fei Mo also tugged on his leash, and kicked his dog.

"Are you blind? He's a male too!"

Thinking there was a hidden meaning in Fei Mo's comment, the young woman glowered at him.

"Disgusting!"

She walked on, dragging her dog behind her, just as Yu Wenjuan got through to Fei Mo.

"Old Fei?" she blurted out. "Where are you?"

Fuming over what had just happened, he failed to recognize the voice.

"Who's this?" he asked. "I'm walking my dog."

On the other end, Yu Wenjuan asked:

"Walking your dog? This is Yu Wenjuan. Where's Yan Shouyi?"

"Yan Shouyi . . ."

Now that his brain was working again, Fei Mo recalled that Yan Shouyi had returned home that morning to get his cell phone, obviously troubled, which meant that something had gone wrong. His brain kicked into high gear as he rushed to Shouyi's aid, first hemming and hawing for a moment.

"I think he had something planned for this evening. Ah, that's right, the CEO of a mobile phone company invited him out to dinner. I think that's what I heard him say after this morning's taping."

To his surprise, his comment was met with silence.

"Did you hear what I said, Wenjuan? What's wrong?"

This time his comment sparked a clipped laugh.

"This morning, you say, a mobile phone company called him before dinner, and he told me he was with you, that the two of you were going over program topics."

She hung up.

Sometime later, Li Yan revealed that Wenjuan told her that when she hung up the phone, she was nearly overcome with rage. For Yan Shouyi to tell such a baldfaced lie meant it had to be something major. So she picked up the phone and started dialing his number, over and over for two solid hours, without getting through. By then the water in her basin was cold. Snapping out of her rage-induced fog, she shivered and lifted her dripping wet feet from the basin, then began walking aimlessly around the room, barefoot, like a headless housefly. When she finally looked down, she saw that the floor was covered with wet footprints, which changed shape as they began to dry, fragmenting the floor. At the sight of all those fragments, she burst into tears.

7

While Yu Wenjuan was crying, Yan Shouyi had just dropped off
Wu Yue and was in his car heading home. Fei Mo later told him
that he'd tried calling him a dozen or more times to warn him of
trouble and give him time to figure out how to deal with it; but
Yan's phone was off. Fei Mo, still holding the leash with the family
dog in tow, could not bear going back up to the apartment, fearful
that Li Yan would know what the phone calls were all about, which
could only complicate matters. So he walked the dog for a full two
hours. Finally, with mounting anger, he kicked the poor animal.

"Stupid!"

Meanwhile, Yan Shouyi was concerned not about his cell
phone, but about how he reeked of perfume. Earlier, when the
dogs were barking, he hadn't noticed the odor. But when Wu Yue
climbed out of the car, the powerful smells of her and her perfume
lingered in the car and on him. He was afraid his wife would smell
it on him when he walked in the door or detect the odor the next
day in the car. He cursed the now absent Wu Yue:

"Stupid!"

So as he drove along, he lowered all four windows, hoping the
wind would sweep both him and the car clean of the perfume, even
though it was the tail end of winter, with biting winds making him
shudder from the cold. He had no choice but to slip on his parka as
he drove, then pull the hood up over his head. One after another,
cars with their windows up sped past, and he watched as a man and
woman in one of them laughed at the bizarre sight. He saw they
were talking about him, and he was pretty sure the woman said:

"Madman!"

The man seemed to be saying:

"What a nutcase!"

From their gestures, it then appeared that they recognized him
just before they sped away. Yan Shouyi was so angry he snapped

open his phone and dialed Wu Yue's number.

"You nutcase, the car and I reek of your perfume. Are you trying to ruin me?"

"Come on back then. My mother moved over to my aunt's house."

"I'm driving with the windows down, and I'm freezing in this wind."

Wu Yue burst out laughing.

"Then you'd better take a spin around Beijing, or maybe drive to Tianjin and back. That'll get rid of the smell."

"Slut! Go get yourself married, and stay the hell out of my life!"

Wu Yue greeted this outburst with more laughter. Yan Shouyi hung up and, as suggested, drove round and round Third Ring Road for half an hour. After his call to Wu Yue, fearing that Yu Wenjuan would call to get him to come home, he turned the phone off again. Once he was confident that neither he nor the car still smelled of perfume, he drove home. But then, as he stepped out of the car, it occurred to him to scroll through the day's incoming calls and purge the readout of Wu Yue's number; he flipped open his phone and did just that. He was about to turn off the phone one last time when on second thought he realized it would look better if he didn't. So he didn't. How was he to know that this decision would ensure that a layer of frost would quickly cover that day's troubling snows?

Yan sensed nothing out of the ordinary when he walked into the flat. The entryway light was on and he could hear the TV in the bedroom; no different from any other night. He self-consciously sniffed his sleeve, and when he detected no trace of perfume, he was relieved enough to confidently change out of his shoes. He had no idea that this was all part of a trap carefully laid by Yu Wenjuan. He walked into the living room just as she came out of the bedroom, barefoot. With a smile she said:

"You're home. How did the planning session go?"

Yan Shouyi began weaving his web of deception:

"Ah, Fei Mo and I wrangled half the night. He's a good guy and all that, but sometimes he can't stop talking."

Yu Wenjuan said, still softly:

"You must be tired."

"I need a shower."

Wenjuan stepped up, put her arms around his neck, and kissed him tenderly on the neck, the cheek, and the lips. This did nothing to put him on his guard, since that was how she greeted him every night. She kissed him before they went to bed, and once they were in bed, she held his head. In the past, this was all in the name of getting pregnant. How could he possibly know that this time she was like a detective hot on someone's trail? As a man with a guilty conscience, he was terrified that she'd detect the lingering odor of Wu Yue's perfume; and yet, it was his guilty conscience that kept him from pushing her away. Suddenly an idea occurred to him. As if recalling something important, he said:

"Oh, that, um, I have to find it!"

He wrenched free of Wenjuan's embrace and ran over to the coffee table, where he searched frantically through a stack of newspapers and magazines. She followed him, stopping to lean against the bedroom doorway; looking straight at Shouyi, she said:

"What are you looking for?"

He muttered as he continued digging through the stack:

"That whatchimacallit, you know, that laser disk. Little Ma has been after me to get it for her, but I keep forgetting."

In a calm, measured voice, Wenjuan said:

"Shouyi, your mouth, it doesn't smell like you tonight."

Whump! An explosion went off in Yan Shouyi's head. He looked up at Wenjuan, only to see the tender look on her face gradually darken. That was the moment he knew that trouble was in the air. But how bad it was, and how he ought to deal with it, he couldn't be sure. So as he bent over the stack of newspapers and magazines, he held out his hands, palms up, and, with a slight stammer, asked her:

"Then, then whose smell is it?"

He could have slapped himself for not rinsing out his mouth while he was airing out the car and his clothing. He thought back to when he and Wu Yue were in the stand of trees, and how he'd taken her earlobe in his mouth and found it to have a bitter taste. It must still have been on his lips, and Yu Wenjuan had detected it. He had to come up with something quick to stall for time. He'd had some bitter melon for dinner? He'd sucked on a throat lozenge that afternoon to soothe his throat? No, neither of those produced this particular smell. His thoughts were interrupted by the ringing of his phone, which he'd decided to leave on. An incoming call. In that quiet of night the ring was unnerving. He was afraid that Wu Yue, assuming he was still driving around town, had decided to call. So, as he tried to suppress a growing sense of terror down deep, he took the phone out of his pocket and, without looking to see who it was, answered in a practiced fit of annoyance:

"Who the hell is this, calling at all hours? Well, I'm not in!"

But before he could turn off the phone, Wenjuan stayed his hand.

"Here, I'll take it."

With that simple sentence, all Shouyi's routes of escape closed. Turning off the phone was not an option, but neither was *not* turning it off. Meanwhile, it kept ringing, and when he saw Wenjuan reach for it, his initial reaction was to draw his hand back. In the end he handed it over to her, but not before taking a quick look at the name of the caller. It was Fei Mo, not Wu Yue. He breathed a sigh of relief, only to realize that a phone call from Fei Mo at this particular moment could be worse than one from Wu Yue. After Wenjuan opened the phone but before she said a word, he heard Fei Mo, panic in his voice:

"So, you finally turned on your phone, did you. Are you still out there enjoying your hanky-panky? I've been trying to get through to tell you that Wenjuan called me two hours ago, asking where you were."

He heard every sentence, every word. Without any response, Wenjuan closed the phone and glared at him.

"Didn't you say you were with Fei Mo all night?"

This was serious, and he knew it. Time to do whatever he could to put things right. Trying his best to look both upset and remorseful, he said:

"That was a lie, I admit it. I wasn't with Fei Mo tonight. One of our financial backers took me to dinner. Then he treated me to a sauna and a massage by a young masseuse. I knew you'd be upset, so I didn't tell you."

At that point, the situation might well have been saved. Wenjuan would indeed have been unhappy to learn that he'd been rubbed down by a young masseuse, and she'd make life miserable for him, for a while. Not that she'd yell at him—she never did that—rather, she'd ignore him for a week or so and not let him touch her. In the past, he'd explained away his extramarital shenanigans with a similar excuse, and after a week of being ignored, he'd gradually worm his way back into her good graces. But then, wouldn't you know it, his phone chirped—an incoming text message. Wenjuan opened it. It was from Wu Yue. A message of concern:

It's cold out. Hurry home. I gave you a hickey in the car, so don't take off your undershirt when you go to bed.

After reading the message, Wenjuan held the phone up so Yan Shouyi could read it. *Whump!* Another cranial explosion. This time it had really hit the fan.

"Shouyi, take off your shirt for me, would you?"

He froze. He couldn't take off his shirt, but he couldn't *not* take it off either.

"Take it off. I want to see."

Yan Shouyi's road had come to an end. He racked his brain for an excuse not to take off his shirt, but none rose to his aid; now she had him. He hesitated for as long as he thought he could before taking off his shirt. More hesitation as he stood there in his undershirt. Seeing Yu Wenjuan wait patiently, he finally took that off and stood before her naked to the waist.

Yan Shouyi was slightly pigeon-chested.

Yu Wenjuan examined his chest carefully. Then she said softly: "Turn around, would you?"

By this time, his mind was a blank, like his first time in front of the camera as host of "Straight Talk" years before. He woodenly turned around. In the light of the lamp, a row of bite marks stood out on his shoulder blade.

Yan Shouyi turned back and saw the tears in Yu Wenjuan's eyes, pooling at first, then slowly running down her cheeks. He wanted to say something, but felt an itch in his nose, and—*ah-choo!*—he sneezed. The chilly air on his bare skin.

Yu Wenjuan draped his shirt around his shoulders and put her arms around him again. His head felt about the same as it had that time he lay in the hospital—totally befogged. Wenjuan, tears still flowing, said with measured calmness:

"Shouyi, when I asked you to take off your shirt, it was as if *I* had stripped naked in front of a crowd."

Then she pushed him away and let her rage take over. The words tore from her mouth like bullets from a machine gun:

"Yan Shouyi, I added it up just now. I've been with you for ten years and three months. I was twenty-six when I married you, now I'm thirty-six. Never once in those ten years did I consider being unfaithful to you, and I never imagined that you would one day be unfaithful to me. I don't know who this Wu Yue is, nor do I care to know. What angers me isn't so much that you've been unfaithful, but that you kept it from me. In your eyes, I'm a fool, a woman without a clue. You know that, don't you? All these years of complaining that you never talked to me, and now I know that's because you had someone on the side. If you thought you and I had nothing to talk about, you could have told me. I never dreamed you had somebody else to talk to. Your whoring doesn't anger me, but the idea that you've picked up with someone else makes me your whore. Don't you know that? Just thinking about what you might be saying about me when you're with that other person is like having a stake driven through my heart..."

Given the fact that Yu Wenjuan had always spoken in slow, measured tones, always prefaced by a smile, this unprecedented change of pace had Yan Shouyi standing there in stunned silence. He opened his mouth, wanting to say something, but after hemming and hawing for a moment, all he could say was:

"That's not it."

Hard to say if he meant he wasn't carrying on with somebody else or that he never talked about Yu Wenjuan when he was with that somebody else, but with that comment, she returned to the Yu Wenjuan of old. Looking him straight in the eye, she said in slow, measured tones:

"Shouyi, you've lost me."

Her comment finished, she smiled.

8

A simple mistake had led to Yan Shouyi's divorce. Calm seas had accompanied him as he left home in the morning; an exploding land mine greeted him when he returned that night.

During all the time he'd been with Yu Wenjuan, he had believed that so long as *he* didn't seek a divorce, they would stay together forever. The idea that one day *she* would do the asking, and with steely determination, had never occurred to him.

"You'd better think it over. Don't be rash. It was only a few times."

Hard to say if he meant only a few times with Wu Yue or if he hadn't stepped out on Yu Wenjuan more than a few times.

"Then let it be my fault, because I'm so fragile. A few times? Once would have been enough to cut out my heart. You're not the reason I want a divorce. It's just that my life is over. You know that, don't you?"

Yan Shouyi stood there in a daze. Wenjuan seemed like a total stranger. Ten years of living together, and he realized he didn't understand her one bit.

Yu Wenjuan, it turned out, was barren. When they emerged from the district office, having completed the divorce formalities, she seemed somewhat unsteady as Yan stared at her back, and he was tempted to catch up to say something. But try as he might, he couldn't come up with a thing.

9

Three months passed.

During that time, Yan Shouyi often phoned Yu Wenjuan. But when she saw it was his number, she refused to answer.

It would be a long time before he heard her voice again.

10

After the speed of trains was increased, the trip from Beijing to Changzhi, which had once taken more than twenty hours, was reduced to a little over ten. Summer had arrived, and when his train reached Hebei Province, he looked out the window and saw peasants bringing in the wheat. A young woman in a flowery kerchief rode her motor scooter up to a young man who was working in the field. She untied a cardboard box from the seat behind her and took out a little pot; she'd brought her husband his lunch. Yan Shouyi saw steam rising from the pot, but was too far away to smell what was inside. Then a gust of wind bent the stalks of wheat like a wave and carried their fragrance to him, it seemed. His heart lurched, as he was reminded of Yu Wenjuan. Back when they were together, they could never find anything to talk about, but now that they had been divorced for six months, there were all sorts of things he'd have liked to say to her. The smell of wheat brought back memories of that time in 1999 when he'd fallen into a feverish sleep, and she'd held his head in her arms; this was the smell her body had given off.

Three days earlier, Shouyi had received a phone call from his cousin Black Brick, telling him that it had rained nonstop for three days, following a particularly dry spring season, and that the surrounding hills were soaking up the water. But the wall around their grandmother's house had begun to crumble under the onslaught of rain, and he'd asked Shouyi what he should do about it.

"Why ask me? Have it repaired."

"That's what I said. But Granny won't let me."

"If she's worried about the expense, I'll wire the money today."

"I'm just calling to let you know what's what. I'm not asking for money."

As it turned out, Yan Shouyi had some free time, since several episodes of "Straight Talk" had been taped, so he told the people at the TV station that he was taking a few days off to go home. Besides taking care of the crumbling wall, he could visit his grandmother for the first time in six months or so. Shouyi's mother had died when he was very young, and his father had been a man of few words and extremely stubborn. His grandmother had raised him, from his days in diapers all the way to manhood. He recalled a time when, as an eight-year-old, he and Lu Guoqing, Jiang Changgen, and Du Tiehuan had climbed a poplar tree to get to a crow's-nest built on the tip of one of the limbs. The other kids had climbed about half way before turning and shinnying back down, but the boastful Yan Shouyi had gone all the way. Just as he was reaching out for the nest, a loud *crack* accompanied the snapping of the branch, and sent him crashing to the ground. His leg was broken. Lu Guoqing and the others took off running, shouting for Shouyi's father, who ran down the mountain, his hoe slung over his shoulder. With one look at Shouyi's leg, he reached down and gave his son a vicious slap.

"I'll be fucked!"

In the end, it was Yan Shouyi's grandmother who carried him piggyback a hundred li down a mountain path to the county town, where a traditional doctor who also treated fractures set the bone and applied medicated salve for fifteen yuan. On the way back to the village, with him in pain, nothing to eat, and no money to buy food, his grandmother, once again carrying Shouyi on her back, had to beg for food.

"Elder brother, look at the boy's leg. Can you spare a piece of cornbread for him?"

At the time his grandmother was sixty-two.

This time Fei Mo was accompanying Shouyi. Freed of courses that semester so he could advise doctoral students, he was a liberated man; he could deal with the students any way he pleased. His wife, Li Yan, who worked at a travel agency, was off leading a tour group to Singapore, Malaysia, and Thailand, leaving him at home alone. But when first asked to come along, Fei Mo had waved Yan Shouyi off.

"Me? Go someplace where even rabbits won't shit? Why would I do that?"

"When we were talking that time, and the topic 'Making a Phone Call' came up, you said you'd like to have met Lü Guihua. Well, now's your chance."

Again Fei Mo had waved him off.

"The Lü Guihua who made the call is thirty years older now. How old does that make her? Fifty? Older? Her waist must be as thick as a water vat. Your 'alluring beauty' existed back then, but there's no reason to see her now."

Yan Shouyi didn't force the issue. But then, the night before, when he was driving along Fourth Ring Road, he received a call from Fei Mo.

"Buy a ticket for me. I'll accompany you to Shanxi tomorrow."

"You had your chance when I invited you. Now, I'm afraid, you're no longer welcome by the good people of Shanxi."

"The only reason I'm going is to visit the grandmother you're always talking about."

That warmed Shouyi's heart, as a true sense of friendship washed over him. Besides, having Fei Mo along meant he wouldn't be bored on the train ride.

And it wasn't just the two of them. Shen Xue, the instructor at the Drama Academy, also came along for the ride. During her first lecture for TV hosts, she and Yan had clashed over his use of a cell phone. He'd then written a self-criticism on the blackboard to head off a disaster. When he first encountered her, she'd been a stickler for discipline. On the first day she'd taken the roll, on the second she'd had the "students" choose a class leader. Owing to his blow-up with her, the other TV hosts had unanimously, and mischievously, chosen him. So after class, Shen Xue had asked him to stay behind to discuss responsibilities: he was to help maintain discipline in class and keep track of their ideological trends. Yan Shouyi's impatience quickly surfaced.

"Miss Shen," he blurted out, "every student in this class is older than you. Their worldviews and attitudes toward life are well established. On the road of life, let them make their own decisions. If we get in the way, we're just asking for trouble."

That brought her up short, and he raised both hands to keep her from blowing up.

"If you want to talk, fine. But somewhere else."

"Like where?"

"I've been invited to dinner tonight. Why don't you come along?"

Shen Xue's eyes widened as she gazed out the window.

"The viewers of this country must have been blind to turn their TV stations over to the likes of you people."

She glanced at him out of the corner of her eye, then doubled over in laughter. He took delight in seeing her shed her schoolmarmish façade and reveal her true nature. Now that he and Yu Wenjuan were no longer married, he'd moved out of the apartment and into a bachelor pad. Hating the idea of being alone in unfamiliar surroundings, he accepted any and all dinner invitations. So that night, Shen Xue joined him for dinner, where he drank too much, owing to all the troubling domestic matters on his mind. After dinner, as he was driving her back to the Drama Academy, he was stopped by the police. He stepped out of the car, and nearly fell flat on his face, shocking the policeman until he realized who he was.

"Mr. Yan," he said with a laugh. "Where have you been, getting drunk like this?"

A cold wind caused the alcohol to rush to his head. As his eyes glazed over, he pointed to Shen Xue.

"With her."

The policeman looked in the window at Shen Xue and directed his anger at her.

"I take it you're his wife. How could you let him drive in his condition?"

The policeman was getting on in age, probably in his fifties, graying at the temples, and Yan Shouyi felt a little sorry for him, having to be out on a cold, windy night. He was either incompetent or had traveled a rough and bumpy road through life. He looked a little like Niu Sanjin, the coal miner at the Number Three Mine in Changzhi more than thirty years before. Shouyi walked up and took the man's arm.

"Don't blame her, my friend, it's my fault. Drinking puts me in a foul mood, but then so does not drinking."

He'd expected this to soften up the old cop, and was surprised when he flicked his hand away, glared at him, and roared:

"Do you really think this is only about moods? I ought to run you in!"

In the end, Yan Shouyi's car was confiscated, forcing him and Shen Xue to take a taxi. At the Drama Academy, he stumbled along trying to stay awake, and she had no choice but to let him sleep it off on her sofa. Much later, she revealed that while they were negotiating the stairs, he'd brushed his lips against her face—maybe by accident, maybe not—for which he'd received a resounding slap. He had no memory of the incident, recalling only that when he woke up the next morning, it felt as if his head were about to explode. He wasn't surprised that he'd spent the night in her flat. But something did surprise him.

"You knew I was drunk last night," he said. "By getting into my car, weren't you afraid you might wind up dying along with me?"

Shen Xue stared at the ceiling.

"So what if I did?"

He felt a stirring in his heart. In the wake of that evening, they went out to dinner two nights a week. The other TV hosts knew that Yan Shouyi and the instructor were dating, and couldn't have been happier. For now that she was involved with Yan, class time was less off-putting. No more roll calls, no more demands for discipline, and no more talk about ideological trends. The class ended two months later, and everyone "passed with distinction." The ecstatic "students" crowded around Shen Xue to have a graduation picture taken with her.

Once the training sessions ended, Yan Shouyi and Shen Xue ate together every night. They still hadn't been to bed, but hugs were the norm when they said good night. As time passed, his view of her underwent a change. At first he'd assumed she was pretty much like Yu Wenjuan or one of the TV newscasters—a fine presentation of an inedible dish. But he actually enjoyed listening to her talk. That isn't to say she was a fount of wisdom; rather, what she said was often so goofy he had to laugh, like the dimwitted serving girl in *Dream of the Red Chamber*—like, but not the same. Some dimwitted people are no fun to be around, but there's something about a goofy person that's endearing. And it dawned on Yan that while goofy talk may appear to be stupid, it often carries wisdom, the silver lining around a cloud. It is what set Shen Xue apart from Yu Wenjuan and Wu Yue, the two women involved in his divorce, in which he thought he'd gotten a raw deal. All along he'd only been looking for a little excitement, something to quench his thirst, a bit of a disinfectant, and he'd never dreamed it would turn out the way it had, with him getting dumped into the mud. The divorce proceedings had made him feel dirty inside, and now he needed to lay things out in the sun to get clean. On the eve of leaving for his hometown, he'd phoned Shen Xue to tell her what he was doing. More or less in jest, he'd said:

"Why not come along? I'd like my grandmother to meet you."

Having meant it as a joke, he was surprised when she replied: "Sure. That way I can see where you grew up."

And so they were traveling together.

Yan Shouyi was aware that Shen Xue and her boyfriend, one of the other teachers at the Drama Academy, had broken up after dating for two years. A colleague of hers, Xiao Su, told Yan that the relationship had ended because the guy didn't like the way she spoke her mind, and that she was on the daffy side, in other words, not worldly enough. Yan Shouyi had to laugh at that. What is it they say, one man's meat is another man's poison? To his way of thinking, the world was big enough to accommodate one daffy performance teacher. Besides, how daffy could she be?

Yan Shouyi, Fei Mo, and Shen Xue booked a sleeping compartment on a local train; the scenery between stations and their conversation kept them in a good mood. Seeming to take to Shen Xue, Fei Mo was especially talkative. Cooling himself with a fan, he talked from Beijing all the way to Shijiazhuang, with anecdotes about every district and county along the way, and when he'd finished with that, he talked about the train they were riding. From there, somehow he moved on to the TV show, telling Shen Xue how making a TV show was much the same as riding a train: The train's interior remained constant, while the scenery outside never stopped changing, which forestalled boredom for the rider; how boring it would be if the train stopped at only one station. Yan Shouyi, who was thinking private thoughts about Yu Wenjuan as he looked out at the passing wheat fields, wasn't paying close attention to what Fei Mo was saying. He knew only that the conversation had moved from the train to talk about their destination, and to the people of Shanxi—how they were tightfisted, prone to jealousy, and provincial. Shen Xue took off her stockings, half knelt alongside Yan Shouyi, and told a joke about a Shanxi man:

"A hopelessly spineless fellow from Shanxi who was always the target of bullies did pushups at home every day. His father said, Son, what are you doing that for? The son replied, I'm building up my chest muscles, like I've seen on TV. The father reached out and boxed his son's ears. You're wasting your time. You'll never be as big as your sister!"

Fei Mo snorted with laughter. Yan Shouyi gave Shen Xue a playful kick. He was about to say something when his cell phone rang. He looked at the read-out: it was Wu Yue. She had planned to get married before his divorce, but it hadn't panned out, not because of the divorce, but because the prospective groom had abruptly taken off for America. With Yan's divorce, the two of them were free to move in together, but he'd lost interest in a long-tem relationship with Wu Yue. It had nothing to do with the fact that he'd met Shen Xue, but was a result of a change in attitude toward Wu Yue. She was the perfect person to slake his sexual thirst, the necessary purging, but the thought of spending the rest of his life with someone like her terrified him. It was not so much a case of "once bitten, twice shy" as it was a concern that all that dirty talk in bed, night after night, would cease to be thirst quenching and could end up poisoning the relationship. You might think that a dish of abalone in a nice restaurant is quite a treat, but have it every night at home, and dinner becomes a fearful meal. By now he was ready for some home-cooked food and a bowl of corn porridge. That was another reason he'd taken up with Shen Xue. He'd recently come to realize that he was a pretty ordinary man, someone who professed love for what he feared the most. A divorced man plays a unique role in society, and since he wasn't interested in marrying Wu Yue, he began to distance himself from her. Besides, he was with Shen Xue now, and didn't want her learning too much about his past. She knew that Wu Yue had played a role in his divorce, but wasn't sure how involved he'd been with her. He'd told her that it had all been a misunderstanding, for he decided that the less a decent young woman knew about the more seamy side of his life, the better. No one else would have believed this line, but Shen Xue did; she even accused Yu Wenjuan of being small-minded. You had to like her for that, and he did. But Wu Yue had no intention of going quietly out of his life. It had been all right for her to keep him at a distance after Lushan, but now he was trying the same thing, and that was not all right. It was sort of like teasing a clam that ignores you until you're ready to leave, and then it clamps down on your finger. She wasn't about to get down on her knees and beg him to marry her, but now that her fiancé had left her, she needed her thirst quenched from time to time, an occasional purging. When you're hungry you eat, she'd said, and when you're thirsty you drink. She wanted things back the way they were; marriage was not something she had on the front burner. But the harder she pushed, the more Yan Shouyi shrank back, afraid of wallowing in the mud again, so when he saw the name Wu Yue on his phone readout, he had no desire to pick it up, especially since Shen Xue was there beside him. But precisely because she was there, not picking up would make it seem as if he had something to hide. So he picked up, hesitantly. An angry Wu Yue exploded into the earpiece:

"What the hell is going on, Yan Shouyi? Why haven't you been answering my calls? What are you hiding for? Afraid I'll bite you or something..."

Knowing she was just getting started, Yan Shouyi decided to put on an act.

"Hello... say something, I can't hear you! Speak up! Can you hear me? We've got a bad connection... I'm on a train, on my way home... hello..."

Wu Yue hung up. Fei Mo pointed his fan at Yan Shouyi.

"A good act," he said. "Maybe you couldn't hear, but I could."

As he closed his phone, Shouyi smiled sheepishly. "A bit of foolishness can cure lots of illnesses," he said.

"If you have nothing to hide, a drink of cold water won't bother you."

Yan took a look over at Shen Xue, then pointed to Fei Mo and said:

"Fei Lao, you're supposed to be the kind one."

Shen Xue, who had no idea what they were talking about, kicked Yan Shouyi with her bare foot.

"Say, Shouyi, when we get to your home, how will you introduce me to your grandmother?"

"You're my teacher. You and Fei Mo, you're both my teachers."

Obviously not liking his answer, she glared at him before moving to the bunk across the way, where she took Fei Mo's arm, shook it, and said:

"I'm a good girl from a good family, Fei Lao, and I don't like to give people ideas. So we'll just tell them I'm *your* girlfriend."

Fei Mo reached out and, with a smile, patted her on the head.

"Well, now, I like the sound of that. But if we're not careful, I'll be in hot water."

11

Bad news greeted Yan Shouyi on his arrival at the village. Du Tiehuan, the childhood friend with whom he'd stolen the melons and raided the crow's nest, had died barely a month before. He'd been fine during Shouyi's last visit, over New Year's; in fact, they'd gone out drinking. But he wasn't around any longer. As a boy, Tiehuan had been skinny as a monkey, but by the time he reached middle age, he'd put on a lot of weight. Never tall to begin with, once he started filling out horizontally, from a distance he took on the look of a medicine ball. He had a booming voice, and he reacted to minor events like a house on fire. A month earlier, he'd taken a load of grain to town on his tractor. The purchasing station was crowded that day, and after he'd sold his load, he drove his tractor over to buy a piglet. When someone tried to stop him from cutting in line, instead of the brake, he stepped down on the gas pedal and, swerving to avoid a donkey cart, crashed into a post. *Wham!*—he was flung into the steering wheel and knocked unconscious. They carried him to the town's hospital, where he came to, rubbed his chest, and said to his wife:

"I'm fine."

Not much later, he said:

"I feel sick. I'm going to throw up."

A half hour later he was dead. His heart had burst, a massive hemorrhage. The news hit Shouyi hard. Fei Mo and Shen Xue had never met Du Tiehuan, but Fei Mo sighed and said:

"Life can be fickle."

"Something like that makes you wonder what the struggle's all about."

But his other childhood friends were still around. Lu Guoqing had a restaurant in town, while Jiang Changgen, true to his simple nature, worked the family farm. He'd married young, and had become a grandfather only the month before. Both childhood friends came to see Shouyi when they heard he'd come back.

That night they stayed up talking until Orion was off in the western sky, and Shouyi realized that their conversation seldom strayed from their childhood; when it did, it went nowhere. When it was time to go to bed, he slept in his grandmother's room, while Fei Mo went home with Lu Guoqing.

"I've got a spare room," Lu said, "but the blanket is dirty—kids, you know."

Fei Mo waved him off.

"People don't wash blankets every day."

Shen Xue slept at Black Brick's house, sharing a room with his wife, while Black Brick spent the night at Jiang Changgen's.

The next morning, Shouyi talked to Black Brick about repairing the wall. Since it would have to be torn down and rebuilt from the ground up, he suggested that they build a new arch over the gate while they were at it. Black Brick calculated the costs:

"The wall: bricks, mortar, sand. The arch: wood, bricks, mortar, sand, nails, and mud. Materials alone will cost thirty six hundred. It'll take eight or nine men three days to do the work, and they'll need three meals a day. Food will cost six hundred. Cigarettes, beer, tea, that's another three hundred. Altogether forty-five hundred. I'll put up two thousand, you put up twenty-five hundred."

Yan Shouyi took five thousand yuan out of his wallet, laid it on the table, and pushed it over to Black Brick.

"What's that for?" Black Brick groused. "If Granny knew, she'd accuse me of taking advantage of you."

"I put up the money, you do the work, and I won't breathe a word to Granny. How's that?"

Black Brick took the money and was about to say something when his hip chirped like a bird, startling Shouyi. Black Brick opened his shirt to reveal a black leather pouch, in which a cell phone was cradled. Shouyi knew it had to be the one Lu Guoqing had gotten rid of several months before. Black Brick unsnapped the pouch, removed the phone, and took the call. It was an old model with a pull-out antenna. Black Brick raised one leg and shouted:

"I'll be fucked, who's this? No time . . . can't talk now . . . waste of money."

Shouyi was puzzled. "Who was that?" he asked.

As he put the phone back into the leather pouch, Black Brick said:

"No one you know."

"It sounded like a woman."

Black Brick turned and looked into the yard, then said softly:

"A girl who works at the public bath in town. A northeasterner . . . won't leave me alone."

"Can't you just ignore her?"

Patting his cell phone, Black Brick sighed and said:

"I never think about it when I don't have it, but I hate to have it and not use it."

Yan Shouyi wasn't sure if he was talking about the cell phone or the girl.

"Don't let your wife know," he said.

Black Brick proudly patted the phone again.

"Her—all she knows is how to slop the pigs. She'd never believe there could be a girl hidden inside this."

Yan Shouyi scratched his head.

Work started in the yard that afternoon with a dozen young village men under Black Brick's supervision. Jiang Changgen was in charge of materials—bricks, mortar, sand, wood, and nails—while Lu Guoqing brought over two cooks from his restaurant. They set up a stove in the yard. The meat, vegetables, steamed buns, and condiments all came from town. The old wall had been built when Yan Shouyi was a child; the arch also dated from his childhood, and both had outlived their usefulness. All it took was a push by several of the men with poles for both the wall to crumble and the arch to topple to the ground. Yan Shouyi's grandmother, who had bound feet and walked with a cane, found all those people running around in her yard, all that activity, even a temporary stove, annoying. Looking away, she said:

"Are you people trying to drive me into my grave?"

But they knew it was the cost that concerned her, so they didn't let her comment bother them. By late afternoon, the men were cleaning up the debris from the wall and gate. Shouyi's grandmother was sitting in an armchair under a date tree, still looking unhappy. Fei Mo tried to make her feel better.

"It won't cost much, and Shouyi can afford it."

The old lady nudged him with her cane.

"He's not building a wall. To him this is just one big prank!"

But then she smiled.

"Our little Stone," she said to Fei Mo, "is always saying that you write what he says on TV. As a child he was always pulling pranks. Since I can't be around him, you watch him for me."

"I've been wanting to visit you for a long time," Fei Mo said, "but he refused to bring me along. He's always saying how you raised him since he lost his mother when he was small, and how you had to sell a pair of bracelets to put him through school."

The old lady smiled.

"That was my mistake. Now he's flown far away, and I don't get to see him much."

"You can see him on TV."

The old lady looked off to the side.

"I don't understand anything he says up there. He's a different boy."

Abruptly, she turned and pointed at Fei Mo.

"Young man, you don't look very healthy."

Pointing to his chest, Fei Mo said:

"Grandma, I feel bad here some of the time."

Out in the yard, Shen Xue was excitedly helping the cooks around a big-bellied, coal-burning stove with a set of bellows to keep the fire blazing. Wearing an apron and rolling up her sleeves, she chopped the vegetables and meat. She also personally cooked up a dish of braised pork. But when she lifted the wok off the stove, she accidentally knocked a bowl of pork stock onto the ground. Yan Shouyi ran over and yelled at her:

"I'll be fucked, the more you help, the worse things are. Go somewhere and make yourself useful!"

One of the cooks Lu Guoqing had brought from town was fat; the other was skinny. The fat one held Yan Shouyi back.

"Let her stay, elder brother. I like the smell."

Pleased, and obviously proud of herself, Shen Xue said:

"Hear that? The chef likes the way my food smells."

The skinny cook said:

"He doesn't mean he likes the smell of your food. He likes the way *you* smell. What are you wearing?"

They all laughed.

Once the food was ready, Shen Xue scooped boiling water into a basin and said to Fei Mo:

"Fei Lao, time to eat."

Then she turned to the men who were cleaning up the debris and, in the local Shanxi dialect, shouted:

"Wash up—the water's hot!"

The night before, when they arrived at the Changzhi station, a row of water basins had greeted them as they exited the platform; greasy towels hung at the sides of the basins. Local women stood in front and shouted in the local dialect:

"Wash up—the water's hot!"

The wash-ups cost fifty fen. Shen Xue was now standing in the middle of the yard shouting in a passable Shanxi dialect. The men laughed and stopped work, ready to wash up and eat. The old woman joined in the laughter as Fei Mo helped her out of her armchair, and as her gaze swept across the spacious compound, she muttered:

"All this bother. I'm ninety-four. I wonder how many more days I've got."

Tying her apron around her, Shen Xue scooted up next to the old woman and said, "Granny, you look more like forty-nine to me."

Everyone in the yard laughed again. Fei Mo rapped Shen Xue on the head with his closed fan.

"You've got a bit to learn about ass-kissing."

An incident occurred after they'd finished eating. Du Tiehuan's eldest son had come to help out, and when everyone was about to leave, he decided to take the lumber from the razed gate home to build a pigpen. In a careless moment, he gashed his face with one of the nails, barely missing his eye; the wound bled freely. Shen Xue rushed inside and dug through one of her bags for a bandage. Then, taking the injured youngster in her arms, she placed the bandage over the wound. The first attempt was wide of the mark, so she peeled it off and tried again. Du's son hadn't complained when he hurt himself and was bleeding profusely, but now that he was standing up against Shen Xue, with her perfumed, feminine fragrance, his chest began to heave; he was getting aroused. When Yan Shouyi saw how the aroused youngster's forehead was beaded with sweat, he thought back to his own youth, when sharp weeds had poked him in the face and made it bleed, and Lü Guihua had held him up close. He had to laugh.

12

Work began on the new wall on the second day, now that the debris had been cleared away: first, a foundation was laid with water, cement, mortar, and sand. Meanwhile, a carpenter began building the arch over the gate. Black Brick acted as foreman for all the work, leaving nothing for Yan Shouyi to do but take Fei Mo out back to stroll among the foothills, where farmers were irrigating hillside fields planted with wheat. Wheat crops in Hebei had already been harvested, while the local grain was not yet fully mature. The crops here were one season behind. When the farmers saw the two of them approaching, they straightened up from their irrigation work to greet them. Spring corn was by then a foot high. After passing by the fields, they walked up to an abandoned brick kiln. From there the village spread out beneath them; they could see Yan's compound, where the figures of men building the wall and the arch were moving busily back and forth. Undergrowth was a nesting place for mosquitoes, which kept Fei Mo busy shooing them away with his fan. Yan's cell phone rang; it was Wu Yue again. Since he'd put on an act with her on the train, he couldn't do that again, so he took the call. She was livid, and he mollified her as best he could:

"I wasn't putting on an act . . . that's right, I'm here with her . . . you knew damned well what I was doing, so why the harassment? What? You've hit the nail on the head. I am serious about turning over a new leaf . . ."

The conversation was intermittent at best, but as soon as Yan Shouyi hung up, Fei Mo, who was still swatting mosquitoes, said:

"Wu Yue, right?"

Yan Shouyi nodded.

"I used to think that Yu Wenjuan was the only person you hurt. But I guess you've done the same to Wu Yue."

Yan Shouyi held his tongue.

"You've now hurt two women," he said in earnest, "one after the other. I'd hate to see you hurt a third."

"Who am I hurting this time?"

Fei Mo pointed toward Shouyi's house down in the village. The compound was faintly visible from where they were standing. Shen Xue, wearing a red short-sleeved blouse, was taking water to the farmers building the wall, which was waist-high by then. Yan Shouyi lowered his head, deep in thought.

"Old Fei," he said, "she's quite something. A bit goofy, but other than that..."

"Shouyi, don't get me wrong, but I know your failing. Your affairs start and end with incredible speed."

With a long look at Fei Mo, Shouyi said:

"This time I'm serious about becoming a new man."

"What concerns me is, you'll revert back when the chips are down."

Yan Shouyi just looked at Fei Mo and said nothing.

Three days later, the wall was up and the arch was in place. Yan Shouyi had the two chefs prepare an outdoor meal to express his gratitude. Black Brick went out and bought a string of firecrackers, which he hung from the arch. *Pi-pi pa-pa* explosions encircled a dozen men sitting around the two tables, smoking cigarettes. Fei Mo was seated at the head of one of the tables, and the cooks managed to get Shen Xue to sit next to him, but he stood up to give his seat to Shouyi's grandmother, who was sitting beneath the date tree in the yard. She smiled and shook her head. Now that the wall and arch had been built, she stopped complaining about all the trouble. Shen Xue also tried to get her to take her seat.

"Granny doesn't drink," Black Brick said, "so there's no need for her to sit at the table. Just give her a bowl and some food when it's time to eat, that's all she needs."

Although Shouyi was paying for everything, he chose not to sit at the table, since Black Brick was there; instead, he put on an apron and helped the cooks serve the food. Before the meal began, Black Brick waved ceremoniously to quiet everyone down. Then, in his role as host, he said:

"Building a house and putting up a wall are major events. You villagers have pitched in as good neighbors. Now it's time to take it easy, so I won't say any more. Time to drink!"

But instead of following that up with a toast, he picked up a bottle, walked over to the second table and poured some liquor into the bowl in front of Fei Mo.

"Mr. Fei, you've come from Beijing to our poverty-stricken, out-of-the-way village. I'm an uncultured villager who hasn't been as attentive to you as I should have been, thanks to all the running around the past few days. I hope you'll do me the honor of overlooking that and this meager spread."

The others laughed at the out-of-character elegance of his little speech, but Fei Mo jumped to his feet.

"Brick, I can see you're a better talker than Shouyi. He should be back here tilling the fields and you should be hosting the TV show."

Black Brick was thrilled.

"Finally, someone who understands me. I had less schooling as a child, but I've got a better noggin than him."

By then the liquor had reached the rim of the bowl, which he picked up and held out to Fei Mo.

"Out here, I am Shouyi's elder cousin. In Beijing, it's you. So, Cousin, drink up!"

Now Fei Mo was an accomplished drinker, but this outburst so startled him that he held out his teacup instead.

"My dear Cousin, I accept your good wishes. But since I don't drink, let me toast you with this tea."

Black Brick insistently held up the liquor.

"You will dishonor me if you insist on it. Or maybe you're afraid I'll drink up all your liquor when I come to Beijing."

Shouyi walked up with a steaming bowl of stewed chicken and mushrooms and placed it on the table. He came to Fei Mo's rescue:

"Cousin, Fei Mo really doesn't drink. I'll drink for him."

That enraged Black Brick, who responded by kicking Yan Shouyi.

"Get lost! Who the hell do you think you are?"

An awkward tension filled the air until Shen Xue rose to her feet and, in the best Shanxi accent she could manage, said:

"What would you say if *I* drank for him, Cousin?"

Black Brick's anger was instantaneously transformed into delight.

"I'd say that's fine. A young lady drinking with me makes me look pretty good."

So Shen Xue took the overflowing bowl from him and—*glug glug glug*—drank it down, for which she received approval from the village men, who applauded loudly, cigarettes dangling from their lips. Black Brick filled the bowl a second time and held it out to Shen Xue, who grew visibly anxious.

"Are you trying to get me drunk? You're not drinking."

"You have to drink three times first. That's our custom."

Shen Xue turned to the old lady sitting under the date tree and said:

"Granny, our cousin here is taking advantage of me!"

The old lady stood up and took a swing at Black Brick with her cane.

"Damn you!" she said. "The girl can't drink, so stop trying to force her."

"Don't you worry, Granny, she knows how to drink!"

Shen Xue took the bowl from him and—*glug glug glug*—drank it down.

Black Brick filled it up yet again, but this time Fei Mo said to Shen Xue:

"Xue, my girl, don't do it. There's no need for you to show off."

She stiffened her neck and said, in obvious high spirits:

"I can drink, and when I do I proudly represent Beijing."

She drank down the third bowlful—*glug glug glug*—and now that she'd opened the door, others rushed in. Once Black Brick had completed his toasts, it was Lu Guoqing's turn. After that came Jiang Changgeng; by then Shen Xue was clearly drunk. Without waiting for the next person, she got to her feet, picked up the bottle, and reeled her way over to the stove to toast the two cooks, barely covering the distance before crumpling to the ground like loose clay. Annoyed by the scene in front of her, the old lady stood up and brandished her cane.

"How dare you get our guest drunk! Am I next?"

She hit Black Brick with her cane. Fei Mo tried to calm her down.

"Granny, we're just having a good time."

Meanwhile, Yan Shouyi had picked Shen Xue up and was carrying her on his back over to Black Brick's house, where his cousin's wife quickly made up a bed for her. After Shouyi laid her down on the bed, Black Brick's wife heated a bowl of brown sugar water and handed it to Shouyi, who held the bowl up to Shen Xue's mouth. She pushed it away, spilling the liquid all over the blanket. Drunk, Shen Xue was a very different person. She glared at Shouyi.

"Who do you think you are? Pour me a drink. Bottoms up!"

Black Brick's wife handed Shouyi another bowlful of brown sugar water, which he once again tried to get Shen Xue to drink.

"Here's your drink. You first."

"*Glug glug, glug glug.*" Shen Xue drank several mouthfuls, then stopped abruptly and looked around the room.

"Where am I?"

"You're home. Now get some sleep."

Black Brick's wife said teasingly:

"Yes, sleep. When you wake up, we'll talk about finding you a husband."

To their surprise, that brought tears.

"You can't do that without my OK," she said. "And who? There's no one!"

Black Brick's wife put on a new blanket.

"How about this?" she said to console her. "If you decide not to get married, you can stay here with me as long as you like."

Shen Xue pointed a finger at Black Brick's wife.

"No," she said. "I have to get married! You've got your husband, but you won't let me have one!"

She ended her tirade with an outburst of giggles, fell backward, and was out. As he looked down into Shen Xue's face, her head wiped clean of thoughts, Shouyi stood there dazed. It was like seeing someone from home.

After five days, it was time to head back to Beijing. The station had phoned to urge them to return the next day. The banquet guests were gone, the yard was neat and clean, and a new wall and arch over the gate stood silently in the moonlight. Leaves from the date tree cast their shadows on the wall, swaying with each gust of wind. Yan Shouyi held his grandmother's arm as they strolled around the yard. Finally, she said what was in her heart:

"They did a good job."

She pointed to the wall and to the arch with her cane.

"Sturdy."

She pointed again.

"Solid."

Shouyi helped her back inside, where she sat on the brick bed and leaned back against the folded quilt. He sat down across from her and took out two thousand yuan, which he laid next to her pillow. Before she could speak, he said:

"It's not from me, it's from Shen Xue. Just a little spending money."

The old lady decided not to say anything, but she didn't pick up the money either. Instead, she took a photograph out of an old cosmetic case at the head of the bed and held it up to the light bulb. It was a picture she'd taken with Yan Shouyi and Yu Wenjuan. She was sitting in her armchair under the date tree, with Shouyi and Wenjuan standing beside her, one on each side. Wenjuan was smiling broadly, giving a clear sign that she and the old lady were getting on well. Because of that, Shouyi hadn't told the old lady about the divorce until two months had passed; he broke the news to her a little at a time. She hadn't said a word when she'd heard.

Now, as she looked at the photograph, she sighed.

"I knew without your having to tell me. I couldn't find fault with her. I blamed you, my own grandson."

Shouyi reached into his pocket and took out a ring. It had been a gift to Wenjuan from the old lady ten years earlier, when they came to Shanxi after the wedding.

"When we split up," he said, "Wenjuan said she wanted me to return this to you. I've been thinking about it the past few days, but didn't dare say anything."

The old lady stared at him.

"I know what she had in mind. She was hoping I'd give you hell."

She poked him in the chest with her cane.

"I expect better from you from now on."

She held the ring up to the light.

"When I was young, my family was so poor we didn't have enough to eat half the time. But my father favored me over the other girls. So the year I was married, he sold his lambskin coat to buy this for me. I came into your family at the age of sixteen, and he died of typhoid fever the next year."

Yan Shouyi looked at his grandmother, still not saying anything.

"My father was a tall man," she said, "but skinny, and never much of a talker. I recall how it was when I was a little girl, how he'd go to the landlord's at night to mill flour, and take me with him. As he turned the mill, over and over, he sang to me. I can almost hear him now."

Yan Shouyi looked at his grandmother without saying anything.

"The deaths of two people have hurt me the most," she continued. "One, when I was only seventeen, was my father. The other, when I was eighty-two, was your father. The two saddest events in my life, and I was there for both of them. I've never told anyone before today."

Yan Shouyi didn't say anything.

She handed the ring back to him, and he assumed she wanted

him to give it to Shen Xue. She surprised him.

"When you get back to Beijing, return this to Wenjuan and tell her she's no longer my granddaughter-in-law, she's now my granddaughter. Tell her I said that you may be thoughtless, but the old witch isn't."

Yan Shouyi laid his head in his grandmother's lap and bawled like a baby.

13

Two months later, someone from home came to Beijing with a bag of dried dates from his grandmother, with instructions to give them to Fei Mo. They were from the tree in her yard, and she'd dried them herself. She said he hadn't looked well, and that dates would be good for him. He held the sack in his hand to feel its heft.

"Your grandmother may be illiterate, but she's no ordinary woman."

Then he looked at Yan Shouyi.

"Eating these dates is a heavy responsibility."

14

After returning from Shanxi, Yan Shouyi and Shen Xue moved in together.

15

Winter arrived.

16

Fei Mo was openly annoyed during a planning session of "Straight Talk." Up until then, his annoyance with the staff had usually been only half-serious. But not this time. He was annoyed not because he didn't like the topic of conversation or because they'd said something to injure his self-esteem again, but because of the atmosphere and surroundings.

The offices of "Straight Talk" were divided into two rooms—an inner and an outer office. The outer office was equipped with five phone lines. Two receptionists were kept busy answering the phones and recording incoming calls. The two young women called themselves "call girls," since they spent the whole day answering calls. Once the ratings for "Straight Talk" went through the roof, the phones never stopped ringing. Some callers were critical of a particular show, others called to offer their congratulations; some called to point out errors, others called in with bizarre questions, such as: "Since it's OK to raise dogs in the city, why can't we raise pigs?" "Zhang Chunsheng went into Beijing to find a job, and while he was away, the village head slept with his wife. What should he do?" "A fellow named Liang found five thousand yuan, which he returned to its owner. But the two men fought over whether or not a thousand-yuan reward was appropriate." "We're a cooking oil and grain products producer in Changzhou. Last week we registered the name 'Straight Talk' for a new line of stuffed buns. You have to change the name of your show or you're in violation of copyright." Then there were the girls who offered to send their photos to Yan Shouyi and asked for his cell phone number.

The production staff of "Straight Talk" occupied the inner office, which was slightly larger than the outer office, and was furnished with a dozen or so randomly placed, partioned desks. The center area, which was left open, was where production meetings were held, with the staff seated around a circular conference table. Yan Shouyi had started out as the host only, but once he took over as head of the production team, he moved into a small office with a connecting door to the inner office. Fei Mo's desk was there as well.

The staff was meeting in the larger office, going over the script for the next show, the topic of which was "Why Do People from Henan Lie So Much?" But before the meeting began, when he was still at his desk, Fei Mo's anger surfaced. He told Yan Shouyi he had something to say. That "something" had nothing to do with why "people from Henan lie so much," but involved the programming for the past several shows. In his view, the show had been on the decline, with nothing but frivolous, rambling chatter. When it should have been tight, it was too loose, and when it should have been loose, it was too tight. If they didn't stop and take stock, there was no telling how far they'd slip. The more he talked, the angrier he got. The sight of Fei Mo getting agitated worried Yan Shouyi, but he couldn't tell if Fei Mo was truly dissatisfied with the show, or if he was venting again after a fight with his wife the night before. And because he was puzzled, the best strategy was to follow his instincts. In the long run, it was better to be dissatisfied than satisfied, since dissatisfaction opens the door for improvement. In the end, an unintended consequence of a fight between Fei Mo and his wife was that it helped "Straight Talk." So before the meeting got underway, Yan Shouyi clapped his hands and announced:

"Quiet down, everyone. I want to start today's meeting by talking not about people from Henan, but, thanks to Fei Lao, about us. Our work in recent weeks has failed to meet his expectations by a mile, and it's time to ask him to shorten that distance."

Everyone quieted down to hear what Fei Mo had to say. Except for one rattan chair from Hunan, which was reserved for him, they all sat in leather chairs. After taking his seat and lighting a cigarette, Fei Mo began to speak:

"The programs over the past couple of months can be characterized by one word: backsliding. With the exception of the show on dowries for women of Mizhi, which wasn't bad, if a little clumsy, and wasn't an attempt to be clever, the others were so bad they made being clumsy a virtue. I've said it before, and I'll say it again, putting a show together is like a train ride, with stops along the way. But these stops are all at stations. Now, instead of stopping at stations, we've been racing along and stopping without warning wherever we feel like it. People don't mind racing along when scenery's passing by. But we've pulled down all the shades . . ."

The more he talked, the more agitated he became:

"Is it nighttime? No, it's the middle of the day, but when you pull down the shades, it's as if you're hiding something shameful, right? Then there are the tracks. Our tracks are the threads of conversation. By abandoning our tracks, we've got a runaway train, thundering along and going nowhere. It won't be long before it crashes and flips over. It's like people. If they seek nothing and set no goals, passing aimlessly through life, with no long-term plans, that's an insult to life itself. Are you aware of that? If you keep backsliding the way you've been doing, you're hurting yourselves. And not just you, but me too! Have you ever taken a train . . . ?"

Yan Shouyi could tell what this outburst was all about. A storm had raged at Fei Mo's place the night before. But, as he thought a bit more, he realized that the storm, which had triggered Fei Mo's anger, might mean that it had also gotten him thinking up new ideas for the show. But then producer Big Duan's cell phone rang, slicing through Fei Mo's anger. He stopped in mid-sentence as he watched Big Duan take the incoming call. Now, if the call had been a short one, no problem. Unfortunately, it went on for three, maybe four minutes. Big Duan kept his head down the whole time and hardly spoke, listening unhappily, occasionally tossing in a word or two, more like muttering than talking:

". . . yes . . . um . . . OK . . . oh . . . um . . . aiyo . . . I heard."

The weird conversation got everyone's attention. He finally rang off, raised his head, and discovered that they were all looking at him. One of the other producers, Hu Keqing, fired up by the call, forgot all about Fei Mo.

"Had to be a woman," he said.

Before Big Duan had a chance to deny the accusation, Hu Keqing silenced him with his hand.

"I'll translate."

Then, alternating between a man's and a woman's voice, he said:

" 'Are you in a meeting?' 'Yes.' 'Can't talk?' 'Um.' 'Then I'll do all the talking.' 'OK.' 'I miss you.' 'Oh.' 'Do you miss me?' 'Um.' 'You were a bad boy last night.' 'Aiyo.' 'Give me a kiss. Can't do it? Then I'll give you one. Hear that?' 'I heard.' "

The others cried out in unison:

"I heard!"

Laughter filled the room. Yan Shouyi, who laughed along with the others, was thrilled. Until, that is, he saw that Fei Mo was not amused. He looked angrier than ever. He raised his hands to quiet them down, then turned to Fei Mo and said:

"Go on, please."

Fei Mo glared at the others before he would continue. Then, once he'd vented his anger, he turned his attention to the program.

"That's all I'm going to say about trains. Now let me tell you about turnips, common vegetables whose peels most people throw away. But if you prepare them right, they can appeal to refined tastes. Here at 'Straight Talk' we started out preparing turnip peels, but now we're preparing ginseng! The problem is, it's not real, it's plastic!"

He'd barely finished when the cell phone belonging to the recording secretary, Little Ma, went off. Having learned from Big Duan's experience, she went out onto the balcony so she wouldn't have to take the call in the office. But, to everyone's surprise, Fei Mo stopped speaking anyway. Yan Shouyi reached out, took Little Ma's notebook, and said:

"You can continue, Fei Lao. We won't wait for her."

Fei Mo lit a cigarette and stared at the ceiling.

"No, we'll wait. I'm not about to repeat myself to every one of you."

Yan Shouyi shouted out to the balcony:

"Hurry up, Little Ma! You're holding up the meeting."

She quickly ended the call and ran back in to take notes. Fei Mo continued:

"That's enough about turnips. Now let's talk about black bears. Black bears know enough to throw the corncobs away after they've eaten the corn. But we keep repeating ourselves, show after show. The contents seem different on the surface, but they're the same old corncobs. We're not even the equal of a bear. I've put up with this for a long time now..."

Yan Shouyi's cell phone went off. Having learned a lesson from his two predecessors, he flipped it open and, without looking to see who it was, spat out:

"I'm in a meeting!"

He was about to close the phone when he saw it was Wu Yue, who, as it turned out, was calling from downstairs.

"Why didn't you tell me you were coming to the station?" Then he added, "Wouldn't you know it? I'm out on business, I'm not at the station."

Anything to avoid Wu Yue. But she said the security guard had told her he'd shown up at the station bright and early that morning. Caught in a lie, and worrying about the length of the call, which would increase Fei Mo's anger, he could only say:

"Hand the phone to the security guard."

"This is Yan Shouyi," he said to the guard. "Show her to the reception room."

He snapped the phone shut. Just his luck that Big Duan decided to gloat a bit:

"Looks like you've been busted."

"Had to be a woman," Hu Keqing said. "Want me to translate?"

Once again they all laughed, but Yan Shouyi quieted them with hand gestures—he'd seen Fei Mo's face darken as he rose out of his chair, picked up his briefcase, tucked it under his arm, and started for the door. Knowing they'd gone too far this time, Yan rushed over to stop him from leaving.

"I want you all to turn off your cell phones and give Fei Lao your undivided attention," he announced. "This is a business meeting, so act appropriately!"

Fei Mo tossed his briefcase onto the conference table.

"Now where was I?"

Little Ma flipped through her notebook.

"So far you've talked to us about trains, turnips, and black bears."

Then she looked up and gazed at Fei Mo, confusion in her eyes.

"Fei Lao, what is it you're trying to say?"

Everyone felt like laughing, but forced back the impulse. Fei Mo sat down.

"I wish I knew!" he said.

Then it all came back. He pointed at each of the gathered staff and said:

"What I think is, we should put together a show called 'Cell Phone.'"

He turned to Yan Shouyi.

" 'I'm not at the station,' indeed. You open your mouth and out come lies."

Then he turned to the others:

"As I see it, it isn't people from Henan who lie all the time, it's you people! Just how much crap and how many lies have you spewed into your cell phones? Chinese is supposed to be a succinct language, but no one speaks honestly anymore. How many unspeakable things are hidden in those cell phones of yours? At this rate, there'll come a day when your phones become grenades. So I think the best thing to do is open them all up and reveal their secrets!"

As the monologue progressed, his anger vanished and was replaced by mounting excitement. He slapped the armrest of his chair and announced:

"That's our next show—not liars from Henan, but cell phones!"

Overcome by the crescendo of excitement, he clutched at his chest. Little Ma rushed over with a glass of water.

"Fei Lao, please don't get too excited."

But he pushed the glass away, swept the gathering with his eyes, and said with unhurried candor:

"What are you all afraid of?"

Looks crisscrossed the table. They were all unwilling to say they weren't afraid of anything and just as unwilling to admit what it was they were afraid of, as Fei Mo had intended, for that gave him a free hand to develop his idea. He sat up straight, a gesture that signaled serious discourse, a sign that Yan Shouyi immediately recognized. What was coming would surely take half an hour, or more, and Wu Yue was downstairs waiting for him. If she tired of waiting, it would not be out of character for her to come barging into the conference room. That would be a live grenade indeed. So he leaned over and whispered to Fei Mo:

"You go ahead, Fei Lao, and I'll go find the station boss."

Fei Mo glowered at him.

"In the middle of a meeting? What do you need him for?"

"This is an explosive plan, so I'll go whip up some enthusiasm for it. If what you're proposing is doable, we can start work today."

He then turned to the others.

"There's nothing to be afraid of. Secrets in our cell phones that need to be made public will be. We'll be suicide bombers, and, in the process, sanitize society!"

He fretted that his lie lacked the power to convince, and that Fei Mo would see through it. But Fei Mo just frowned and sent him on his way. As anticipated, before Shouyi even reached the door, Fei Mo had linked the use of cell phones to primitive society and the grunting sounds they made when moving logs: Back then there were no lies. Why? Because monkey-like primitives didn't know how to talk. The reason you love to lie these days is because you've learned how to talk . . .

No one dared even smile in response, although Yan Shouyi had to cover his mouth to keep from laughing out loud.

17

Yan Shouyi found Wu Yue in the reception room. He'd anticipated the meeting with trepidation, but after greeting her, he was relieved to learn that her reason for coming to see him was unrelated to their past, had nothing to do with thirst or purging, but was something new, something involving Fei Mo. This was the first time Yan Shouyi had seen Wu Yue since his divorce, and what struck him most compellingly was the fact that her appearance hadn't changed over the intervening months. Her attire, her hair, her face, even the basketballs on her chest, were just as they'd been that night in the grove of trees by the stream. The next thing that surprised him was that when they were face to face, her tone of voice carried no reminders of how she'd spoken to him over the phone. Back then, she'd been petty, but now she was casual and straightforward, and he instinctively knew that their months-long battles had ended in a truce. The passage of time had worked to his advantage. But before broaching her reason for coming to see him, she asked where the ladies room was. He saw her to the door and waited until she came out and walked to the sink to wash her hands. That done, she said:

"Yan Shouyi, you really are a small-minded person!"

He was leaning against the door, holding her overcoat and handbag.

"Now what'd I do?"

"You wouldn't take my calls for months, and today you said you weren't at the station. In your eyes, I'm like a hooker who's been delivered to your door, aren't I?"

Yan Shouyi felt his heart slip down into his stomach. Sucking air in through his teeth, he said:

"I wouldn't dare. I'm not worthy of that."

He added, softly:

"I'm in the middle of a meeting, and Fei Mo's in a foul mood."

"It was also at a meeting, on Lushan, when you came sneaking into my room a couple of years ago."

Somewhat embarrassed, Yan Shouyi sputtered:

"Ah . . ."

Wu Yue turned off the water, walked up to Shouyi, and without warning, wiped her wet hands on his sweater. Then, again without warning, she leaned over until her face was touching his. Mistaking her intent as wanting to kiss him, he stopped her with the palm of his hand on her forehead.

"Be cool."

She sniffed the air.

"Yan Shouyi, you disappoint me. You've fallen so low you've taken to wearing perfume, haven't you?"

All thanks to Shen Xue, who had mischievously sprayed him while she was putting on her makeup that morning. Sort of an insurance policy, she'd said. Like a dog that sprays its territory as a sign for other dogs to stay away. At the time, he didn't know whether to laugh or cry, and now he needed to create a diversion. But he'd no sooner opened his mouth to say something than a light bulb went off in Wu Yue's head. With a scowl, she said:

"Hey, why did you push me away just now? Think I wanted to kiss you? Well, maybe I will!"

Yan Shouyi looked around and leaned toward her.

"OK, but just once."

Wu Yue pushed his face away.

"You disgust me! You say you've turned over a new leaf since you hooked up with that drama teacher. So, when's the wedding? I'll be her maid of honor."

With a look of insouciance, Yan Shouyi said:

"Fine with me. I'll let you know when it happens."

He then escorted her to the third-floor coffee shop. On the way up, she snorted disdainfully.

"You don't have to worry that I'll mess things up for you. I'm here on business. Fei Mo has written a book we're going to publish, and the publisher wants you to write a foreword."

Yan Shouyi suspected she was trying to be funny.

"Write a foreword for Fei Mo? You're barking up the wrong tree, I'm afraid. I am not an educated man. Now if *you* wrote a book, I'd be happy to oblige."

Wu Yue stopped walking.

"All right—I'm hard up enough to do it. I'll call it 'Straight Talk,' and use it to expose all your repulsive affairs. I'll print a warning on the cover: 'Not for children.' "

Seeing there was no one on the stairs, Yan Shouyi put his arm around her shoulder.

"I think it ought to be titled 'I Gave You My Youth' or 'Bullshit'!"

Wu Yue shrugged free.

"Fei Mo's book has already been typeset. When can you have a foreword done?"

"You really want me to write a foreword? Does Fei Mo know?"

"Not yet. I'll tell him after it's written."

Yan Shouyi thought for a moment.

"You have to handle this very discreetly, since he might consider it a loss of dignity."

"You're going to have to write it, whether it's a loss of dignity or not. The book is hard to describe. He's calling it 'Speaking,' the one thing he's unable to do, as I see it. From Aristotle to Confucius, from the UN to a college classroom, even that 'Straight Talk' of yours, a range that includes just about everything, and each utterance is more profound than the next, not to mention all the foreign words he uses. But in the end, nothing he says is clear, which is pretty much the same as saying nothing!"

Yan Shouyi thought about Fei Mo, up in the conference room musing over primitive societies, and he had to laugh.

"But if you people hold him in such contempt, why publish his book? Does your boss have shit for brains?"

"He doesn't have shit for brains. His daughter is Fei Mo's grad student."

Yan Shouyi understood.

"He wants you to write a foreword, not because he thinks you're a better writer than Fei Mo, but in an attempt to spice Fei Mo's book up a bit. And not that your writing can accomplish that, but your name should bring some publicity. Otherwise, we're afraid we might not sell a single copy."

She pinched Yan Shouyi on the arm.

"That's the whole story. I've done my part. Now, whether you write the foreword or not is up to you!"

Yan Shouyi pulled back his arm and scratched his head.

"I can write it, that's no problem. But this business with Fei Mo, something doesn't seem quite right."

Wu Yue glared at him.

"I guess things were quite right with our business, is that it?"

Embarrassed once more, he sputtered:

"Ah . . ."

They were relaxing, drinking their coffee, when he glanced at his watch.

"Oh, my, it's already 11:30. We have a taping at one this afternoon. I need to get over to makeup."

Wu Yue saw through his deception. She stood up and made as if to spit in his face.

"Until now I never realized how calculating you are."

She added:

"I bet you thought I wanted to have lunch with you, right? Well, I've already got a date, with my new boyfriend."

Yan Shouyi knew that was a lie, but he grinned and said: "Ah, good for you. Bring him by some day and let me have a look at him."

Wu Yue walked out. When she reached the entrance, she stretched a bit, hiking up her short jacket enough to expose a line of snowy white skin. The sight had an immediate effect on Shouyi, which gave way to a sense of loss. Now that peace had been restored, he felt that the thirst quenching and purging of the past hadn't been as fearful as he'd once thought. Together he and Wu Yue had explored the darkest language the world has to offer. By comparison, Yu Wenjuan and Shen Xue felt like little more than casual acquaintances. He went to the window and looked down as Wu Yue walked across the compound, alone, heading toward the gate. All of a sudden, threads of loss and isolation seemed to float in the air around him, heading not toward Wu Yue, but toward him. He took out his cell phone to dial her number and have her come back. But, thinking better of it, he closed his phone and put it back in his pocket.

18

After he and Shen Xue began living together, Yan Shouyi grew anxious as soon as night fell. The reason was simple. As an instructor at the Academy of Dramatic Arts, she enjoyed taking him to evening drama performances. He'd never balked at traditional fare, such as *Thunderstorm* or *Teahouse* or *Hamlet*, or even Peking Opera, which he could tolerate. But these were not on Shen Xue's agenda—she considered them passé, humdrum; instead, she took him to see representatives of performance art and experimental drama. One day she dragged him all the way to Tongzhou to watch a man hang himself from a locust tree, then cut open his arm and let the blood drip into a fire on the ground, each drop sizzling in the flames and forming puffs of smoke. On another occasion, she took him to Huairou, where a man smeared his upper body with honey to attract ants that swarmed in clumps on his skin. Then there was the time she took him to an artists' colony in Tongzhou to stare at a huge vat filled to the brim with Coca Cola. A naked couple emerged from behind a curtain and jumped into the vat to bathe like a pair of ducks. The audience was captivated, all except Yan Shouyi, who couldn't make heads or tails of what he was seeing. He had no idea what they were doing or what they were saying. He did know that this was supposed to be avant-garde and postmodern, but why couldn't they say something people could understand, even in the name of the avant-garde and postmodern, instead of trying to be so convoluted?

On this particular evening, Shen Xue took him to an abandoned textile mill to watch an experimental play called *8½*. Shouyi had been apprehensive about going.

"Teacher Shen," he'd said, "I've seen plenty of your performance art and experimental dramas, so how about letting me skip the performance of *8½*? We can split up for tonight—you go to the play and I'll stay home and rest."

She put her arm in his.

"No. Whether you watch it or not is your business, but you're going with me."

Then, assuming the pose of his classroom teacher, she said:

"You have to study, young man. If you don't, how will you ever improve?"

He smiled wanly, knowing he had no choice but to accompany her to an abandoned textile mill in Beijing's western suburbs. They left just at the height of rush hour when Third and Fourth Ring Roads were jammed—bumper to bumper traffic turning a short trip into an hour of stop-and-go driving. The play had already started by the time they arrived. The mill was packed with men and women, including a good many foreigners, all standing, some of whom were taping the action with video-cams. A stack of plywood lay in the center of the stage, and every few minutes a laborer walked up, removed a sheet, and nailed it over one of the windows on the four walls. After two long hours, most of the windows had been covered with the plywood, reducing the light inside to a mere glimmer. By then, Yan Shouyi's legs ached from standing, and he was getting sleepy. He was about to yawn, but one look at Shen Xue, who stood there captivated by the show, was all it took for him to stiffle it. Eventually, all but one window were covered, letting in only a tiny sliver of light. Then, one final sheet was nailed to that window, throwing the mill into total darkness, just as a light went on overhead and a man dressed like a foreman, wearing a hard hat, walked to the center of the stage and announced:

"Altogether there are forty-eight windows, plus eight doors. Ninety-eight sheets of plywood, at 95 yuan apiece, were used, for a cost of 9,310 yuan. Six and a half jin of nails, at 13.50 per jin, comes to 87.75. Twenty-eight workers, at 50 yuan apiece, comes to 1,450, for a total expenditure of 10,847.75 yuan."

He removed his hard hat, revealing a shiny bald head, and, in a different voice, said:

"I directed this play. My name is Hu Lala."

That was greeted by thunderous applause. Since Shen Xue clapped excitedly, so did Shouyi, as a worker-type with a microphone started asking the audience what they thought of *8½*. The first to be asked looked like a businessman; he had a large, round head and a gold chain draped around his neck. What was he doing there? His response was terse and direct:

"I didn't understand it. It was ridiculous, a complete waste of time."

The worker said nothing as he passed the microphone to another member of the audience, a young, bearded man wearing Ben Franklin eyeglasses. Shen Xue nudged Yan Shouyi.

"That's Zhang Xiaowu, a famous avant-garde critic."

Naturally, Yan had never heard of him. Zhang gave his opinion in a somber tone, cocking his head and speaking slowly into the microphone:

"It had tension and remarkable substance. The performance of this play was an indication that China's experimental drama has moved from postmodernism to neo-realism. At the same time, it constituted a refraction of the light of existentialism and new wave . . ."

Yan Shouyi didn't understand a word of what the man was saying. But then one of Shen Xue's colleagues, a woman named Xiao Su, elbowed her way over to them, followed by her boyfriend, a second-rate soccer player named Mai Zhuang. Seeing them work their way through the crowd meant that he was about to be with someone he could relate to, someone he could talk to. Intentionally ignoring Mai Zhuang, he spoke to Xiao Su as if they were old and dear friends:

"Teacher Su, I hear you're getting married tomorrow. The news nearly broke my heart!"

He reached out to put his arm around her waist, but she swatted it away.

"None of that!"

She turned to Shen Xue.

"Why don't we all get married tomorrow?"

"Sure. That way we won't have to go searching for bridesmaids. I can be yours, and you can be mine."

She looked at Shouyi, who knew that he'd inadvertently opened a Pandora's Box. Not once since they'd begun living together had either of them brought up the subject of marriage. He had only recently walked out from under the shadow of divorce, and had no interest in remarrying, at least not yet. As for Shen Xue, when she moved in with Yan, like all modish young women, she was interested only in being happy; as for marriage, she didn't seem to care, one way or the other. But now, six months later, signs of change—in what she said, in the look in her eyes, in her attitude—were beginning to emerge, as if cohabitation was not her goal, but a prelude to something else. It too had become a sort of experimental drama, where avant-gardism and experimentalism are merely a veneer over something else; now, for her, experimentalism and lyricism were on the way out. But having brought up the subject, Yan had to find a way to make light of a serious topic. Turning to Xiao Su, a mischievous grin on his face, he pointed to Mai Zhuang and said:

"Fine with me. Tomorrow there'll be two brides, but only one groom, me or him, take your pick."

With a laugh, Xiao Su slapped him, which also made Mai Zhuang laugh. He walked over and threw an arm around Yan's shoulders. Xiao Su said to Shen Xue:

"That damned school of ours is relentless. I'm getting married tomorrow and I still have to make the rounds tonight. Dean Han says it's for my own good, since evaluations are due next month, and this will give me a chance to show what I can do."

"Don't listen to him," Shen Xue said. "Go home and get some sleep. Forget about making the rounds!"

"I can't. Dean Han is worried about students who stay out all night."

"I'll take your watch."

Xiao Su laughed. "Just what I was hoping you'd say."

Meanwhile, now that the avant-garde critic was finished, Yan Shouyi heard someone call his name as the microphone was thrust under his nose. Lights from news cameras lit up the place, giving him a fright.

"How about a comment from you, Mr. Yan?"

Yan Shouyi tried to avoid the lights.

"You'd better ask somebody else. I don't know a thing about drama."

"Then just tell us what you think, your first impressions."

Desperate to find a place to hide, he felt a nudge in his ribs and heard Shen Xue say under her breath:

"Say something, anything. We're Hu Lala's guests tonight."

Yan Shouyi had no choice.

"Good, it was quite good. It's a scene I'm familiar with. I recently went back to my native home in Shanxi, where we put up a wall around the compound, and the place was buzzing with activity. My cousin was the foreman, and he was every bit as meticulous with his calculations of lime and sand. But we didn't call it *8½*, we called it building a wall . . ."

Shen Xue kicked him in the shin. He quickly corrected himself:

"But to me, tonight's performance was more profound than real life. It was about life, but larger than life. It was one thing, but then it was something else. That's why my cousin is a farmer, while Hu Lala is an extraordinary director. Seeing a play like this once isn't enough. Too bad, since according to what I've heard, this place is to be torn down tomorrow, and the play won't have a second showing. Good, really good. I can't wait to go home and let it all sink in."

The audience applauded as Yan Shouyi and the lights moved away.

"Can we go now?" he whispered to Shen Xue.

But she was clearly annoyed about something, maybe unhappy with how he'd treated the issue of marriage a while earlier. Her anger surfaced:

"What's up with you? I bring you to a play to help the guy out, and what do you do? You repay him with sarcasm, then you want to split. Well, you listen to me, this play is just getting started. The audience is an important part of the cast."

"Oh!" Yan Shouyi feigned enlightenment, and stayed pat. Then his cell chirped. He took it out of his pocket, looked at the readout, and saw it was an incoming text message. He opened it.

I'm Kim Yushan from Korea, remember me? I'm back and I'd like to see you.

The name didn't ring a bell, but he knew it was a woman. Since Shen Xue was standing beside him, he quickly closed the phone and stood there, an oasis of silence in a noisy, densely packed crowd. But he kept thinking, and finally it came to him. Three years earlier, a Korean student at a language school had been a huge fan of the show. One night, after a taping, he'd walked out of the station and found her waiting for him at the exit. Like all Korean females, the girl was somewhat short and stocky, but she had a pretty face. She'd dyed her hair, one half red, the other half green, and when she saw him walk out the door, she said in barely adequate Chinese:

"I from Korea. I like your show and you. Are you angry?"

Jokingly, Yan Shouyi said:

"I'm never angry at pretty girls, no matter where they're from."

The girl smiled, which turned him on. Since it happened during his profligate phase, it was only natural that he take her out for a late-night snack. After that, he drove her back to her college dorm. Parked by the entrance, he kissed her, and when she responded enthusiastically, he went upstairs with her. Over the next six months, he saw her a few times. Then, six months after that, she went home to Korea. The fact that she reappeared three years later came as a complete surprise. If he hadn't figured out who had written the message, he'd have quickly put it out of his mind. But, having recalled who she was, he grew apprehensive. When he looked over at Shen Xue, he saw that she was on her tiptoes, engrossed in the play. Now that the audience interviews had been concluded, Hu Lala and his workers had stripped to the waist and were running around shouting: "Wula, wula!" They kept bumping into one another. Yan Shouyi lowered his head, took out his phone again, and furtively erased the message.

19

The play ended at 10:30, and they didn't arrive back at the academy dorm, where they had set up housekeeping, until 11:30. By that time, snowflakes were dancing in the air, and since she'd agreed to make the rounds for Xiao Su, Shen Xue told Shouyi to go on in, and she'd be along when she was finished.

"Will you be checking the girls' dormitory?" he asked as he was parking.

Unaware of what lay behind the question, she said: "Yes."

"I'll come along."

She gave him a scorching look.

"How come you're so interested in girls' dormitories all of a sudden?"

"You dragged me along to suffer through that damned play, and now you want me to go home alone while you nab truant girls. Well, if it's an experimental play you want to watch, then I've got just the thing for you. Let the drama begin!"

By offering to accompany her while she checked the dorms, Shouyi hoped to make up for revealing his attitude toward marriage during the performance. In the car on the way home he could tell that Shen Xue was unhappy. Now, it appeared, she was appeased.

"You think it's a great task, don't you? You've got a dirty mind."

"Just the thought of nabbing truants gives me a rush. It reminds me of how we used to steal melons as kids."

Shen Xue went around to the back of the car and took a flashlight out of the trunk. He fell in behind her as she started making the rounds. First they checked the boys' dorm. No problems there, except that some of the lights that shouldn't have been on, were, so the residents could play poker. The losers' faces were dotted with slips of paper. In one of the rooms a noisy game of mahjong was in progress, with some ten-fen notes on the table. Shen Xue's arrival threw the players into a panic; they scurried to clear the table of telltale signs of the game. But they didn't concern Shen Xue, who simply told the man in charge of the power plant to turn off the electricity in that dorm. It was immediately enveloped in darkness and the resultant silence. Then it was off to the girls' dorm, where the problems were more serious. No poker and no mahjong, and all the lights were out. But, just as Xiao Su had said, many of the girls were missing. One or two of the beds in each of the six-girl rooms was vacant. The most serious offenders lived on the third floor; when Shen Xue opened a door and trained her light on the beds, she discovered that none of them had been slept in. Except for one. When the beam of light landed on the face of a girl who had just sat up in bed, Shen Xue turned on the overhead light and asked sternly:

"It's midnight. Where is everybody?"

The girl rubbed her eyes.

"I don't know."

"Why are you here?"

"I'm sick, Teacher Shen."

Since it was a girls' room, Yan Shouyi waited outside the door. Shen Xue stepped out of the room.

"Go to a restaurant off campus and bring back a bowl of soupy noodles."

Shouyi gave her a thumbs-up.

"A model of virtue, always concerned about her students."

With a quick glance into the room, Shen Xue pinched him on the arm.

"Knock it off."

So he tramped through the snow to buy a bowl of noodles at a diner just beyond the Academy gate. At that late hour there wasn't another customer in the place, which was barely lit by a tired, naked bulb hanging from the ceiling. Both cook and waitress were sitting at tables, fast asleep. Yan woke up the cook, handed him some money, and asked him to prepare a bowl of noodles. The waitress raised her head, squinted at Yan with one eye, then laid her head down on her arms and went back to sleep. Just then his cell phone chirped. An incoming text message. He flipped open the phone. It was Kim Yushan, the Korean student.

Can I see you tomorrow? I've been thinking a lot about you.

Shouyi grumbled about the girl's immaturity—a typical foreigner, who didn't understand this country at all. It was midnight. If he'd been home in bed, next to Shen Xue, this text message would have had danger written all over it. But since the last thing he wanted was to provoke her, he needed to end it before it began. He walked over to the restaurant entrance, where snowflakes danced in the pale light, and called Miss Kim, who picked up immediately, excitedly:

"Is that you? I'm so happy. Can I see you tomorrow?"

Time for Yan Shouyi to play the innocent.

"What a pity, you're in Beijing, while I'm off taping a show. I'm in Xishuang Banna. That's in Yunnan. It's a show about which animals people can eat and which they can't. Oh, really? Snowing in Beijing? How long will you be staying?"

"Six months. I'll be here six months."

That was deflating news to Yan Shouyi, who nonetheless pretended to be thrilled:

"Really? That's wonderful. I'll be back in Beijing in a couple of weeks. I'll call you then."

After closing the phone, he stood there a while, pondering, before taking the noodles from the cook and heading back to the Academy.

By then, the girl had gotten out of bed so she could eat the noodles. Just as Shen Xue had planned. Before she'd finished, the girl choked up with sobs.

"I'm really sorry, Teacher Shen."

Maintaining her stern look, Shen Xue just stared at her.

"I know where the other girls went," she blurted out.

"Where?"

"They went to a karaoke joint with some boys."

Shen Xue walked over to the window and stared silently at the snowflakes swirling in the streetlight. The girl kept eating, but by now was weeping openly.

"I'm really sorry, Teacher Shen."

Shen Xue spun around to look at the girl, who said:

"While I was still in bed I sent them a text message, telling them you were checking the room."

"When will they be back?"

"Any minute."

"Through which gate?"

"Usually through the west gate, because there's no guard there."

Shen Xue left the room and walked past Yan Shouyi, who caught up with her in the hallway.

"You're brutal, Teacher Shen. A five-yuan bowl of noodles is all you need to make someone spill their guts."

Shen Xue snickered.

"Wait and see how I deal with the others!"

Just then a thought occurred to her.

"Oh, right, yesterday I was tidying up your bag, and a bunch of photos of pretty girls fell out. What's that about?"

"We're on the lookout for a replacement host. Straight talk, that's all I do, day in and day out, and I'm tired of it."

"Have you found one that suits you?"

"Not in that batch."

He turned serious.

"Teacher Shen, if you don't mind, I'd rather you didn't go through my bag from now on. It's a bad habit to get into."

"You can go through my bag any time you want to. Why don't you?"

Yan Shouyi sighed.

"After all this time I finally found a truant officer."

The snow was falling more heavily now and forming a thick blanket of white on the ground. By the time Shen Xue and Yan Shouyi reached the gate, a Mercedes 600 was pulling up, its headlights on. The front door opened, and a girl climbed out, followed by another. One of them opened the rear door to let out more girls, one after the other. Altogether, nine of them climbed out of the Mercedes. It was clear from the car and its driver what the girls had been up to. The car turned and drove off, while the girls swarmed toward the gate, where Shen Xue lay in wait.

Nine students were lined up in front of the gate, all hanging their heads.

Shen Xue, hands clasped behind her back, paced in front of them. Without warning she stopped in front of one girl, bent forward, and sniffed.

"You drank your share, I see."

Yan Shouyi, staying out of sight in a grove of trees, had to hold his hand over his mouth to keep from laughing out loud. This was far more entertaining than stealing old man Liu's melons as a kid. All of a sudden, his cell phone chirped. Assuming it was the Korean girl again, he dug it out of his pocket to turn it off. But he saw that the caller was Fei Mo, which was even scarier than if it had been Miss Kim. Fei Mo was calling from a hospital. He told Yan Shouyi that Yu Wenjuan was in the maternity ward and that she'd just had a baby.

Whump! Yan Shouyi felt as if his head had exploded.

How could she . . ." he blurted out. "Whose is it?"

Fei Mo was clearly upset by the question:

"Who do you think? It's yours!"

Shen Xue walked by, leading a line of girls as if they were her prisoners.

"Who was that on the phone?" she asked him.

"Fei Mo," he said offhandedly. "About tomorrow's meeting."

20

Yan Shouyi couldn't sleep all night. Back home after catching the truant students, Shen Xue forgot her displeasure over the experimental drama incident and, as soon as she climbed into bed, chattered on excitedly about catching students. Xiao Su had caught some students once, she said, and when she saw how nicely they were dressed, she took them straight to the rehearsal room and, in the middle of the night, had them do pushups. You've got an abundance of energy this late at night, she told them, so start using it. Yan forced himself to hear her out, as she talked on and on until she fell asleep holding his arm. But he lay there wide-awake, thinking about the mess God had put him in. He could not get his head around the idea that, now that they were divorced, Yu Wenjuan had gone and had a baby, something denied her while they were married despite all her plans to get pregnant. Out of the blue, dropped into her lap from the heavens. He couldn't believe it was his until he began to count back; it couldn't be anyone's *but* his. But that was no reason to be happy, not in his state of confusion. This wasn't a gift from God, it was more like God's revenge. This was life-changing. His life of the past had wedged its way into his life of today. Time was in God's hand. God could make it possible for time to rid you of all your worries, but he could also draw time out to make things hard on you. Yan Shouyi knew that his life was about to get complicated. This child, who had made an abrupt appearance, was like a new hormone introduced into a bucket of raw material, altering its makeup. Just about all the world's problems have simple remedies. If a marriage is in trouble, there's divorce; but the abrupt appearance of this child held out no promise of an easy resolution. This was not something he could hide from, and being kept out of the loop made things even worse. How, for instance, did Yu Wenjuan feel about it? The next morning, Yan Shouyi said he was going to the office, but drove instead to Fei Mo's house to get his read on the situation. Before he could say a word, Fei Mo frowned.

"This is a fine time to show up," he said angrily. "You should have gone straight to the maternity ward the minute you hung up last night."

"I was confused," Yan said frankly.

With Fei Mo and his wife to accompany him, he drove to the clinic. On the way there, Fei Mo told him it was a boy.

"It looks like the Yan family has its heir now," Li Yan joked.

Yan Shouyi did not think that was funny.

They met Yu Wenjuan's young uncle in the waiting room. A classmate of Fei Mo's, he had made a great deal of money in computer software, some of which he'd invested in horses, opening a riding club in Changping, and followed that with a golf course in Shunyi. Yan, who'd shared many meals with the man, called him Little Uncle. On one occasion, after getting drunk together, they'd thrown their arms around one another and called themselves brothers. But that ended with the divorce.

Wenjuan's brother, a typical southerner—slight, fair-skinned, and taciturn—had also come, all the way from Nanjing. He greeted Yan with a nod only. But not Wenjuan's young uncle, who was wearing riding boots.

"Yan Shouyi," he shouted, "you've broken the law, you know that, don't you?"

"What law is that?" Yan asked, caught by surprise.

"The marriage law. You can't get a divorce when your wife is pregnant."

"I didn't know," Yan said with a wave of his hands to show his innocence. "I really didn't know."

While Li Yan and Yu Wenjuan's brother went inside to look after the new mother, Fei Mo and the young uncle led Yan Shouyi over to the nursery to see his son, one of dozens of similar tiny new beings in cribs, none of whom looked quite human; with their pruned faces and doughy skin, they looked more like newborn, curled-up rats. Some were asleep, some were squirming, their eyes closed, and some were bawling, their faces obliterated by their gaping mouths. A nurse was weaving her way through the forest of cribs with a feeding-bottle cart. Fei Mo and the young uncle led Yan up to one of the cribs, whose unfamiliar occupant lay there quietly with his eyes closed, making not a sound. After a sleepless night, Yan Shouyi had a headache, and as he gazed down at the infant, for the second time in as many days he had the feeling that the world had spun off its axis. With a quick look at the young uncle, Fei Mo pretended to be upset with Shouyi:

"Wenjuan insisted that we not tell you about this, but after thinking it over last night, I decided you ought to know, which is why I called you first thing this morning. To your credit, you came right away, but all in all, you're not treating this business with the seriousness it deserves."

With his eyes still glued to the infant, Yan did not respond. A nameless anger toward Wenjuan was building inside him—again. Not just because she'd gone childless during their decade together, only to have a baby after they were divorced—how had that happened? herbal medicine? breathing exercises?—but also because she hadn't revealed her pregnancy to her husband before the divorce was final, leaving him in the dark for nine whole months. Instead of the sympathy he might have felt toward her, in his eyes she came across as malicious.

Fei Mo tried to explain:

"Wenjuan told Li Yan she knew something was different prior to the divorce, but wasn't sure what it was. She was going to break the good news to you when, unexpectedly, things turned sour.

Yan Shouyi merely smiled bitterly. Then the baby woke up, eyes wide. No crying. He stuffed his fist into his mouth, then glanced Yan's way without, apparently, taking note of him. But the effect of that glance on Yan was immediate and powerful—he was chilled to the bone. He turned to Fei Mo.

"Should I go see Wenjuan?" he asked tentatively.

"Yes. Childbirth takes a lot out of a woman."

The young uncle offered a different opinion:

"Do you really think that's a good idea? I think seeing the baby is enough."

Then he added:

"In her weakened state, that could easily turn into something unpleasant. She had a Caesarian birth, and the incision hasn't healed."

But Fei Mo thought differently.

"He's already here," he said to smooth things over, "and he ought to go in to see her."

He turned back to Shouyi.

"But remember, this is not the time to bring up what can't be changed, like the fact that she hid her pregnancy from you all that time."

Yan Shouyi sighed.

"She was punishing me."

The three men left the nursery together on their way to Wenjuan's ward. But they'd no sooner arrived outside the room when Yan Shouyi blurted out:

"Hold on a minute."

He ran out of the clinic, threaded his way through traffic across the street, and went into a shop to buy a phone for Wenjuan. She hadn't used one all the time they were together, calling them nothing but trouble, since there wasn't anyone that eager to get in touch with her.

Back in the clinic, once he'd caught his breath, Yan Shouyi entered the room. And there she was, in her hospital bed, head covered by a postpartum cap. Not surprisingly, she looked drawn, and while most women still appear slightly heavy right after the birth of a child, with her it was the opposite, as she lay there, stretched out flat, looking quite a bit thinner than before. Reminded of young uncle's comment that the incision hadn't healed, Yan felt a sudden sadness. That time before, when he was in the hospital, she'd wrapped her arms around his head. But this time, it seemed to him that he'd entered in the middle of a discussion that had imprinted a look of anger on Wenjuan's face. She turned her head away as soon as she saw him. Her brother, who had been saying something in his Nanjing dialect, accompanied by hand gestures, stopped in mid-sentence, and an awkward silence settled over the room. Yan Shouyi didn't know what to say. After an uncomfortable pause, Li Yan broke the silence by walking up to the head of the bed and removing the lid from an earthenware pot.

"Wenjuan," she said, "put everything else aside and drink some of this. I had a Caesarian myself, and I know how important it is to build up your strength. Besides, breast feeding is best for the baby."

Yu Wenjuan ignored her.

Once again, Fei Mo stepped in to smooth things out.

"Wenjuan, last night I came up with a name for the child. I'd like to know what you think. Since it's a boy, you can call him Yan Shi, you know, the *shi* that means substantial or solid. That works on two levels—physique and behavior.

Still no response from Wenjuan, and the sense of awkwardness intensified.

At that point, Yan Shouyi felt it was up to him to do something. So he walked up to Wenjuan and took a ring out of his pocket, the one his grandmother had told him to give to Wenjuan that time he'd gone back home to Shanxi. He'd brought it along today to do just that. He laid it beside her pillow.

"I went back home to Shanxi a while ago," he said, "and gave this to my grandmother, like you told me to. But she wanted me to bring it back for you. To her, she said, you're not a granddaughter-in-law, you're her granddaughter."

He saw that there were tears in Yu Wenjuan's eyes.

Relieved by the sight, he took out the cell phone he'd just bought, the newest model, eye-catching red, and laid it next to the ring.

"I got this phone for you," he said. "I'm at the other end any time you or the baby need anything. From now on, my phone is always on."

"That's a good idea," Fei Mo said helpfully. "Raising a child is too much for one person."

Finally, after drying her eyes, Wenjuan said to Li Yan:

"Can I ask a favor, Yan?"

Li Yan quickly got to her feet.

"Anything."

"Come take that phone away, please," she said. "It's dirty."

Now what? Li Yan looked over at Yan Shouyi, who stood there like a statue, painfully aware that things were not turning out the way he'd hoped. Li Yan then turned to look at Wenjuan's brother and young uncle. They looked around without saying a word, leaving it up to her to find a way out of her predicament. So she glanced at her husband, who nodded that it was OK to do as she was asked. She picked up the phone and returned it to Yan Shouyi, just as his phone, which was in his pocket, rang. He quickly fished it out and looked to see who was calling. It was Shen Xue. This was no time to be taking her call, but ignoring it would be a mistake. So he instinctively turned his back and took the call.

"Not now," he said, "I'm in a meeting."

But Shen Xue's voice was loud enough for everyone in the room to hear.

"Xiao Su's wedding is about to begin, and you mean a lot to her, so don't be late."

"Got it."

He quickly closed the phone. Yu Wenjuan's eyes were on the snow-covered trees just beyond the window.

She said nothing as her young uncle walked up to Yan Shouyi.
"You should go," he said. "You have things to do."
"No," Yan hastily replied, "I really don't."

21

Xiao Su's wedding was held in a hotel called the "Star Metropolis,"
next door to the Drama Academy. It enjoyed an especially good
reputation for a medium-class hotel with outdated furnishings.
The banquet room, however, had a European theme, its walls
decorated with Renaissance-style relief murals and lion heads.
The tables and chairs, on the other hand, were reproductions of
Ming and Qing style furniture: square tables and armchairs with
carvings of dragons on the back. Merging the two styles was like
a tall, husky European man and a short, dainty Chinese woman
walking hand in hand, a disquieting mismatch at the very least.
But it was that quality that gave the place the appearance of
Western flair and luxury. Privately, Xiao Su had told Shen Xue that
despite the high-class appearance, the hotel offered moderately
priced food. And since the manager, a soccer fan, was a friend of
Xiao Sun's fiancé, Mai Zhuang, a so-so soccer player, he was only
charging them half the regular cost. So that's where the wedding
was going to take place.

Yan Shouyi arrived late. The ceremony was half over by the
time he showed up, and the tables were littered with remnants
of food and drink. The guests were getting the newlyweds to kiss
publicly when he walked up to a scowling Shen Xue.

"Where've you been? You said you wouldn't be late. What a
joke."

Yan was late because he'd gone to the maternity ward to see
Wenjuan and the baby, but even if his ex hadn't just had a baby,
this was not someplace he wanted to be. Why? In part because
social events bored him, but, more importantly, he didn't want a

wedding to give Shen Xue ideas. That was something he did not need. Especially on a day when his ex had had a baby, and he could not decide if he should tell Shen Xue or not, a predicament that had kept him awake half the night. Dawn broke, and he hadn't told her. He figured she'd find out sooner or later, and it behooved him not to wait until she heard the news from someone else. But how would she react? Whatever the answer to that question, now was not the time, not in the middle of a wedding. That decided, he said, sounding unhappily defensive:

"Do you think I wanted to be late? I was in a meeting with the station boss."

Xiao Su chose that moment to flounce her way up to Yan Shouyi.

"Our famous guest has arrived. Time for a picture."

With a quick look at Shen Xue, Yan Shouyi stood up and put his arm around the bride's waist.

"If you don't mind," he said, "I'm happy to oblige."

"The flash went off, drawing laughter from people looking on. One of the Academy's instructors, a middle-aged man surnamed Guo strode up, ponytail swaying behind him, and shoved Yan away from Xiao Su.

"Knock it off, Old Yan. It's time to see the newlyweds kiss!"

He pushed Xiao Su up to the bandstand, to have her and Mai Zhuang kiss in front of a hanging banana. While their lips were together, Guo shouted out:

"One, two, three!"

The guests responded:

"Kiss me to death!"

"One, two, three!"

The guests responded:

"Love me to death!"

Shen Xue joined in the excitement; Yan Shouyi made an attempt to go along. Bride and groom kissed three times in all, then the groom took a bite out of the banana and delivered it into the bride's mouth, ending the ritual to the raucous applause of their guests. Old Guo, who appeared to have had too much to drink, staggered up to Yan Shouyi.

"When everybody was shouting the slogans," he said, "Old Yan held back. I wonder why that was. Is he waiting until he and Shen Xue tie the knot to really shout?"

That comment proved the statement that you always pick up the teapot before it boils. It hit Yan where he lived. But he jumped to his feet and, to lessen the damage, put up a phony defense to match the fake surroundings:

"You're right, I did hold back, because what I wanted to shout was: I'm jealous to death!"

That was greeted with enthusiastic applause and laughter. Xiao Su doubled over, giving Yan the chance to change the subject.

"I heard Shen Xue say that Xiao Su has a special way of dealing with students at night. If she catches them out of bed she makes them do pushups. As far as I'm concerned, from now on, Xiao Su should be responsible only for dealing with our iron defender and leave the students to me."

More laughter. The iron defender, Mai Zhuang, the groom, hurried over and, with a laugh, clinked glasses with Yan, who emptied his.

Yan was feeling the effects of all he'd drunk by the time the wedding party ended, but he was not too drunk to see that his performance had pleased Shen Xue. They were back at the dormitory by midafternoon, and as she helped him climb the stairs she made it sound as if she was unhappy with him:

"How come somebody else's wedding gets such a charge out of you? You kept emptying your glass, while everybody else sipped their way through the toasts."

"Not easy, I tell you," he said with a shake of his head, "not easy at all."

She helped him off with his shoes when they were back in the flat.

"We pulled something off," she said. "I was able to switch a bottle of water for one of liquor, and Xiao Su put on a terrific act. She wasn't really drunk. Could you tell?"

Yan Shouyi waved his hand.

"Nobody could tell what was really going on."

Shen Xue helped him into the bedroom.

"Xiao Su said that when it's my turn, she'll do the same thing for me."

Yan Shouyi was sober enough to realize what she was saying, something he had to steer clear of. And so, pretending to be drunker than he really was, he repeated himself:

"Not easy, not easy at all."

With that he fell onto the bed, pretending to pass out. Two minutes later, he was out.

Night had fallen by the time he woke up, still groggy. The first thing he saw were the contents of his bag, strewn all over the bed. The bag itself was on the far edge of the bed. Shen Xue was rummaging through the contents.

"Why must you always tidy up my bag?" he said unhappily.

The words were barely out of his mouth when he saw that she was holding the phone he'd bought for Yu Wenjuan earlier in the day. That sobered him up completely. She looked puzzled.

"Shouyi, since when did you start carrying two cell phones?"

He could have kicked himself for being so careless. Telling her about Yu Wenjuan and the baby now would look like he was forced into revealing it to her, so he made up a story:

"Fei Mo's phone crapped out on him, so the production team bought him a new one."

Shen Xue laid the phone down and turned her attention to other things.

"Who bought it for him?" she asked as she moved the contents of his bag around. "And why get Fei Mo such a fancy model?"

Then something occurred to her and she picked the phone up again. She made a face.

"No, Shouyi, this is a girl's phone."

Now she was glaring at Yan Shouyi, who started to get nervous. She flung the phone down on the bed.

"I knew there was something wrong with you today," she said. "You were late to the wedding this morning, a meeting, you said. Well, dogs don't get out of the habit of eating shit. Which slut did you buy this for, that's what I want to know!"

She spun around and went out onto the balcony, leaving Yan to smack himself on the forehead. He already had a headache, which probably meant that today's liquor had been a local knock-off. He quickly dressed and followed her out onto the balcony. From that vantage point he saw the capital city all lit up. Shen Xue was just standing there, so he put his hand on her shoulder and made up his mind to tell her everything.

"Here's the truth. That phone wasn't something they bought for Fei Mo. I bought it for Yu Wenjuan, who had a baby yesterday."

The news hit Shen Xue like a thunderclap. She stood there, mouth open, as if she wanted to say something, but immediately forgot what that something was. Then after a long pause, she said:

"How can that be?"

Yan Shouyi assumed the same tone:

"You're right."

Anyone would think they were of one mind, that the child had no right to exist.

Shen Xue turned to face Yan Shouyi.

"I was wondering why you got so drunk today. Maybe overjoyed to finally have a son. You're a better actor than Xiao Su!"

"Overjoyed? More like depressed."

A thought occurred to her.

"What do you plan to do?"

Yan Shouyi wrung his hands and sucked in a mouthful of air.

"That's a problem," he said.

"What do you mean, a problem? With me out of the way, you can go back to her. What's wrong with that? A wife *and* a son, one big happy family!"

"That's not what I meant when I said it's a problem. The baby's here, and I can't refuse to have anything to do with him, can I?"

"You're a liar, Yan Shouyi," Shen Xue said angrily. "All the time I've been with you, you haven't said a word about this."

He threw up his hands.

"I tell you, this was news to me. Like you, it took me by surprise. But I'm telling you, that's how things are, and, like it or not, you're going to have to accept it. Use your head."

She stood there, dumbstruck, so he continued:

"Let me put it this way. Let's say I already had a kid before the divorce, then you and I got together. Stuff like that happens all the time."

Then, in an abrupt shift, he added:

"A Caesarian, the incision isn't healing well."

By then, Shen Xue was crying.

"How come it seems that everybody's lying to me?"

"Who's lying to you? No one."

"How come I feel like I'm all alone?"

Leaning over the railing, she cried.

Yan Shouyi knew he should say something, but had no idea what. And that reminded him of what it had been like with Yu Wenjuan, when he had nothing to say. Without warning, he suddenly felt the alcohol again, as the city lights began to swirl at their feet.

22

After the baby's first month, Yu Wenjuan's brother took her back with him to Nanjing to recuperate. She stayed six months, to Yan

Shouyi's great relief. Twice during that period he sent money, and both times it was returned.

23

Spring arrived.

24

According to Wu Yue, the fatal message she'd sent to Yan Shouyi from Lushan was a spur-of-the-moment thing. Beijing swelters in August, and she'd accompanied a trendy novelist to Lushan, where she wanted to revise her manuscript. Wu Yue had no use for the novelist, since her narrative relied solely on nonsense, and, if that weren't enough, it was filled with typos and misprints. Her favorite expression was "tears trickling down the cheek," tears that trickled three times a page. But she emphasized writing with her body, in particular, her lower body, which was what lofted her onto the bestseller charts. She herself was a squat woman with a melon-shaped face and a compact body with no discernible figure. Wu Yue's publisher handed her the assignment, which she immediately refused.

"Just the sight of her makes my skin crawl. I won't go. Besides, I've been to Lushan, and I don't like the place."

Old He, who had a thin and, to him, much beloved, comb-over that crept from one side of his head to the other, laid his hand on Wu Yue's shoulder.

"No, you have to go," he said. "This is work, not a vacation."

Wu Yue began backing down.

"Why does it have to be Lushan? If the heat bothers her, what's wrong with Beidaihe?"

Old He tapped her shoulder with one finger.

"She wanted to go to Xishuang Banna, and I talked her into

Lushan."

Wu Yue reached up and removed Old He's hand.

"Shit!"

In Lushan, she and the novelist checked into adjoining rooms in the Lushan Hotel, and Wu Yue didn't spot anything out of the ordinary until after dinner, when she went to open the door of her room and she saw that it was 102, the same room she'd had two years earlier, during that conference, the night that Yan Shouyi had quietly opened the door and walked in. Just then the novelist knocked at her door and invited her to go for a walk to Guling.

"I've heard," she said, "that there's a street in Guling where the prostitutes hang out. Let's go see."

"I've got a headache," Wu Yue said. "You go."

After the novelist left, Wu Yue lay down on the bed to watch TV. As she surfed the channels, there, all of a sudden, was Yan Shouyi. "Straight Talk" was on the air.

"Bastard!" she said with a laugh.

She stripped down to her bra and panties, stacked one pillow on top of another, and slipped under the covers to watch. Grinning from ear to ear, Yan bowed to her.

"Good evening, folks, I'm Yan Shouyi, and this is 'Straight Talk.' The discussion topic of tonight's show is 'Is It OK to Lie?' From the moment we wake up in the morning to the time we go to sleep at night, we speak on average twenty-seven-hundred sentences. That doesn't count you people who talk in your sleep . . . add another thirty or so "

The studio audience laughed. So did Wu Yue. In later days Yan Shouyi would recall that he had originally called the episode "Why Are People from Henan Such Liars?" But the station boss had thought the Henanese would be offended, and broadened the topic to include everybody. If it had only been the Henanese, the discussion would have taken a different slant, and Wu Yue wouldn't have acted so rashly. On the screen, Yan Shouyi walked toward his audience.

"Is it OK to lie?" he asked. "I don't have enough experience to answer that question. Even when I was little, I tried to tell lies, but was never very good at it. All you folks in the audience and those watching at home are probably more experienced than I in this regard. So let's hear what you have to say."

More laughter. Wu Yue watched as an elderly man took the microphone.

"I don't see what there is to talk about. Is it OK to lie? The answer's obvious. I've sold candy in a shop for forty years, and I've never cheated a customer, whether they bought two pounds or two ounces . . ."

"I can tell just by looking at you that you're an honest man," Yan said. "But outside of selling candy, have you ever lied in your personal life?"

The old man filled the screen as he thought about that.

"I told a lie once, when I was young and in love. I was afraid to tell the girl I wanted to marry that I sold candy for a living, so I said I worked for a labor union."

"So what you're saying is, it's OK to tell a lie when you're in love, but only then?"

The audience laughed. Wu Yue didn't.

A middle-aged man stood up.

"I won't talk about falling in love, I'll talk about buying a house, since that's the best way to view social mores. I searched half of Beijing when I was looking for a house, and I never heard an honest word. Ads in the paper? Hah! Tall trees, nice lawn, nothing but come-ons. If you call them on it, they say you're too literal."

"It doesn't sound to me like they were lying," Yan said. "The trees are real, so are the lawns, just in a different location."

At that moment, Wu Yue felt as if a needle had pricked her heart. A woman stood up. She looked like a mill worker. She pointed a finger at Yan Shouyi.

"Here's what I think. A liar is anyone who opens his mouth to speak. The question is, who? Take us, for instance, when we're borrowing money, we'll lie to friends and family. But famous people like you are different. When you lie, the effect is nothing to laugh at . . ."

The audience applauded.

"I think I know what you're getting at. If you and I go out, you can lie to me, but I can't lie to you."

The audience roared. Wu Yue got out of bed, still in bra and panties, opened the door to the balcony and walked out, where she gazed up at Incense Peak, which was shrouded in evening mist. *The trees are real, so are the lawns.* Two years ago, this is where they grew. TV noise reached her outside. She would later tell Yan Shouyi that it was that sentence that reminded her of so much of what had happened in that room two years earlier. They had talked a lot that night before he put his arms around her, two sweaty bodies, and in his frenzy he had said over and over:

"I love you . . . I love you . . ."

When they were finished, he fondled her breasts and said:

"Green water flows far."

It was getting nippy out on the balcony, but she hardly felt it. She was crying, and in the midst of her anger, she sent him that message.

At the time, Yan Shouyi was at a foot-washing salon with Fei Mo, Shen Xue, and Li Yan, all having their feet washed. Yan, who disliked the practice, was there only because Fei Mo was so insistent. Yan had invited Fei Mo and Li Yan to a birthday dinner for Shen Xue. On their way home after dinner, they passed a shop called "Good Family Foot-Washing," and Fei Mo said he wanted to drop in. Yan wasn't so sure. Back when he and Yu Wenjuan were together, not only had she soaked her feet every night, she'd made him do it as well, something he'd never done before. Not that it was something he disliked—he knew it was good for tired feet—

but it was too involved a process for him, a real pain. He wouldn't even do it at home, and at a salon it would take a whole hour out of the day. First came the rubbing, by short, unrefined village girls—their more attractive sisters all worked in nightclubs—some of them, the newly arrived, still smelling like the countryside, to the discomfort of their clients. Noting Yan Shouyi's hesitation, Fei Mo nudged him with his elbow and made a barely noticeable gesture toward his wife.

"Let's go in," he said. "If we don't, she'll start surfing the internet as soon as we get home, and that really bugs me. These days, I don't ever feel like going home. I'd rather hang around outside."

Yan Shouyi had little choice but to go on in with his friends. The salon had only been open a short time, and the furnishings were still new. But the smell of fresh paint had Yan Shouyi thinking of beating a hasty retreat until he saw Fei Mo settle into one of the easy chairs and let the attendant take off his socks. He decided to put personal desires aside and sit down next to his friend. Once the washing began, Fei Mo could see that Yan Shouyi was not in a good mood, and hastened to start a conversation. Pointing at the sign on the wall that said "Good Family Foot-Washing," he said:

"The owner of this place obviously didn't have much of an education. The name is all wrong."

Yan Shouyi gave him a quizzical look.

"What's wrong with it?"

"He shouldn't have called it 'good family.' That makes you wonder."

The girl in front of Fei Mo, who had already begun kneading his feet, bore down with her fingers and spoke up—the accent pegged her as Sichuanese.

"That's not what the owner meant. It refers to the four goods."

"What four goods?"

"Good girls, good hearts, good service, and good impressions."

"A perfect example of a coverup."

Fei Mo asked the girl:

"What if I don't feel good about the service?"

Before the attendant working on Fei Mo could answer him, the one working on Yan Shouyi looked up at Fei Mo and blurted out:

"You have to feel good about it. If you don't, the owner will deduct something from our wages."

They all laughed at that. Li Yan, who was sitting next to Shen Xue, pointed at her husband and said:

"That's just like him, making people unhappy wherever he goes."

With a *ping*, Yan Shouyi's cell phone announced the arrival of a text message. Unconcerned, he took out his phone and saw it was from Wu Yue. Now was not the time to see what it said, not with Shen Xue around, so he shut the phone.

"Who's the message from?" asked Shen Xue, who was sitting across from him.

Yan put the phone back into his pants pocket and replied:

"Big Duan, more of those stupid dirty jokes. I'm not interested."

Now, this episode could and should have gone no further, but Yan Shouyi was a little too clever for his own good. He waited until Shen Xue wasn't paying attention to take the phone out again and, with the foot-washing attendant between them, switched the ringer to vibrate. That way, if anyone called, it would go unnoticed. He could have turned the phone off, but in the wake of the birth of his son, he wanted to be reachable in case Yu Wenjuan needed to contact him. As promised, he kept it on 24/7. The fact that Yu Wenjuan had never called him on his cell phone made no difference; if anything, that seemed like an even better reason not to turn it off. Now that it was on vibrate, he settled back to have his feet washed. The sensation of having his feet rubbed and kneaded seemed to improve the flow of blood throughout his body, and he dozed off for about ten minutes. The vibrating phone jolted him awake. Afraid it might be Wu Yue calling, he pretended not to notice. Leave it to the girl washing his feet to ruin everything. Of course that wasn't what she meant to do when she pointed to his pants pocket and said:

"Wake up, Uncle."

Feigning ignorance, he opened his eyes.

"What is it?"

"The phone in your pocket, it's vibrating."

Suddenly he experienced a flop sweat. He sneaked a quick look at Shen Xue. She wasn't paying attention, so he took out his phone and looked at the read-out. It wasn't Wu Yue. He didn't recognize the number, so, with a sigh of relief, he answered:

"Hello, who's this?"

The vibrations had gone on too long. The party had hung up. So he put down the phone and said to Fei Mo—though it was really for Shen Xue's ears:

"A reporter, probably. The topic on today's show was 'Is It OK to Lie?' With them it's always something."

He'd have done himself a favor by not saying anything, but he had, and it put Shen Xue on her guard. Trying to sound lighthearted, she reached out and said:

"Here, let me see the number, so you don't try to put something over on me. You wouldn't be afraid to answer unless it was some girl."

Ever since their recent arguments, she'd kept a close eye on Yan. First of all, she'd found that stack of photos of women in his briefcase and wasn't sure she believed his story that they were candidates for a hostess on "Straight Talk." The second reason had to do with Yu Wenjuan—she was afraid that the embers from the marriage had not died out. He handed her his phone. What else could he do?

"Go ahead, it's not a number I know."

Shen Xue studied the number. No name, just numbers, and so there was no way to identify the caller. She closed it and was handing it back to Yan Shouyi when a thought struck her. She opened it again.

"Your phone rang a while ago," she said, "so why is it on vibrate?"

Yan Shouyi saw that Fei Mo was looking at him, as was Li Yan—wide-eyed. With a nonchalant shrug, he said:

"I didn't want to disturb anyone, especially when we're relaxing and having our feet washed."

That, he figured, ought to do it, but then Shen Xue started scrolling back, and there was Wu Yue's text message. Her reaction to what she read was immediate and violent: she kicked over the basin in which her feet were soaking, drenching the attendant and staggering everyone in the room.

"I knew you were covering something up, that you were playing games with me. Here, read this."

Li Yan, a busybody by nature, jumped out of her seat, barefoot, and rushed over to see what the message said. She was aghast as she handed the phone to Fei Mo, who also read the message; he was nearly as surprised as his wife. Yan Shouyi took the phone from him and read what was on the screen:

Yan Shouyi, you can lie to me if you want, but I can't lie to you. I'm at Lushan, in our room. You told me that green water runs far. Crap!

Yan broke out in a cold sweat. The woman's an idiot! Later on he would complain to her:

"OK, the place reminded you of old times, and that pissed you off. But because all you could think of was yourself, you really screwed me."

But for now, his hand shook as he said to Shen Xue:

"She sent that, not me. I don't know what she's talking about."

Shen Xue was so angry her chest was heaving.

"You don't know what she's talking about? Your memory's that bad? You always said there was nothing between you and Wu Yue, and that Yu Wenjuan overreacted. But this woman wrote about the 'room' and 'green water runs far.' What could be clearer than that?"

Things were getting out of hand, so Yan Shouyi lowered his head and charged ahead:

"So what if something happened? That was years ago, before I met you."

"If it happened in the past, who's to say it isn't still going on? Why else would she send the message?"

Fei Mo stood up to try to make peace.

"We all agree that she wrote their 'room' and 'green water runs far,' but we're forgetting that she followed that with 'crap.' Obviously angry. And even if she was trying to win him back, I know he'd refuse."

He put on slippers, walked over to Shen Xue, and laid his hand on her shoulder.

"Shen Xue," he said, "he and I are together all the time, and I know he's a man of character. If there was something in his past, those embers died long ago."

Shen Xue pushed Fei Mo's hand away, put on her shoes—without her socks—and, drying her tears, headed out of the foot-washing salon, but not before firing off one last shot.

"Yan Shouyi, I never dreamed you could be so dirty!"

If the episode had stopped at this point, the damage would have been minimal. But after Shen Xue stormed out in anger, the others lost interest in having their feet washed. So they dried their feet and put on their shoes and socks.

"Let's go try to smooth things over with her," Fei Mo said to Yan Shouyi.

Yan shook his head.

"Wait till she's cooled down a bit," he said.

"He's right," Li Yan said. "She needs to be alone. Anyone else would be adding fuel to the fire. Besides, Shouyi wouldn't be able to sweet-talk her."

Fei Mo looked over at Yan Shouyi and sighed.

"It's my fault. If I hadn't insisted on getting our feet washed today, none of this would have happened."

Yan said good-bye to Fei Mo and Li Yan and went home, where Shen Xue was inside taking a shower. The bathroom's glass door was fogged over. But Yan saw movement on the other side, which meant he'd probably come through OK this time. Besides, he'd told her the truth, it had all happened years before, and there was no talk of rekindling embers; he was doing everything possible to avoid Wu Yue. Even if he had tried to hide this part of his history from Shen Xue in the past, it wouldn't have been any different than the old man who sold candy in the segment "Is It OK to Lie" that was broadcast that day: it was for love, which made lying virtuous.

After her shower, Shen Xue came out of the bathroom in her pajamas, a towel wrapped around her head, and stony-faced. She ignored Yan Shouyi, but at least she didn't pick up where she'd left off. She went straight into the bedroom and slammed the door behind her. Yan Shouyi knew she'd given that text message some thought and saw that she'd overreacted. He'd later say to Wu Yue:

"Thank God you added the word 'crap' to your message. Without it I'd have really been sunk."

Yan relaxed as he sat lethargically on the sofa, prepared to let time take the edge off Shen Xue's anger and resentment. In fact, why not spend the night on the sofa and see what tomorrow brings? But then he was reminded of the phone call he'd missed at the foot-washing salon. At the time, there'd been so much going on that the number hadn't registered. But now, in the quiet of his own home, he wondered if maybe he hadn't seen it somewhere. Now where was that? Then it hit him—it was Yu Wenjuan's brother's cell phone. After she'd gone to Nanjing to rest and get her strength back, his only source of news about her and the baby had come via her brother, a decent fellow who didn't mind occasionally letting Shouyi know how they were doing. He hadn't entered the number in his contact list to keep Shen Xue from knowing about it. Up till then, Yan had always initiated the call, not the other way around. This was a first, and he worried that something might have happened to Wenjuan or the baby. Panic set in for the second time that night, worse than his reaction to Wu Yue's text message. He instinctively glanced at the bedroom door. Her getting upset with him had turned out to be a blessing in disguise. By staying clear of her, he wouldn't have to worry that she'd have anything to do with him. So he tiptoed into the bathroom, shut the door quietly, and sat down on the toilet seat, where he scrolled down to the number and pressed the send button.

What he heard was:

We're sorry, but the phone at this number has been turned off.

That was good news. By turning off his phone and not calling again, the brother was effectively letting him know that Yu Wenjuan and the baby were fine, at most a bit of fever. What concerned him was that by not returning the call until tomorrow her brother might be upset enough to not answer, which would cut off his sole pipeline to news about Wenjuan and the baby. So he decided to send a text message to explain why he hadn't answered the call. Still sitting on the toilet, he tapped out:

I was in a meeting when you called and had left my phone in the car. Yours was off by the time I called back. I'll try again tomorrow.

Imagine his surprise when the bathroom door suddenly opened, and Shen Xue walked in. After her shower, she had trimmed her toenails. While admitting to herself that the word 'crap' in the message probably meant they'd had a falling out and were no longer involved, she was still so angry she'd split one of her toenails and had come back to the bathroom for a bandage. She ignored Shouyi, who was still sitting on the toilet, so shaken by her entrance that he instinctively shoved his cell phone down between his legs. But after she'd found what she was looking for and shut the medicine cabinet door, she noticed how tense he looked in the mirror. Suddenly suspicious, she turned to him.

"What are you doing in here?"

Instinctively, he stood up.

"Using the toilet."

The words were barely out when the cell phone fell noisily to the floor.

"With your pants on?"

Then her gaze fell on the phone, and she was ready to explode again.

"Who were you calling? Wu Yue again?"

Yan Shouyi bent down to retrieve his phone.

"No."

She stepped on the phone. By now flames seemed to shoot from her eyes.

"I'm warning you, Yan Shouyi, this time you'd better tell me the truth."

They argued till three in the morning. Eventually, he told her everything, that he was phoning Yu Wenjuan's brother not Wu Yue.

"That's the truth," he swore.

Shen Xue didn't waste a second.

"If that's the truth," she said, "then what you told me before, all lies?"

He handed her the phone, so she could see what he'd written. But he hadn't finished the message and it was open to interpretation. It could have been intended for someone else, but it also could have been intended for Wu Yue. His explanation took half the night. In the end, he managed to convince her that there was no longer anything between him and Wu Yue, and that he'd been writing to Yu Wenjuan's brother. He'd kept the "Ho Chi Minh trail" leading to Yu Wenjuan's brother from her. After her anger had abated, she began to cry.

"How many secrets are you keeping from me, Yan Shouyi? Sharing a life with you is too hard. I'm a simple woman, but you're too complicated, and I can't handle that. I can't keep living with you."

Yan Shouyi just threw up his arms. He didn't know what to say.

25

On his way to work the next morning, Yan Shouyi phoned Yu Wenjuan's brother from his car. The phone rang for two minutes before he answered. His voice sounded the same as always, and Shouyi breathed a sigh of relief. Then he told Shouyi that he'd called the day before to let him know that he'd accompanied Wenjuan and the baby back to Beijing, and that he wanted to see Shouyi before returning to Nanjing.

"I'll come right over."

"No," her brother whispered. "I'm on the balcony, and I don't want her to know I'm talking to you."

Yan Shouyi paused to let the news sink in before saying:

"Come to the TV station, then"

"Not the TV station," her brother said. "Let's meet at the nanny market. I'm leaving tomorrow, and I need to find her a nanny, since she's now a single mother."

The nanny market was in a large tent, like a farmers' market, near Beijing's South Station. Hundreds of girls from the countryside sat on long benches, holding their plastic bundles, as residents of the city walked among them, calling out their choices. The sight reminded Yan Shouyi of eighteenth-century slave markets in the American South or Thailand's red-light districts. When he spotted Wenjuan's brother, they went first to a quiet corner of the tent, where they sat on a nanny bench to talk. They had not been close when he and Wenjuan were together, even when they'd traveled to Nanjing to meet him. Since he had little to say, Shouyi thought he might be a bit of a wimp. His wife, a Yangzhou woman, had once railed at him in her native dialect in front of Shouyi and Wenjuan over some meat he'd bought at the market. He'd just stood there, head bowed, and taken it. At the time, Yan Shouyi could not have predicted that years later this seemingly useless man would play such an important role in his life. He was Shouyi's Ho Chi Minh trail, the string of Shouyi's kite, the sole link between him and his ex and the baby. The first thing he said to Shouyi on this day was:

"You've put on weight."

What was Shouyi supposed to say to that? He just smiled. Then Wenjuan's brother said:

"Your eyes are red. Work must be keeping you too busy to sleep."

Shen Xue had kept him awake the night before. Again he just smiled. Then Wenjuan's brother said:

"I received the money you sent, but I didn't dare let Wenjuan know."

Then, in a soft voice, he said:

"My wife either."

Yan Shouyi nodded.

"The baby can sit up," her brother said, "and when your show comes on the TV, if Wenjuan isn't around, I let him watch."

That was unexpected. *This guy's not bad after all.*

Her brother laughed. "But he can be a little devil. When he wakes up at night, if his bottle is five seconds late coming, he bawls and makes a fuss. On his hundredth day, I laid out a pen, a computer disk, and one of those MashiMaro stuffed rabbits to see which one he'd pick. He went straight for the rabbit."

That made Yan Shouyi laugh.

"I was a handful as a baby too."

Wenjuan's brother heaved a sigh.

"She wasn't happy in Nanjing. You probably didn't know that she never got along with our mother, even as a little girl."

Shouyi did not know, and was surprised by the news. He thought back to that night when he found her talking to a toy puppy and felt a chill run down his spine.

Her brother lit a cigarette and didn't say anything for a long while.

"I hadn't planned to call you this time, but Wenjuan's got a problem, and I'm hoping you'll be willing to help out."

Yan Shouyi looked up. "Of course."

Her brother puffed on his cigarette.

"I was going to go see her young uncle at first, not you. He has some connections. But you know how he is, he thinks his wealth gives him the right to say anything he pleases, and I never liked that."

Yan Shouyi nodded.

"Wenjuan's realty job was secure when she left for Nanjing," her brother said. "But while she was gone, the company went out of business. Is there any way you can help her find work?"

Yan Shouyi was speechless.

"And she mustn't know you did it," her brother made clear. "If you find something, let me know, and I'll tell her an old schoolmate of mine found it for me. You know how she is, smiling on the outside, but stubborn as hell. If she found out you had anything to do with it, she'd make life miserable for me."

Yan Shouyi nodded.

"Keep in mind that she can type," her brother added.

Again Yan Shouyi nodded. Wenjuan's brother looked at him and sighed.

"I know you're divorced and you don't have to do this. Just pretend you're doing it for me."

Yan Shouyi was moved by this slim southerner's comment.

"It's really you who's helping me."

Wenjuan's brother shook his head, flipped away his cigarette, and took a photo out of his pocket.

"I took this before we came to Beijing," he said as he handed it to Yan Shouyi.

It was a picture of Yu Wenjuan holding a husky little boy in her arms. He'd gotten a lot bigger since Shouyi had seen him in the nursery. Wenjuan was smiling, but he wore a frown, like an unhappy boy.

"I know you'd like to see him, but now isn't the right time. I'll work on her, but it'll take a while. We'll just take this one step at a time, you know."

With his eyes on the photo, Yan Shouyi nodded.

"She registered him under her name, Yu. I'll work on that too."

Yan Shouyi nodded.

They stood up and went looking for a nanny, settling on a nineteen-year-old girl from Gansu. She had a ruddy face, but looked like an honest girl. Her name was Ma Jinhua. She was carrying a printed cotton bundle. After they took care of the paperwork, Wenjuan's brother left for home with the new nanny, while Yan Shouyi headed for his car. He took out the photograph. What had so disturbed him was his own lack of emotion. The same thought that had occurred to him six months earlier at the nursery—that the child was nothing but a burden, trouble he did not need—recurred. He forced it out of his mind, since holding on to it would shame him terribly.

26

Yan Shouyi spent the next week quietly looking for work for Yu Wenjuan, during which time his relationship with Shen Xue, following a stormy period, gradually returned to normal. A three-day cold war ended one evening at the dinner table, when he noticed that she had bought some sheep's trotters for him. It was one of his favorites, as Yu Wenjuan had known, and now so did Shen Xue. The trotters opened the door for him to explain a few things to Shen Xue, starting with his relationship with Wu Yue. That, he insisted, was over, and any talk to the contrary was crap!

She held her tongue while he went on to talk about Yu Wenjuan and the baby.

"Like I've said many times, life is tough for a woman and a child alone. On those infrequent occasions when I'm in touch with her, it's to ask about my son, not to get back with her. What would people say if I just washed my hands of them?"

Shen Xue bent over her food and said nothing.

"Stop worrying," Shouyi added. "With Yu Wenjuan it's a case of spilled water. Even if I wanted to gather it back up, which I don't, she wouldn't be interested. I can't even ask about the boy without going through her brother."

Now Shen Xue looked up. She was beginning to come around, but slowly.

"I'm not saying you can't have anything to do with them. What makes me mad is the way you do things behind my back."

"Like what?" Shouyi threw out his arms.

"Like everything. Instead of laying things out in the open and telling the truth, you hide them from me, with careful scheming."

Shouyi's reaction was an embarrassed smile.

"I hide them because I care about you. If I've done anything behind your back in the past, count it as a case of a small-minded man trying to guess what a high-minded woman wants. From now on, transparency will be the watchword in this government."

"That's still not it!" she said, glaring at him. "I can't help feeling that your heart is starting to wander."

"Who, me?" Shouyi laughed. "My heart's not going anywhere."

"I'm not afraid if it is," Shen Xue said. "Don't fool yourself that I can't live without you. In fact, over the past few days I've been asking myself if now isn't the time to leave you."

"You're right," Shouyi remarked between bites of a trotter. "It's me who can't live without you."

Back to normal. He'd probably meant it when he promised transparency, and there were definitely things he did out in the open. But finding work for Yu Wenjuan could not be one of them. That he had to keep from her. If she found out, a blow-up would follow. He could almost hear her spiteful words:

"Only the child, you said, not Yu Wenjuan!"

So he kept it from her, and not just her, but Yu Wenjuan as well. When a rat gnaws its way into a bellows, air comes at it from both ends. Yan Shouyi didn't know whether to laugh or to cry.

What really frustrated him was his lack of progress in finding work for Yu Wenjuan. He'd thought that, with his name, finding a job for her would be relatively easy. How wrong he was. First, she had few marketable skills. In fact, outside of her stubborn nature, about all she was good for was typing. That narrowed the search. He phoned the heads of some of the organizations he was familiar with, as well as the CEOs of local companies. Their thrill at receiving a personal call from the famous Yan Shouyi was short-lived, lasting only until they heard that he was trying to find a job for a friend. Almost every organization and business was already staffed to the bursting point. The change in attitude was manifested not in open refusals, but in the expression "I'll see what I can do." Which meant, of course, wait till the year of the minotaur and the month of the unicorn, as they say. Making a follow-up call the next day would be impolite. A famous name, he realized, has no standing. These people could treat him with respect to his face, but since he had nothing they wanted, no quid pro quo was even remotely possible. He told Old Fei how much trouble he was having.

"A scholar's feelings are thin as paper," Fei Mo said with a sigh.

"Empty fame," he continued, "a false reputation. Now you see how much it's worth."

Wu Yue, who had returned from Lushan, phoned Shouyi to pressure him to write that foreword for Fei Mo's book. He lashed out at her over the phone, telling her what an idiot she'd been to send that text message from Lushan, the one that had caused all the trouble. She just laughed. But then she explained that she'd been moved by the familiar surroundings and her memories of what had happened there. While she was talking, it dawned on Shouyi that he could use the requested foreword as leverage to get Yu Wenjuan a clerical job at the publishing house. She knew how to type, after all, so it was a good fit. Needless to say, he'd have to swallow his pride, given what each side was getting out of the deal, but at this point, his hands were tied. By getting him to write a foreword they were using him, weren't they? If Old He's daughter hadn't been Fei Mo's grad student, his book would never see the light of day. Given this state of affairs, he had few options. And it was all Yu Wenjuan's fault! Her stubborn streak had cost him plenty of face. But he couldn't say all this to Wu Yue over the phone; they'd have to meet. And that thought brought Shen Xue back into the picture. What would she be doing over the next few days? As it turned out, she was scheduled to take students to see an experimental play the next night. The title, she'd said, was *A Peck of Rice*, and it comprised spreading a peck of rice over the stage and picking it up one grain at a time. Since it was a class, Yan Shouyi was not invited. How many grains of rice in a peck? He wondered. Had to be at least a hundred thousand, several hours' worth of picking. Just right, he felt, so he decided to invite Wu Yue for dinner.

"Let's have dinner tomorrow night. I'm not quite sure what your boss wants me to write, so bring him along."

"It's a date," Wu Yue said, obviously pleased.

They decided on a hot-pot restaurant near the Sijiqing Bridge on Fourth Ring Road, a place he and Wu Yue had visited when they were romantically involved. When he arrived the next night, Wu Yue was alone. Her boss hadn't come along.

"Why isn't Old He coming?" Yan asked.

"What do we need him for? It's only a foreword. I can tell you what we want."

This was a discouraging development. But there was nothing he could do about it, and they had to eat, so they went inside, where a private room was waiting for them. But before they reached it, one of the waitresses recognized Yan Shouyi and asked to have her picture taken with him. That was just the beginning, as another waitress walked up with the same request, and before it was over, paper-hatted cooks were filing out of the kitchen to be photographed with Yan Shouyi, followed by several of the diners. Yan was not pleased. First of all, he could kick himself for forgetting to wear his dark glasses, and second, he knew he couldn't make his displeasure known.

"Let's take a group picture," he said with a sweep of his arms.

No dice. They wanted individual photos with the famous man. Half an hour later, they finally made it into the room, where Wu Yue put her face up next to his and said:

"That should have satisfied your vanity."

"To hell with vanity," he said. "I want more than that from you."

When the hot-pot made it to their table, he told her his plan for trading the foreword for a job for Yu Wenjuan. He would not have been so direct if Old He had joined them, but with Wu Yue he did not have to mince his words. When he finished, she pointed at him with her chopsticks, from which hung slices of lamb.

"I tell you, Yan Shouyi, you're going backward in your old age. You even have conditions for writing a foreword for a friend."

"I'm just taking pity on an orphan child and his single mother," he quipped.

Then he sighed and said seriously:

"I don't have a choice. Talk to Old He and tell him I'm not asking him to hire her in his office."

"Then where do you want her to be hired?"

"He knows his way around the publishing industry. See if he can come up with something."

Wu Yue stuck the lamb slices into the boiling water.

"I don't understand," she said.

Not willing to be completely truthful, he made up an explanation.

"If I write your foreword and she's hired at your place, that would be too obvious. Not only that, since you were the cause of my divorce, that could make things awkward."

What really worried him were the possible consequences of the arrangement. If either Yu Wenjuan or Shen Xue found out what he was up to, this drama would play out in ways that would make life miserable for him. Wu Yue took out her cell phone and dialed her boss's number.

"Here, talk to him yourself. I don't want to have anything to do with this. You divorced Yu Wenjuan, but didn't marry me afterward, so I don't owe her a thing."

Yan's cell phone chirped. He checked the read-out. It was Shen Xue. He immediately held his finger to his lips so Wu Yue wouldn't say anything.

"Hello . . . the play's over? Me? I'm at the Atlantic City Hot-Pot Restaurant . . . some people from the publishing house . . . about that foreword for Fei Mo's book . . ."

He hesitated for a moment, but then made happy sounds.

"Sure, come on over."

Yan put his phone away, suddenly a nervous man. Shen Xue had told him that the play had ended and she'd missed dinner. When she said she'd like to join him, under different circumstances, he could easily have fended her off. But he didn't, thanks to a guilty conscience. The damned play had ended earlier than he'd expected—most of the time, experimental plays seemed never-ending, with meaningless dialogue that could last three or four hours. Wouldn't you know it, this playwright had decided to be pithy! How in the world had they picked up a hundred thousand grains of rice in so short a time? Afterward, he asked Shen Xue that very question.

"It wasn't just a few actors taking their time picking it up," she explained. "The audience joined in. And they only threw out one peck of rice, but wound up with three or four when it was over. Know why?"

Yan Shouyi shook his head.

"Because the director allowed the audience to toss small coins into the containers and changed the title of the play on the spot to *Three or Four Pecks More*."

Yan Shouyi got his answer. But that was then. At this moment in the restaurant, that play was the last thing he wanted to think about. He couldn't have Shen Xue run into Wu Yue, not here.

"Trouble," he said. "Shen Xue's on her way over."

"Great," Wu Yue said, unconcerned. "Let her find a job for Yu Wenjuan. She got a good deal, so she ought to do her part to help out the victim."

"I think it's best if you leave," he said, looking straight at Wu Yue.

"If anyone's going to leave," she replied testily, "it should be you. I'm staying right here. You may be afraid of her, but I'm not."

Then, pointing her finger at him, she said:

"You should see the look on your face. You poor, mistreated thing."

"I'm not afraid of her," he said, more than a little abashed. "I just know how awkward you'd feel in one another's company." But, since getting her to leave wasn't going to work, he said:

"When you see her, please don't say anything about finding a job for Yu Wenjuan."

A quarter of an hour later, Shen Xue, handbag in hand, showed up at the restaurant. "Where is everybody?" she asked when she saw that Shouyi was alone.

"In the restroom," he replied. "Wu Yue's here."

Seeing the startled look on Shen Xue's face, he continued:

"I know what you're thinking, but this is strictly about Fei Mo's foreword. You know I can't keep putting that off. The truth is, she hasn't been involved in Fei Mo's book, it's her boss at the publishing house, Old He. Actually, it's not even him, it's his daughter, who happens to be Fei Mo's grad student . . ."

There was a bit of incoherence in his explanation, which came to an abrupt end when Wu Yue appeared, drying her hands on a paper towel. To her credit, she stuck out her hand to welcome Shen Xue.

"You must be Shen Xue," she said. "I'm Wu Yue, from the publishing house."

Shen Xue quickly recovered from a momentary start by taking the hand.

"Ah," she said, "so you're Wu Yue. I've heard Shouyi mention your name."

Yan Shouyi breathed a sigh of relief, happy to witness the genial meeting. Now that the two women were in their seats, he called out to the serving crew:

"Another place setting!"

He turned to Shen Xue. "Something came up, and Old He had to leave."

Wu Yue decided to be helpful:

"He has an early flight tomorrow morning. A book fair in Xi'an."

She followed her little charade by kicking Yan Shouyi under the table. He lurched and pulled his leg back, drawing a quizzical look from Shen Xue, who took a package out of her handbag. It was a baby's outfit. She smiled at Yan Shouyi.

"Before I took my students to the play," she said, "I stopped by the mall and bought this for your son. I hope it fits."

That was the last thing in the world he expected. Shen Xue had never shown any indication that she cared a whit about his son. Maybe she'd changed. He was touched by this unexpected turn of events.

"It'll fit, I'm sure it will."

As Shen Xuen dipped slices of lamb into the boiling water, she smiled at Wu Yue.

"I wasn't going to come, but the words 'hot-pot,' made me hungry," she said.

Wu Yue returned the smile.

"Me, too," she said. "It's addictive."

Thinking he detected an edgy undercurrent in the conversation, Yan quickly laid down the baby outfit and shouted out the door:

"Bring us some fried duck's blood."

He turned to Wu Yue.

"It's one of Shen Xue's favorites."

As Yan Shouyi drove home after leaving the restaurant; he could tell that something was bothering Shen Xue, which created a pall in the car. Feeling a need to break the silence, he said:

"Fei Mo's book is called *Speak*, so I've titled my foreword 'Intimate Words Are Hard to Speak.' What do you think?"

A stern look had settled over Shen Xue's face.

"Tell me, Shouyi, how many people were in that room before I came?"

"I told you, there were three of us, and Old He had to leave early."

"How do you explain the fact that there were only two place settings?"

Taken by surprise, Yan realized that she hadn't changed after all. Shen Xue would always be Shen Xue. He had to come up with something, and quick.

"The waitress took his away."

She sneered.

"You're insulting my intelligence, Shouyi."

He let this comment pass and concentrated on his driving. But a moment later he sighed and said:

"You're right, there were just the two of us, but it was about my foreword and nothing else. I made up a story to keep you from getting suspicious."

"What upset me was how she went along with it by saying that

Boss He had to be in Xi'an tomorrow. A seamless bit of deception. I can only imagine what went on in there before I arrived, but you made sure to keep me in the dark. Exactly what is going on in that head of yours?"

With his back solidly up against a wall, Yan Shouyi's only course was to take the offensive:

"What's in my head? That's what I've been wanting to ask you. I've given you plenty of face, haven't I? For days you've made me feel like a sneak thief, with all your suspicions. It's gotten to the point where I'm afraid to meet with anybody. I'm telling you, what I'm looking for is a wife, not an FBI agent!"

He screeched to a halt by the side of the road, now truly worked up.

"You can do what you want. If you don't want to be with me any longer, you can get the hell out of my car!"

Yan Shouyi had never gotten this angry with Shen Xue in all the time he'd known her. She looked at him in total shock, unable to speak. Fully expecting her to open the door and get out, the last thing he anticipated was that she'd bury her head against the dashboard and burst into tears.

"What do you expect me to say?" she said after composing herself. "All I want is for you to stop lying to me, is that so much to ask?"

More tears.

"I saw what a tramp she is at first sight, and what's wrong with my wanting you to keep your distance from her?"

"I haven't been close to her," Yan said, softening his tone. "This was business."

After starting up the car again, Yan was comforted to see that the crisis had passed, and reached the conclusion that backing off wasn't always the answer to his problems. Sometimes losing your temper worked to your advantage. In the past he'd never been one to speak harshly to people. Maybe it was time to change.

27

Fei Mo's book appeared after the October First celebration. Yan Shouyi had, as promised, written the foreword. Wu Yue told him that after he'd agreed to write it, the publisher had passed this information to Fei Mo, who'd had no reaction to the news. The next morning Yan broached the subject with Fei in his small office.

"Fei Lao, asking me to write the foreword was like piling dung on the Buddha's head."

Fei Mo merely sighed and said frankly:

"I know all about it, how it made things difficult for you and for others."

Yan Shouyi tried to clear up the situation with a light touch.

"Having my name associated with yours raises my cultural level at least one notch."

In truth, Fei Mo's book was not something Yan Shouyi could relate to. When they sent him the galleys, he found it was way beyond his understanding, which could only mean that it was filled with considerable wisdom. Trouble was, it was virtually unreadable. Reading it, one indigestible sentence after another, was like chewing wax. Academics who write books that purport to "speak" unfortunately cannot form a single sentence that a normal human being would utter. How could Fei Mo, a man with a keen sense of humor who had supplied "Straight Talk" with so many good ideas, be such a boring writer? Confucius was a wise man who wrote stuff that didn't leave the common man scratching his head. Trying to read Fei Mo's book reminded Yan Shouyi of looking at performance art or watching experimental plays with Shen Xue. The objectives were different, as were the means of expression, but though they took different routes, they wound up in the same place. He thought about talking to Fei Mo about this, but could see that this book was his friend's baby.

"Eight years," Fei Mo said, holding up the fingers of both hands, "this took me eight whole years!"

Knowing he needed to tread carefully, Yan Shouyi had to pretend to be a fan of a book he did not understand and hold his nose as he wrote the foreword.

On the big day, the publisher held a well-publicized press conference for a book everyone knew would lose money. Yan Shouyi would be joined by ninety-five percent of the population in their inability to understand it, and submitting to torture was not on their list of fun things to do. Truth of the matter was, people only bought the book to read Yan Shouyi's foreword, since no one knew who Fei Mo was. But Wu Yue had told Yan that the publisher's daughter was finishing up her doctoral dissertation and was about to graduate, which is why Old He was so eager to hold a book launch for Fei Mo—as an expression of thanks to his daughter's teacher. Yan Shouyi showed up that day in suit and tie. Before she set out early that morning, Shen Xue found it strange to see him knotting his tie in the mirror.

"Isn't that going a little overboard for a book launch?"

"It's Fei Mo, after all, which requires a bit more formality."

"You're wearing a tie for Fei Mo? Wu Yue will be there, I know, so maybe that's who you're decking yourself out for."

Being able to joke with him about Wu Yue proved that she'd finally put that hurdle behind her. A deep freeze in their relationship had followed Yan's outburst for three days before the thaw set in. Trying to hide everything or dealing with someone insincerely created only suspicion, so it was better to get everything out in the open, like emptying beans out of a bamboo tube. Back when Yan Shouyi was still living with Yu Wenjuan, he was incapable of quarreling. But now, the way he saw it, raising a row was the best way to solve a problem. That, in essence, was Yan Shouyi's most recent, and most rewarding revelation.

"You got that right," he quipped. "A gentleman acts on behalf of an understanding friend."

The press conference was held at an international VIP hotel. It was a typical press conference, except that it allowed Yan Shouyi to discover one of Fei Mo's secrets, one that shocked him, bigtime. Yan arrived at 9:30, thirty minutes early, only to find that the parking slots in front of the hotel were all taken. He drove around the lot twice, growing increasingly frustrated, until he spotted a car backing out of a space, which he claimed for himself the minute his predecessor drove off. As he sat in his car surveying the scene in front, he spotted a parked little Suzuki Alto with a girl in the driver's seat. He seldom gave more than a passing glance to just any girl, but this one, who wore her hair in braids, caught his attention for the aura of purity and simplicity she radiated, as if it were 1969 all over again. He caught himself staring. And that is when he noticed the fat passenger. The girl's braids were set in motion by her gestured conversation with the man, and she abruptly leaned over and kissed him on the cheek before the man opened the door with a smile and got out—with difficulty, given his bulk and the cramped space in the little car. Imagine Yan Shouyi's astonishment when he realized that it was none other than Fei Mo!

Like a criminal who's been caught in the act, he felt a *whump* in his head. He'd always seen Fei Mo as a principled old-school intellectual who followed the rules. Sneaking around like this was totally out of character. Did this erase the moral difference between them? Yan's initial shock was quickly replaced by a sense of gloating. And not just in regard to Fei Mo, but to the world at large. This is what they mean when they say that hot and cold are shared all around the world. But knowing how important face was to Fei Mo, this was something Yan knew his friend would not want anyone to know, so he stayed in his car until the girl drove off in her little Alto.

And yet, Yan Shouyi's excitement was not so easily suppressed. Once inside the banquet hall, he went looking for Fei Mo, whom he spotted on the escalator. He ran to catch up, claiming a spot on the moving staircase, which was packed with journalists and publishers' representatives who had come for the press conference. They greeted Yan, who returned their greetings before turning to deal with Fei Mo.

"I called you this morning, but you told me not to pick you up. How'd you get here?"

Seemingly oblivious to the tenor of the event, Fei Mo was wearing a casual jacket, which made Yan Shouyi appear overdressed.

"Something came up, so I grabbed a taxi."

Yan Shouyi stifled a laugh.

"I don't think so. You got a ride with someone. Not much of a car, but she wasn't bad."

With a gulp of surprise, Fei Mo felt his face stiffen. Yan Shouyi, the hunter, had caught the wily fox by the tail. Fei Mo was, fair to say, clearly embarrassed. There was no mistaking the evasive look in his eyes behind his glasses.

"A graduate student at the Social Sciences Institute, studying aesthetics, sort of worships me. But I'm telling you, our relationship is strictly platonic, no funny business. So don't get any crazy ideas."

"No funny business, does that include the lips?"

With a laugh, he pointed a finger at Fei Mo and went on:

"You've always told us the only way to stay out of trouble is to be careful. I guess you decided not to take your own advice."

With a frown, Fei Mo took a look around and pointed a stubby finger at Yan Shouyi.

"Old Yan, that was a cruel thing to say. I expected you to be kinder than that."

"All right," Yan Shouyi said, nodding over and over, "I saw nothing, OK?"

With his arm around Fei Mo, Shouyi went with his friend into the banquet hall, where the press conference was about to start.

A podium with a microphone had been set up in front of the main hall, on whose four etched panels were hung large posters of the book, featuring life-sized photos of Fei Mo, with the book's cover on his forehead. Above the four panels, a red-silk banner proclaimed:

Grand Launch Ceremony
for
Fei Mo's New Book, *Speak*

The press conference started on time, at 10:00 sharp. In line with Western custom, not Chinese, there were no tables or chairs. Everyone had to stand, each attendee clutching a copy of the book, given to them when they registered, in one hand, and a drink in the other. Wu Yue, the mistress of ceremonies, was nicely decked out for the occasion, with silver lipstick and a yellow Chinese dress that accentuated her full, jutting breasts. In the past, she'd always preferred short: a short jacket that revealed a strip of skin in the back. But all that changed this morning, and Yan Shouyi was impressed. Video cameras were recording everything. First to speak was Old He, the publisher. He was followed by the sales manager, a middle-aged woman named Gao, who rambled on a bit. But she had only good things to say. Once she stepped away from the microphone, her place was taken by Wu Yue, who said:

"Now that Chief He and Manager Gao have demonstrated their optimism regarding sales of the book, I think it's time to ask the author, Professor Fei Mo, to say a few words."

The room was not as orderly as one might have hoped, since Chinese aren't used to listening to speeches while they're standing. Little by little, drinks in hand, some of the guests began talking among themselves. A polite round of scattered applause greeted the announcement. Maybe he knew why this was happening, maybe he didn't think much of the whole business, maybe all those little groupings got under his skin, and maybe he was still feeling the effects of having his secret discovered by Yan Shouyi, but instead of going up to the microphone when Wu Yue said his name, Fei Mo stayed where he was and shook his head. She gestured for him to come up; he waved her off, the expression on his face hardening noticeably. Poor Wu Yue was in a bind, and showed it. But, blessed with the ability to make the best of a bad situation, she moved on.

"We must assume that Professor Fei would rather not speak, since everything he has to say is right there in the book, something we can take home and enjoy at our leisure. So let's ask the author of the foreword, Yan Shouyi, to make a few comments."

No one had said anything about having him speak at the event, which threw Shouyi off his stride. But he felt a sense of responsibility to the suddenly silent Fei Mo, both to publicly show support for a friend and to display his remorse over bringing his secret into the light of day. Saving face was important to Fei Mo, and had he thought of that, Yan Shouyi would have turned a blind eye to what had occurred. And so, wine glass in hand, he strode energetically up to the microphone. Given his fame, the thunderous applause underscored the anemic handclapping that had preceded Fei Mo's refusal to speak to the gathering. The applause died down and the audience stood in hushed anticipation. No more small groupings. The moment had arrived, and Yan Shouyi had no idea what he should say. Something about Fei Mo's book, of course, since that's why everyone was here. But what? What was the book about? He didn't know, and that would be obvious to anyone who read his foreword, which went round and round without saying anything. The same strategy would have to suffice now.

"Mr. Fei prefers not to say anything, so I guess it's up to me, since on the show I am his mouthpiece. Let me begin by saying that on the escalator a few minutes ago, Mr. Fei was critical of how I was dressed today, a bit over the top, he said. I was understandably concerned, until, that is, until I found myself standing next to Ms. Wu Yue. What could be more appropriate than a suit alongside a *qipao*? At the very least, this underscores the significance of today's event in our lives."

His opening comments were greeted by applause and laughter, just like a taping of "Straight Talk." Wu Yue, who was standing nearby, smiled appropriately.

"In my view," Shouyi started out, "books can be divided into two types—refined and vulgar. Ask me to write a book, and the result will be a casual diversion. But every word and every sentence in Mr. Fei's book functions as guidance toward greater self-understanding..."

Not only was Yan unhelpful in indicating just how that was to occur, he knew that this sort of roundabout talk sooner or later had to give way to something substantial. Then, in a moment of desperation, a light bulb went on. He was reminded of Fei Mo's fit of anger over cell phones months before in the office, and how that had led to a commentary on primitive society, something that then found its way into his book. Now he could deal with specifics.

"Of course functions of guidance are manifest in many aspects, but the one that comes closest to touching the human soul is the relationship between mouth and mind, something I understood only after reading Mr. Fei's book. Why are our lives getting more and more complicated? Because we are getting better and better with words. Before our ancestors had learned how to talk, they spoke with their bodies, which made getting your idea across very difficult, requiring something akin to prolonged gesturing. Lying was even harder. You could hop around all day and still not be able to pull off a deception. Speech changed everything. All you had to do to deceive someone was open your mouth..."

Wu Yue, still stinging from Yan Shouyi's snide comment about her dress, saw an opening to get revenge. Like him, she hid a rebuke in what seemed like an innocuous comment.

"What our Mr. Yan means is, he was so used to lies and deceptions that they didn't even register with him. Now, however, after reading Mr. Fei's book, tendrils of remorse have begun to sprout. But acknowledging one's misdeeds and correcting them in practice are two different things. And so, toward this end, we recommend that the TV program he hosts, 'Straight Talk,' change its format from a talk show to a sort of dance show, and that our Mr. Yan lead us in a dance at the start of each show."

The audience roared. Try though he might, even Fei Mo could not stifle a laugh. And Yan Shouyi? Mortified. But, as a battle-tested TV host, a wealth of experience had taught him to ignore her hidden meaning and target the benign ending of her comment in his counterattack. She had, in fact, done him a favor, for now he knew how to bring his comments to a close and extricate himself from the task he'd been assigned.

"I accept Ms. Wu's suggestion," he replied. "Since we're looking for a woman to take over the hosting duties of 'Straight Talk,' I hope she'll apply, so she and I can dance up a storm in each episode."

Not quite finished, he continued:

"At the same time, we should alert the press secretaries of every government in the world that it is time for us all to change, and that even the White House spokesman must stop talking to the press corps and start dancing for them."

Applause and raucous laughter ensued.

The book launch was a success. Now that it had concluded, the doors decorated with the image of Fei Mo were thrown open to the banquet hall, where a dozen tables groaning under a sumptuous spread sparkled beneath light from crystal chandeliers. With a collective sigh, the journalists and other attendees swept into the room like an onrushing tide. Time to eat.

Fei Mo and Yan Shouyi were seated at the head table, accompanied by the publisher, Old He, Sales Manager Gao, and other ranking publishing and sales personnel. Glasses were raised and formal speeches were given as the meal began, but private conversations were quickly launched at tables, raising a steady buzz in the hall. Seeing that Fei Mo was feeling better about things, Yan took out a photograph and slipped it to his friend. It was the photo of Wenjuan holding the baby, which her brother had given him a few days earlier—she was smiling, he wore a frown. Fei Mo took the photo and scrutinized the baby.

"He's big."

He handed it back to Yan, who said:

"Keep it for me."

"What?" the request surprised Fei Mo.

"I've been keeping it on my book shelf, tucked between the pages of a book. But that's too risky."

With a nod, Fei Mo showed that he understood. But he said:

"It's a fact of life that Shen Xue ought to accept."

"The baby's no problem, it's the mother. Recently I managed to find a job for Yu Wenjuan, and I have to be especially careful."

Fei Mo nodded as Yan took a bankbook out of his pocket.

"She was out of work for a long time and has just started her new job, which means her financial situation is precarious at best. I've put twenty thousand in an account in case an emergency arises. I'd like you to keep this for me too."

Nodding yet again, Fei Mo put the photo and bankbook away.

"I need to tell you something," Fei Mo said. "At first, my wife was not well disposed toward Shen Xue, since she was so fond of Yu Wenjuan, who is now upset because Li Yan has begun spending time with Shen Xue. Li Yan and Shen Xue have talked a lot on the phone in recent days."

Yan Shouyi was not concerned.

"Shen Xue has become a real nag of late."

"That's not what I'm getting at," Fei Mo said as he drew lines on the tablecloth with his chopsticks. "What I'm trying to say is that nothing ruins things faster than alliances."

Reminded of what he'd seen in the parking lot before the press conference, Yan got the message. He nodded and was about to say something when his phone pinged. An incoming text message. He took out the phone and saw it was from Wu Yue. He stole a look at what she'd written:

I'd like to see your body in action. I want to bite you.

Yan shuddered as he quickly deleted the message and looked up to locate Wu Yue. He spotted her back three tables over. With her glass raised—it was red wine—and an audible laugh, she was toasting her fellow diners.

28

Shen Xue would later tell Li Yan that while Yan Shouyi was off attending the book launch, she was interviewing Niu Caiyun, Lü Guihua's daughter, at the Drama Academy. Caiyun had applied to the Academy's Acting Department, and had been staying with her and Shouyi during her three days in Beijing. It so happened that Shen Xue was a member of this year's admissions committee. Caiyun, who had just turned eighteen, seemed bright enough, although, if her conversational skills were any indication, a bit scatterbrained.

The minute he laid eyes on her, Yan Shouyi exclaimed:

"The spitting image of your mother! I never saw her again after she moved to the mining town, and if I ran into you on the street, I'd think I'd been transported back thirty years in time."

"Why do you want to study at the Drama Academy?" he asked her.

She responded in the Shanxi dialect:

"I want to be famous and make a lot of money!"

Shouyi and Shen Xue both laughed at that.

"And you think you can get that by studying at the Drama

Academy?"

He pointed to Shen Xue.

"Aunty here graduated from the Drama Academy, and she's not famous."

Caiyun looked at Shen Xue out of the corner of her eye.

"A teacher opens the door, but the student has to walk in."

She then took a look around the flat and said:

"Actually, it's what my mother wants, not me."

In the best Shanxi dialect she could manage, Shen Xue said:

"What do *you* want?"

"I want to be a TV host like Uncle."

"Think being a host is an easy job?"

"All you have to do is talk!"

Yan Shouyi froze. Later that night, in bed, Shen Xue said to him:

"You saw for yourself what I'm up against. She can't even handle Putonghua, so what makes her think she can study here?"

"Since she's here, what harm can it do to let her try? That'd make things easier on me."

Shen Xue reached out and pinched his nose.

"Your childhood lover. Feeling a little nostalgic, are you?"

Shouyi took her in his arms.

"What kind of talk is that?"

The following morning Shen Xue added Ni Caiyun's name to the list of candidates taking the entrance exam. On the day of the interview, while Yan was attending the launch for Fei Mo's book, Shen Xue accompanied Caiyun to the examination hall, which was packed with student hopefuls. She left the girl in line.

"Don't be nervous during the audition. Just act out your own experiences."

Caiyun nodded, exuding confidence.

The examination was being administered in one of the rehearsal rooms. Academy instructors, all members of the admissions committee, were seated in a row in front of a mirrored wall. The chief examiner was the middle-aged, ponytailed teacher, Mr. Guo, who had called out slogans during Xiao Su's wedding. Xiao Su, who was charged with calling up the student hopefuls, was sitting next to Shen Xue. Ten applicants were admitted at a time and told to stand against the wall across from the instructors. Then, one at a time, they stepped forward to audition. Shen Xue had spoken to Guo and to Xiao Su the day before, asking them to throw their support behind Niu Caiyun. Owing to the exceptional turnout, Caiyun's group was not called until just before noon. Second in line, she immediately searched out Shen Xue, who avoided eye contact. Xiao Su gently nudged her elbow and pointed on the sly.

"Is that her?"

Shen Xue nodded.

First up was a boy who bore rather a lot of resemblance to a monkey. After spending nearly all morning with auditions, the committee members were getting hungry. Mr. Guo pressed Xiao Su:

"Let's speed things up."

So Xiao Su began the questioning.

"What makes you unique?"

The boy's confusion showed in his eyes.

"I can do tumbling."

Everyone laughed.

"Let's see some."

And so he did, right on the spot, an impressive series of cartwheels and somersaults. But before he was finished, Mr. Guo signaled him to stop.

"That's it."

Slightly breathless, the boy stared at Mr. Guo.

"That's it?" he asked.

Mr. Guo ignored him. He turned to Xiao Su.

"Call the next one."

Xiao Su looked down at her namelist.

"Niu Caiyun."

Caiyun pranced confidently up to the examiners and, in heavily accented Putonghua, said:

"Good morning, Teachers."

They laughed.

"It's noontime already," Mr. Guo said.

Xiao Su stopped laughing long enough to ask:

"Niu Caiyun, what does your father do?"

"He's a miner."

"All right, you're a miner's daughter. Show us the first thing your father does when he comes home after a day in the mines."

She added:

"Don't be nervous. Think about it first."

Everyone was stunned by what happened next. Xiao Su's comment still hung in the air when Caiyun turned and walked out of the examination hall. They waited for her to knock at the door, but in vain. Clearly puzzled, Xiao Su looked at Shen Xue. So did Mr. Guo.

"What was that all about?" he asked. "Shall we write her off?"

He turned to Xiao Su.

"Call the next in line."

Niu Caiyun hadn't returned even after all the others in her group had finished their auditions. The next group was called, and half an hour later, still no sign of the girl. Nor did she return when the examiners broke for lunch. Shen Xue walked out of the examination hall to look for Caiyun among the crowd of candidates and their curious family members on the basketball court. She spotted her sitting under a set of parallel bars, off in a corner. She was bending down, engaged in a conversation with someone and seemingly enjoying herself, talking excitedly, complete with expansive gestures. Shen Xue walked up and said, an angry edge to her voice:

"What was that all about? Why'd you walk out of the

examination like that?"

Niu Caiyun looked at Shen Xue quizzically.

"You wanted me to act out what my father did, didn't you? Well, the first thing he does after work is go visiting. He'll be gone three hours sometimes."

That cleared things up for Shen Xue, who didn't know whether to laugh or cry.

"After digging coal all day, doesn't he stop to wash up?"

"No time. He's out of the house and on his bicycle first thing."

"Can't you act out your father saying a word or two to your mother?"

"He's got nothing to say to her."

At that point, Shen Xue didn't know what to do, so she took out her cell phone and as she dialed a number said to Caiyun:

"Talk to your uncle."

She dialed Yan Shouyi's number, and received a recorded message:

We're sorry, but the person at this number is out of the service area.

Shen Xue was puzzled. She'd dialed the right number, and that was the first time she'd gotten that message. He was attending the book launch for Fei Mo, there in Beijing, so how could his phone be out of the service area? But she had other things on her mind, and didn't give it another thought. Then, several days later, in class, she was teaching *Hamlet* and had gotten to the soliloquy "To be or not to be" and ". . . it must follow as the night the day," when one of her students' cell phone rang. The boy tucked his head under the desk to take the call, and when he straightened up again, he was face to face with his teacher, who was giving him an icy stare.

"I'm sorry," he stammered, "that was my father."

"It's OK for your father to disrupt the class like that?"

"He called from England and forgot the time difference."

"Hamlet was in England, and he didn't forget the difference."

By tying the phone call to the lesson, she got a big laugh out of the class. The boy raised both hands:

"See, Teacher Shen, I'm turning it off."

But instead of turning it off, he turned it over, peeled out the battery, and then jammed it shut again. Even in her irritation, Shen Xue had to laugh.

"Turning off your phone and disconnecting the battery, isn't that a bit much?"

One of the other boys couldn't resist the opportunity to tease his classmate.

"You've got it all wrong, Teacher. His girlfriend will be mad at him if he turns off his phone, but by disconnecting the battery, it'll say he's out of the service area when she calls."

The class had a good laugh over that, but not Shen Xue, for she was reminded of her attempt to call Yan Shouyi a few days earlier, when she was with Caiyun on the basketball court, and was informed that his phone was out of the service area. Once again he'd aroused her suspicions.

29

Future developments proved the wisdom of those suspicions. When she'd tried to phone him that day, he'd done exactly what her student had done in class—disconnected the battery. Why? Because he'd drunk quite a bit at the banquet following the book launch and gone with Wu Yue to Room 1108 of the VIP hotel. But before that, when the banquet was about half over, Fei Mo had begun to fidget as his mood soured, and had left early, claiming work at the university demanded his attention. Wu Yue took advantage of his departure to come to Yan Shouyi's table to toast his fellow diners. Sales Manager Gao was a long-winded middle-aged woman who was also a big drinker. Refusing to exchange toasts with Wu Yue, she turned her attention to Yan Shouyi.

Before long, the others at the table joined in, and it didn't take long for him to get tipsy. *Ping!* His telephone announced an incoming text message. It was from Wu Yue, the same message she'd sent earlier, but with an addition:

I'd like to see your body in action. I want to bite you, big fellow.

Immediately aroused, Shouyi looked up and discovered that Wu Yue had walked away from his table. He looked around the room, but didn't see her anywhere. Not yet drunk, he was still thinking clearly, so he held his phone under the table and typed out:

Take it easy, lover girl.

After immediately deleting both messages, he straightened up and picked up his glass, but he had only managed a couple of drinks before he heard another *ping!* He looked down at his phone. Another text message from Wu Yue:

I'm in Room 1108, lover boy.

Now the alcohol was taking effect, and there, swaying before his eyes, were Wu Yue's basketball-sized breasts; and what filled his ears was no longer the buzz of voices in the banquet hall, but their dirty talk of two years before at Lushan. This was no time to give in, so he straightened up again and continued drinking, hoping that the liquor and the lively mood around the table would be enough to suppress the lust that was taking hold of him. But the more he drank, the more the basketballs grew, until they blocked out everything except the dirty talk ringing in his ears like heavy metal rock music. He stood up, finally, and excused himself to go to the men's room, then he stumbled his way past the tables and out of the banquet hall on his way to the elevators. Several people greeted him along the way, including, as he later recalled, Chief He, who was seeing off a guest. He too had had quite a bit to drink, and his comb-over was now flopping out in front. He reached out for Yan's arm.

"You leaving too, Old Yan?"

Shouyi shook the publisher's hand.

"Men's room."

He'd only taken a couple of steps before something occurred to him. He turned and reached out for He's hand.

"Chief He, I couldn't say anything a while ago, too many people around, but I want to thank you for helping her find work."

He put his arm around Shouyi's shoulders.

"That's what friends are for. Working at *Intimates* is no different from working for us. The editor-in-chief at *Intimates* and I are intimate friends."

He thumped Yan on the chest.

"A woman, if you know what I mean."

Yan nodded as he put his lips up to Yan's ear and said:

"Wu Yue told me, and I told the editor at *Intimates,* that Yu Wenjuan is not to know that you had anything to do with finding her work."

Then with an expansive wave of his hand, he added:

"As for anybody else, not a chance."

Yan shook the man's hand with great enthusiasm.

"Thank you. I'll make it up to you one day."

Yan turned and headed to the bank of elevators. Chief He staggered up to him.

"Those are the elevators, Old Yan, not the men's room."

Yan had no choice but to go to the men's room, relieve himself, and come back out, hoping Chief He was gone. He was. Now he took an elevator up to the 11th floor, where he stumbled his way up to room 1108. The sobering-up process was underway by then, and before he entered the room, he took out his cell phone, deleted Wu Yue's last message, then disconnected the battery.

Room 1108 was one of the rooms the publisher had reserved for administrative activities associated with the launch of Fei Mo's book. The floor was piled high with copies of the book and leftover paper bags. Advertisements for Fei Mo's book had been taped onto the room's walls and mirror. Yan Shouyi had barely entered the room when Wu Yue, who'd had plenty to drink, pinned him against the closed door and began kissing him frantically. They hadn't been alone together since their parting amid the barking of dogs in the suburbs the year before, and as their saliva mixed, Shouyi surprised himself with the realization that no matter how hard he looked, he hadn't found anyone who pleased him in the dark like Wu Yue. It was like trying to find yourself in your own shadow; you can look all you want, but you'll never find it. She propped her hands against the door to hold the two of them up. A few moments later, they moved into the room, arms around each other. First they banged into the wardrobe, then the dresser, knocking books and other objects to the floor. Their last stop was the bed, which they fell on heavily, Wu Yue on top. She tore the clothes off him, all but his necktie. Yan followed suit by unbuttoning her *qipao*, under which she was wearing only a bra and panties. He made quick work of the bra; she removed her panties before he had a chance. Out of habit she bit down on his shoulder. Suddenly alert, he reached up and pulled her away by the hair.

"No chewing."

With palpable impatience, she replied:

"OK, no chewing, just screwing!"

She grabbed his tie, scrunched it up, and stuffed it into his mouth.

"That'll shut you up."

All of a sudden, Yan Shouyi, pinned down on the bed, saw a reflection of Fei Mo's image in the mirror, and thought back to what he'd seen in the parking lot. He pushed Wu Yue away.

"This is no good."

But it was too late. She took him inside her, and he instantly felt as if he'd fallen into a raging river.

It was the best sex he'd had in a very long time. A couple of hours later, two sweaty bodies looked as if they'd fallen into a river. All the alcohol they'd ingested had oozed out through their pores, and they were completely sober. The bedding had fallen to the floor. Totally spent, they lay side by side, breathing hard. He spat out the tie she'd stuffed into his mouth and thought about his clothes, which she'd ripped off him on the bed. She picked her cell phone up off the dresser and snapped a few shots of the two of them in bed, then let him see the screen. He saw pictures of them in the nude, slightly distorted and less appealing to the eye than the real thing. Suddenly overcome by fatigue, he began to regret what had just happened.

"We can't do this anymore," he said as he made to delete the images on the screen. Wu Yue snatched the phone out of his hand.

"I can see your new phone has this function," he said. "But why take these pictures?"

"For a keepsake."

Shouyi tried to take the phone from her.

"Delete them, you don't want anyone to see them."

She wouldn't let him have it.

"That's exactly what I want."

There was something different about her, and he didn't like what he saw. Covering himself with his shirt, he touched her head.

"Don't do anything you'll regret. I know I treated you badly, but I can't change the past. Shen Xue and I have been together almost a year."

"I'm not interested in getting married."

He looked her in the eye.

"Then what is it you want?"

"I found a job for your ex, so now you can return the favor."

He didn't know what to make of that.

"You already have a job."

"You're looking for a woman to host 'Straight Talk,' aren't you? Well, I'd like an audition."

She added:

"I can never find anyone to talk to, so now I'd like to talk to the whole nation."

"What I said at the book launch, that was just a joke."

"Well, I'm not joking. This is something I've thought about for a long time."

One look told him that she was dead serious. He sat up and leaned against the headboard.

"What's wrong with your current situation? Why trade it for a hostess job? You'd be a performer, not much more than a call girl."

"A performer, a call girl, sounds good to me."

She pinched Shouyi's nose.

"You're tired of being famous, aren't you? Well, that's what I'm looking for, relying on a TV camera to become famous. I can talk as good as the next person."

"It's not as easy as you think."

"Whether or not I get the chance is your call. Then it's up to me to make it work."

She waved the phone in front of him and pinched him.

"You'd better say yes unless you want to see these in public."

Yan Shouyi tried to make light of the situation:

"That sounds like blackmail to me. What do you have against talking things out?"

"It's not blackmail, it's payback. I learned that from you. I know you too well to fall for that talking things out business."

She snorted at him.

"It's taken me more than two years to realize how selfish you are."

Yan Shouyi buried his head in his arms and kept it there for a long moment before looking up and saying:

"Even if I say OK, I don't make the final decision, the station boss does."

"Don't worry about other people. The station boss will be OK with it. It's you I'm worried about."

That took him by surprise, but before he could respond, the doorbell buzzed, throwing him into a panic. He scooped the blanket up off the floor and covered himself. Wu Yue, on the other hand, was nonplussed. Not bothering to cover up, she lay back as the doorbell buzzed again.

"Who is it?" she called out.

The response was alcohol-slurred.

"It's me. I know you're in there. Open the door."

Yan Shouyi recognized the voice—it was the publisher, Chief He. He reacted to this fearful news by putting his finger to his lips to keep her from saying anything. She ignored him.

"My mother's here," she shouted. "She's taking a shower."

Out in the hall Old He muttered something, then they heard a shuffling sound as he walked off. Wu Yue said:

"Let me tell you, you think it was Old He who arranged the job for Yu Wenjuan, that he wanted to thank you for writing that forword for Fei Mo's book. Am I right?"

Yan Shouyi wasn't sure what to think.

"Then why did he?"

"It was me," she said, pointing to herself. "He just took credit for it."

That led to a flood of tears. Yan Shouyi was stunned.

Yan Shouyi's first stop after leaving the International VIP Hotel was a public bath. He needed to wash the smells off his body before he could drive home. But when he was downstairs, he sensed a funny taste in his mouth, and he recalled nibbling Wu Yue's ear a while before. Her perfume was still on his tongue; it had a bitter taste. Having learned his lesson that time with Yu Wenjuan, he got back in his car and drove to a nearby convenience store, where he bought a bottle of spring water, then took it out into the lane, crouched down, and rinsed his mouth. The convenience store owner, a middle-aged woman, thought something might be wrong, so she followed him outside, and almost immediately recognized him.

"Old Yan," she asked, "is anything wrong?"

He waved her off.

"No, I'm fine."

He returned to his car and drove to a spot behind another high-rise, where he turned off the engine and just sat there. To his astonishment, Wu Yue had abruptly brought up the subject of hosting "Straight Talk" and was forcing him to help her get there. It had taken him till this moment to realize that nobody ever does anything without an ulterior motive. You might start without one, but you'll figure one out sooner or later. He'd always thought that women's ulterior motives seldom went beyond finding a mate. Wu Yue changed that with her desire to become a TV host. Was she obsessed with fame, or was she really interested in a career as a talking head? He'd always thought that she was a frivolous and undisciplined woman, which is why he was surprised to find her so calculating. But what surprised him even more was the amount of behind-the-scenes work she'd done in order to get hired at "Straight Talk." He hadn't a clue. She'd said that the station boss would be OK with it. Had she already talked to him about it? And she'd said that Old He had taken the credit for finding a job for Yu Wenjuan, and was it possible that the boss . . . Yan didn't want to go there. It was a bit like Wenjuan having a baby—the world didn't seem quite real to him. He took out his phone and dialed Wu Yue's number. She picked up.

"Don't do that, my dear, it seems dirty."

"Dirty? You invented dirty."

She hung up.

Around sunset, after a day of auditions, Shen Xue returned home with Niu Caiyun in tow. She opened the door and discovered Yan Shouyi, sitting in a sort of daze on the sofa. His eyes were glazed over. Shen Xue was surprised and concerned.

"What's wrong?"

Yan Shouyi snapped out of it and held his head in his hands.

"I drank too much at Fei Mo's book launch."

Seeing him reminded her of something.

"I called you today, but the message said you were out of the service area. How come?"

"Maybe I was in the elevator."

That was before Shen Xue knew the secret of disconnecting the battery, so she let it pass and began chatting about Niu Caiyun's audition. Caiyun, who was standing nearby, rolled her eyes. Shouyi didn't hear a word Shen Xue said.

30

Trouble for Fei Mo. Yan Shouyi and Shen Xue were at the train station the night it happened, seeing off Ni Caiyun, who was returning home to Shanxi. There at the station they bought some vacuum-packed roasted duck for her to take back for her parents. Caiyun's stay in Beijing had turned out to be a major disappointment. Before boarding the train home she'd said to Yan in awkward Mandarin:

"It wasn't my fault I didn't pass the exam, Uncle."

"Whose fault was it?"

With a glance at Shen Xue, Caiyun said:

"At the audition, Aunty told me to act out real life, and when I did, they failed me."

Instead of defending herself against the girl's unwarranted criticism, Shen Xue said:

"What you did wasn't what we were looking for."

Caiyun muttered, "I won't be so trusting next time."

Yan Shouyi, who had been in a bad mood for days, fired back unhappily:

"Trusting, you say? More like simple-minded, if you ask me!"

With a playful shove, Shen Xue said, "Don't say things like that, she's just a kid."

Then she turned to Caiyun.

"Next year. Come earlier next year, and I'll coach you."

The words were barely out when Shen Xue's cell phone rang. She took the call.

"Who? You're not looking for me? Him? Why don't you call him on his own phone?"

Whoever it was said something in reply.

"OK, here he is."

She handed the phone to Shouyi.

"Why'd you turn your phone off?" she asked him.

He hadn't turned his phone on for a couple of days. He was avoiding Wu Yue. After Yu Wenjuan had the baby, Shouyi had kept his phone on twenty-four hours a day, in case something happened to either of them. But that changed when Wu Yue began blackmailing him with nude photos in order to get hired as host of "Straight Talk." Fearful to begin with, he now had to contend with a fishy scenario that had arisen after taping the show two days earlier. Yan had gone to the men's room, where he'd run into the assistant station boss for adminstration. Once the man had finished his business at the urinal, he shuddered as something occurred to him. He asked Yan how the search for a female host for "Straight Talk" was going. Then, after a bit of small talk, he said casually:

"Oh, right, a girl named Wu Yue applied for the job. Know her?"

Yan nodded. "Yes."

"I've seen her," the man said in a suggestive tone. "Though she's a bit daffy, she's loaded with confidence and knows how to talk. Some real possibilities there."

With a pat on Yan's shoulder, he said:

"Of course, you're responsible for 'Straight Talk,' and we want to hear what you have to say first."

He walked out of the men's room, leaving Yan so perplexed he forgot why he was there. Wu Yue's remarkable resourcefulness was something he hadn't counted on. He'd misunderstood and underestimated her all this time. How had she pulled it off? Of course, those basketballs of hers, that and darkness. There's nothing that can't be accomplished in the dark. That said, nothing—not professional, not personal—could convince him that she was qualified to host "Straight Talk." Professionally, while she might be loaded with confidence, and be a pro where talking dirty in bed was concerned, she certainly wasn't much of a thinker. Episodes dealing with daily life required considerable knowledge. Why else would he have brought Fei Mo into the picture? If she took over, trying to substitute wit and wisdom for dirty talk, the show would be blander than a glass of tap water. On a personal level, if she was hired, how was he going to explain away the common knowledge that she'd once been his lover? On paper, the hire would be the assistant station boss's, but everyone, Shen Xue included, would see his hand in it. Turning official salt into a private stash. A woman like Wu Yue was capable of anything. Yan had phoned her a couple of days earlier and talked for more than an hour. He had hoped to use a roundabout means of saving the situation. In the same way he'd gotten the publishing house to find Yu Wenjuan a job elsewhere, his plan was to put in a good word for her to host a variety show at another TV station, where the second-in-charge was one of Yan's former classmates. No deep thought was required for a variety show, which would allow her to ramble freely and help him avoid being involved. But she dug in her heels. A serious talk show or nothing, which meant "Straight Talk." Seeing the futility in forcing the issue, he turned off his phone and kept it off so she could not reach him and he could hope that the matter would eventually resolve itself. Once again his strategy was to put his troubles in the hands of God and the flow of time. But now that Shen Xue had asked him about it, he had to lay down a smokescreen:

"Oh, I turned it off during today's taping and then forgot about it. Who is it?"

Shen Xue handed him the phone.

"It's Li Yan."

He took the phone from her, unaware that something had happened to Fei Mo, that his affair with the graduate student had been discovered. He would not have answered so lightheartedly otherwise.

"Why in the world would you be calling me, Yan? You can't cover up our little fling by calling me on Shen Xue's phone."

Li Yan responded in much the same tone:

"Does there have to be a reason for us to have a chat? Where are you now?"

Shouyi was walking blindly into a well-concealed trap.

"We're at the train station, seeing someone off."

He added:

"Is there something Fei Lao wants to say to me?"

"He's not home yet."

She followed that with a seemingly offhand question:

"Say, did you two go to some sort of meeting at the Hilton this afternoon?"

All of a sudden, Shouyi sensed that something wasn't quite right, that Fei Mo was about to be in big trouble. He had to think fast.

"Hold on just a minute, Yan, all right?"

Since they were just then seeing Caiyun off, this could help him buy some time to figure out what to say. He raised his voice loud enough for Li Yan to hear on the other end.

"Go on, Caiyun, board the train. Don't forget to give us a call as soon as you're back home. And tell your parents they have a standing invitation to visit us in Beijing. I guess I didn't give her a ride on my bike that time, so when she comes to Beijing, I'll drive her around, and since I didn't help her make that phone call, I'll take her for a ride in an ATV."

Now, what to do about Fei Mo? He hadn't forgotten what had happened between him and Yu Wenjuan. Fei Mo hadn't gone home, which probably meant that he was off somewhere with his graduate student. Time for another smokescreen.

"Sorry, Yan. Yes, we had a meeting at the Hilton, but I left early so I could see someone off at the train station. It must still be going on. You know how Fei Lao is when he's unhappy with what we're doing. He's probably just getting started, and no one's about to call an end to the meeting till he gets it out of his system."

I couldn't have done it any better, he was thinking, until Li Yan's angry retort blasted into his ear:

"Bullshit! He's standing right here beside me. I know all about you, Yan Shouyi. Put Shen Xue back on the phone."

Yan just stood there, phone in hand, zombie-like, having no idea what to do.

"What's the matter?" Shen Xue asked.

Reluctantly, he handed her the phone.

"Li Yan's fit to be tied."

Shen Xue grabbed the phone.

"What is it, Li Yan?" she asked. "Slow down, don't get excited . . ."

With a sideways glance at Shouyi, she moved to a spot down the platform. Shouyi was an emotional train wreck as he waved to Niu Caiyun, who was walking through the train car with her roasted duck, all the while keeping a furtive eye on Shen Xue. The phone call ended, she walked back, a strange look of excitement on her face.

"Fei Mo's in trouble," she said softly to Shouyi.

"What kind of trouble?"

"Li Yan was washing a pair of his pants and found a hotel key card from the Overseas Chinese Guesthouse, and when she asked him why he'd taken a room there, he said you and he had gone to a meeting there. She didn't believe him, and that's why she called you, turning the Overseas Chinese Guesthouse into the Hilton.

And you fell for it. That must mean that Fei Mo . . ."

Yan Shouyi slapped his thigh, knowing he'd screwed up. Suddenly wary, Shen Xue asked:

"What's wrong?"

Conscious of the importance of what he did next, he spoke with feigned indignation:

"How could Fei Mo do something like that? He doesn't seem the type."

"Li Yan wants us to go over right away."

Yan Shouyi was hesitant.

"Wouldn't that be adding fuel to the fire?"

That was not what she wanted to hear.

"The way you're balking makes me wonder if you're not in on it. A minute ago I asked you why you turned off your phone, and you said you were taping a show. But just now you told Li Yan you were at a meeting at the Hilton. Just what are you two up to?"

Yan Shouyi was quick to change the subject:

"Why would Fei Mo let me in on something like this? If he had, he wouldn't be in hot water now."

Before Shen Xue could say anything, he stopped her with a wave of his hand.

"OK, I'll go. Does that make you happy?"

When Yan Shouyi and Shen Xue walked into Fei Mo's flat, it was immediately obvious that a truce had been called in what had to have been a major battle.

Fei Mo was sitting half-dazed on the sofa, head down, glasses nowhere in sight. Without their glasses, near-sighted people's features seem distorted. Li Yan, who was sitting in Fei Mo's chair with her feet on his desk, was smoking a cigarette, not even bothering to dry her tears. The wall behind her was floor-to-ceiling with books, mostly traditional, thread-bound volumes. Their little Pekingese was cowering in a corner, fearfully watching every movement. When Yan Shouyi and Shen Xue walked in, Li Yan erupted anew:

"Liar, you're a rotten liar! You've shown me what you're really like! Say something! What happened to all your fancy quotations and classical allusions? You're always criticizing me, saying how degenerate I am for surfing the Web!"

Mimicing her husband's way of talking, she said:

"Life is short, time is fleeting."

She then jabbed her finger on the pink key card lying on top of the desk.

"You're not worried about fleeting time, you're looking for the good life! A graduate student in aesthetics? A slut is more like it!"

Even though Li Yan had mixed her metaphors, Yan Shouyi could tell that Fei Mo had already owned up to everything, told her all, and that he was now a prisoner of war. With a look at Fei Mo, Shen Xue went over to calm Li Yan down.

"Don't be angry, Yan."

She shot a quick glance at Yan Shouyi.

"Let's talk in the other room, Yan," she said.

She took Li Yan by the arm and coaxed her into the bedroom. As she walked past the sofa, Li Yan spat at Fei Mo.

After the women closed the bedroom door, Yan Shouyi went into the bathroom for a towel and handed it to Fei Mo, who, uncharacteristically, looked like a plucked chicken. He took the towel from Shouyi and managed an embarrassed smile. Shouyi picked the key card up off the desk, sat down beside Fei Mo, and turned it over in his hand as his thoughts took him back to what had happened between him and Wu Yue at the International VIP Hotel only a couple of days before. If she followed through with her threat to go public with the nude photos, he'd wish he'd only been caught with a hotel key card. He broke out in a cold sweat.

With a look at the key card, Fei Mo stammered:

"I forgot to clean out my pants pockets before they went into the wash."

He mopped his face with the towel and said:

"A careless mistake gets me into hot water, and now everything's turned upside down."

Yan Shouyi held his tongue. Fei Mo took a look at the bedroom door and leaned back in the sofa.

"After more than twenty years you get tired of looking at the same scenery."

Again Yan Shouyi held his tongue. Fei Mo, he discovered, was losing his voice.

"But it wasn't just about getting tired. We no longer have anything to talk about."

Brought up short by what he was hearing, Yan Shouyi laid the key card down on the coffee table as Fei Mo sat up straight and lit a cigarette.

"You won't believe me when I tell you that nothing happened."

Yan Shouyi just looked at Fei Mo.

"We did take a room, but all we did was lie on the bed and hold hands. Then we went into the coffee shop, where she listened to me talk."

Yan Shouyi could hardly believe his ears.

"Why?"

"She's in her twenties, I'm nearly fifty. When we lay down on the bed I lost my nerve."

"I got no cooperation from that!" he complained, pointing below. "It's been several years now."

Burying his face in his hands, he began to sob.

Yan Shouyi stood there feeling helpless. Fei Mo looked up, his face wet, and said:

"Living in an agricultural society is better in the long run."

Yan Shouyi missed his friend's meaning.

"What was that?"

Fei Mo shook his head.

"Back then, a man relied on his own two feet to get around. If you went to the capital to take the civil service exam, you were away from home for years, and when you returned you could say anything you wanted."

He poked the cell phone on his desk with his finger.

"But now . . ."

"But now what?"

"Close," Fei Mo said hoarsely, "too close. Suffocatingly close!"

Again, Shouyi stood there trance-like.

31

For Yan Shouyi it was another sleepless night. But for a change he lost sleep not over his own problems, which he was able to put aside for the moment. Now his concerns were focused on Fei Mo; he felt sorry for his friend, who had been caught and found guilty for something he hadn't even done and was incapable of explaining away. The perfect analogy was a clumsy old cat that had never stolen a speck of food, until one day, when no one was around, it secretly got its claws into a tiny little fish, not to eat, but to examine. When it was caught, the immediate assumption was that it planned to eat the fish. Only that one time, but it might as well have been the hundredth. Fei Mo had hoped to get by with Yan Shouyi's help, but Shouyi had been tricked by Li Yan, and instead of helping his friend, he had actually speeded up the process of revelation. Burdened by a welter of emotions, he'd tossed and turned all night without getting any sleep. If only he'd known that he'd get up the next day and discover that the flames from the Fei Mo incident were burning their way toward him. The night before, at the train station, he'd told Shen Xue that he'd been at a taping of "Straight Talk." It was a lie. The taping was scheduled for today. He got out of bed as soon as the sun was up, got dressed, drank a glass of soy milk, and bent down to tie his shoes. But before he could walk out the door, he spotted Shen Xue coming down the hallway in her pajamas, holding something in her hand.

"Your class isn't till nine. Why are you up so early?"

Not until he was standing did he notice the unhappy look on her face. She smacked a photograph down on top of the shoe cupboard.

"You forgot this!"

It was, he was surprised to discover, the photograph of Yu Wenjuan and the baby, which he'd left with Fei Mo for safekeeping. Before he could defend himself, she smacked a bankbook down on top of the photograph.

"And this!"

This emergency fund, in case Yu Wenjuan or the baby needed it, had also been left in Fei Mo's care. His heart sank. This was big trouble. He likely had Li Yan's search of her husband's possessions to thank for this—she'd handed the items over to Shen Xue while they were in the bedroom behind a closed door. The woman standing before him now seemed like a stranger. He'd always thought that Shen Xue was a bit of an airhead who blurted things out as soon as they occurred to her. Shrewd had never been a word he'd associated with her, but she hadn't said a word about this all night, waiting till he was about to leave in the morning to spring it on him, with no chance to make up a story. He wondered if she'd been acting all along or if she'd gotten smarter under his influence. Then there was Fei Mo, whose carelessness had not only led to the discovery of his key card, but to a photograph and bankbook that weren't even his. That was bad enough, but since he didn't know, he couldn't warn Shouyi about the search. Finally, there was Fei Mo's wife, a real shrew who wasn't content to deal with problems at home, and made sure that other people suffered as well. Leaving now was out of the question.

"Let me explain . . ."

She sneered.

"I know you're going to say you asked Fei Mo to hold them for you because you didn't want to upset me. Am I right?"

Now was not the time to shrink from the truth.

"Yes, that was part of it. But . . ."

Shen Xue wouldn't let him finish:

"But what? I'll tell you but what. Did you give any thought to what they'd think of me when you asked Fei Mo to hold them for you?"

"I . . ."

She cut him off again:

"You must really hate Li Yan. When she gave me those things last night, I thought she was just meddling. But now I'm truly grateful to her. And not just to her, but to the whole Fei Mo incident. I was awake thinking all night, and I've come to the conclusion that I'm a real fool. Here I am, trying to console somebody else, while I'm just like them . . ."

Yan Shouyi pleaded with his hands.

"That photograph and bankbook—it only has twenty thousand—they, what do they have in common with what happened to Fei Mo?"

"I'm not talking about the photograph and bankbook, I'm talking about how you were willing to lie for him."

"We're friends, and nobody likes to see a friend get into trouble."

Shen Xue reached out for his arm.

"That's not what I'm getting at. Tell me why you had your phone off at the train station last night."

"I already told you. I turned it off at the taping and forgot to turn it back on."

"Just last night? Your phone's either been off or out of the service area for several days. Why? Yan Shouyi, there's not an ounce of difference between you and Fei Mo. Over the past couple of days I can tell just by looking at you that you're hiding something else from me. Jittery, looking like your soul has fled your body. You and Fei Mo made a pact, I assume. You'll lie to get him out of a jam, then he'll do the same for you. Is that about it?"

Yan Shouyi was starting to lose his temper.

"If that's what you think, nothing I say will make any difference!"

"That's because nothing you say will be the truth."

Now he *was* angry. And he was willing to use this anger to overwhelm Shen Xue again. That time at the hot-pot restaurant, the number of place settings had made Shen Xue suspect something between Shouyi and Wu Yue. A fit of anger in the car later had subdued her. Time for a repeat performance. It had taken the U.S. two wars with Iraq to unseat Sadam, hadn't it? He took out his cell phone, opened it, and smacked it down on the shoe cupboard.

"This is what puts doubts in your mind, isn't it?" he said, one emphatic word after another. "Well, it's on and it's ready for inspection. I'll leave it with you. Forget your class. Stay home and root out all the demons."

Confident that this display would come as such a shock that she'd burst into tears, as she had that last time, he could pick up his phone and head for the door. They could deal with the problem later. Imagine his surprise when she not only weathered his burst of anger, but went on the offensive:

"Leave it. I'm not afraid to do the rooting if you've got the guts to leave it with me. I'm going to start being more like Li Yan!"

Yan Shouyi was facing a real dilemma. He couldn't take the phone with him, but he couldn't leave it with her either. He'd lost control of the situation. Leaving the phone where it was, he stormed out, slamming the door behind him.

By the time he was in his car and on his way, regret began to set in. He wasn't upset over getting angry, but for leaving his cell phone behind. He didn't like the way this drama was playing out. With the phone on all day, what if Wu Yue called? In the past he could have called her on another phone and given her a heads-up. But the way things between them were now, with her threatening him, that was not a call he could make, since it would make it even easier for her to get what she wanted. Besides, the phone was no longer under his control—the wood had already been made into a boat—and going home to retrieve it was not an option, for that would only make Shen Xue more suspicious. His heart felt weighted down, unsettled.

The audience had already been seated by the time he arrived at the TV station, and the studio orchestra was playing an American rockabilly number to warm them up. Several of the musicians had painted their faces for some unknown reason. The drummer, a fat fellow named Zang, was more spirited than usual. Chewing his cheeks—one red and one green—as he laid into his drums, rising and falling with his sticks, the persistent *thump thump thump* nearly drove Yan Shouyi to distraction. He was tempted to cancel the taping, but since the audience was in place and the station's number two man, who produced "Straight Talk," had shown up, he went ahead and let the makeup artist do a quick, light job. After putting on his checkered sportcoat, he steeled himself and took his position behind the host's platform. The stage lights went on. He smiled broadly as the music ended and, with total concentration, started his opening monologue:

"Good evening, everyone, this is 'Straight Talk,' and I'm Yan Shouyi. The theme for tonight's show is 'Illness.' It was developed by our principal adviser, Fei Mo. Mr. Fei studied in Austria, where he was acquainted with Professor Freud. You are all aware that Freud was a contrarian who complicated everything he came in contact with. Well, after getting to know Freud, Fei Mo turned gloomy. He'd be out for a walk and detect illness in nine out of ten people he saw."

The audience laughed. Not a bad beginning. No one could tell how much he had on his mind. The mention of Fei Mo during his monologue hadn't affected him at the time, but a few moments later, his thoughts turned in on himself, and he experienced pangs of severe emotional pain. Forcing himself to endure the discomfort, he said:

"Of course he was talking about mental not physical illness. The main difference between the two is that mental illness doesn't necessarily require hospitalization, and it often manifests itself in daily life. Things like, for instance, anxiety, disorientation, paranoia, incoherence . . . I wonder how many members of our studio audience have experienced any of these symptoms . . ."

Again the audience laughed.

"Why do people develop mental illness? According to our Mr. Fei . . ."

All of a sudden Yan Shouyi's mind went blank. He didn't know what he was saying, forgot everything Fei Mo had put into the script, just stood there dazed. This was the third time something like that had happened to him in the eight years he'd hosted "Straight Talk." The first two instances had occurred early in his career as host, when he came up blank and lost his ability to think. But the audience, thinking it was just part of the show, laughed. But the second-in-charge, who was watching from the wings, frowned and walked out onto the stage. Yan's forehead was beaded with sweat. He turned to the audience and said:

"Sorry, folks, I forgot my lines."

He took Fei Mo's script out of his pocket, turned a few pages, and studied it carefully. Zang the drummer decided to come to Yan's aid by knocking out a drummed *ta-da*. Now that he'd checked out the script, Yan frowned and stayed Zang's hand:

"That's enough, it's making things worse."

Then he turned his eyes to Big Duan in the director's booth.

"I'm OK," he said.

He smiled.

"Why do people develop mental illness? According to our

Mr. Fei, if your life is simple, and you complicate it, or your life is complicated and you make it too simple, illness is inevitable. If that happens, don't be a hero, go to the hospital . . ."

Two hours later the taping was completed, and Yan Shouyi was completely drained. He could feel the sweat around his midriff. He left the stage and went straight down the corridor to his office, in need of a drink of water. But the minute he walked into the office, Xiao Ma exclaimed:

"What the . . . ? What's wrong? Your face is all red!"

She reached out to feel his forehead.

"You're not well."

32

While Yan Shouyi was hosting the show, Shen Xue was in class. She had not taken his cell phone along, having no interest in searching for demons. She'd left it on the shoe cupboard, where he'd smacked it down that morning, without touching it. No sense turning an argument into something worse, she figured, especially since her trust in Shouyi still hung by a thread. The last thing she wanted was to take things beyond the breaking point. What would people say if they knew she'd begun digging around in her man's phone? Shouyi did not learn till later that his phone had spent the day ringing atop the shoe cupboard.

Shen Xue would later tell Li Yan that in class that day one of the boys had opened the back of his cell phone, disconnected the battery, then replaced it so it would appear that the phone was out of the service area. That knowledge rekindled her suspicions regarding Shouyi's phone.

When class was over, Shen Xue went to her office, where she received a phone call from Li Yan. Prepared to hear the older woman ask breathlessly about the photograph and bankbook and how bad things had gotten, she was surprised to discover that Li

Yan was too concerned about the situation with Fei Mo to give any thought to Shen Xue's problem. If there was one act of infidelity, she figured, there must have been more, many more, and she was determined to unearth every one. The graduate student was only the beginning.

"How are you going to do that?"

"I didn't give him a moment's peace last night."

"What did you manage to find out?"

"He played dumb at first, deaf and dumb, but that's not going to stop me."

"So what do you plan to do next?"

"I'm going down to the phone company and check his cell phone record. That'll tell me who he's been talking to, won't it?"

That shocked Shen Xue. Li Yan was a control freak, and was beginning to frighten her.

"Will they give you access to his record?" Shen Xue asked.

"I'm going down there now. I've got his ID card"

She added:

"Want to check Shouyi's record?"

Shen Xue later told Xiao Su that if she hadn't held class earlier that day and seen the student's stunt with his cell phone battery, she wouldn't have gone to the phone company. But after putting that battery stunt together with his jittery behavior over the past several days she made up her mind to accompany Li Yan, but not without some reluctance.

"What if he finds out that I checked his record behind his back?" she asked Li Yan.

That was when Li Yan began to shift the blame for her problem to Yan Shouyi.

"He dealt with the photograph and bankbook behind your back, didn't he? Has he been faithful to you? That's nothing to take lightly. He hid the photo and bankbook, so what makes you think he hasn't hidden other things?"

Under Li Yan's insistent pressure, Shen Xue made up her mind:
"All right, I'll go."

Then another hesitation.

"But I don't have his ID card."

"He's so famous all you have to say is that you're his wife, and
they won't stop you."

So the two women went to the phone company. The business
office was packed when they got there, mostly by people doing cell
phone business. Li Yan handed Fei Mo's ID card and a five-yuan
printing fee to a clerk. A printer spun into action, and a moment
later a woman walked up and slipped a rolled-up copy of Fei Mo's
record through the little window. Following Li Yan's instructions,
Shen Xue said she was Yan Shouyi's wife, and, feigning anger, that
she wanted to see his phone records.

"How could his phone bill be so high this month? You must
have made a mistake!"

Li Yan waved Fei Mo's ID and pointed to Shen Xue.

"We're together."

The top half of the clerk's face wasn't bad, with nice round eyes,
but she had virtually no chin. With a look first at Li Yan, then at
Shen Xue, she woodenly accepted Shen's five yuan.

"Our billing is all done by computer, and computers don't have
an ax to grind with anyone."

The printer spat out another rolled up phone record, which the
same clerk brought up to the window. The two women exited the
business office and went straight to a nearby pocket park, where
they studied the records they'd paid for. The records were so long
they had to sling them over their shoulders, where they fluttered in
the wind, like a pair of Tibetan *hadas* wrapped around their necks.
Shen Xue's eyes glazed over as she looked at the tiny, densely listed
phone numbers.

"I can't make heads or tails out of this," she said to Li Yan. "Have
you found anything?"

Li Yan was concentrating on her search.

"Nothing yet. The problem numbers all belong to that slutty aesthetics student."

But as her search continued, all those calls to one person seemed to make matters worse.

"Look at that, would you? All those calls to that little whore, sometimes four a day! That's more than he says to me in a week!"

Out came the real issue.

"The old son of a bitch keeps saying he can't get it up—with me, that is. With her, since he can put so much fire into his phone calls, he must be a blazing inferno when they're together!"

Shocked by that revelation, Shen Xue stared at Li Yan, who realized that she was being observed. Looking up at Shen Xue, she said:

"Why are you staring at me? Examine your own record."

Shen Xue turned her eyes away, but complained about the difficult task in front of her:

"There are too many different numbers here for me to make sense of."

"Didn't you say he's been acting funny the past few days? That's a good place to start."

So Shen Xue focused on the recent past.

"His phone's been off most of the time lately. He's hardly used it at all. Only calls to Fei Mo and me."

But then a discovery.

"Three days ago he had a call that lasted over an hour. Could that be a problem?"

Li Yan craned her neck to look at Shen Xue's list.

"Anything over five minutes is a problem, guaranteed!" she said categorically.

Shen Xue wasn't sure what to make of it.

"It's not a number I'm familiar with," she said. "Maybe it was a journalist. Their interviews can go on forever."

"Dial the number and see who answers. If it's a woman, see what she sounds like, and you'll have your answer."

That was all the encouragement Shen Xue needed to take out her phone and dial the number on Shouyi's phone record. But she closed it before the call went through.

"Why didn't you do it?"

"It doesn't seem right. What if it's perfectly harmless? What'll the person think of me then? That's it, I'm not going to check up on him. Who cares anyway?"

Li Yan glared at her.

"You make me sick!"

Shen Xue returned home after saying good-bye to Li Yan, and if Yan Shouyi's phone, which had been left on the shoe cupboard, had not rung, she'd have put the events of the day behind her and they could have gone on with their lives together. But while she was changing out of her street shoes, his phone did ring. She picked it up and looked at the digital readout; it said Yu Wenjuan. That made her angry, since Shouyi had told her he had no direct communications with his former wife, that he checked on his son through Yu Wenjuan's brother. Yu Wenjuan had never before answered any call he made to her, so why was she calling *him*? Obviously, he was lying through his teeth. The phone call reminded her of the photograph and bankbook, and really got her blood boiling. Once the ringing stopped, she picked up the phone to check his contacts list against the phone company's list, and searched out the call that had lasted over an hour. There it was. Among his contact numbers, and the name that went with it, was Wu Yue. Her heart lurched. Apparently he hadn't broken off with either Yu Wenjuan or Wu Yue. He'd kept her in a cocoon of deception. Between the two women, Wu Yue was the greater threat; only two days earlier they'd shared an hour-long phone call. What could they have talked about for over an hour? She carried the phone into the living room, where she sat on the sofa to think. A plan slowly formed in her mind: She'd send Wu Yue a text message on Shouyi's phone. Assured that Wu Yue would not know it was her, she made it ambiguous:

What are you thinking at this moment? I'd like to know.

That would not put the woman on her guard, no matter what the relationship. If she was his lover, it would say "I'm thinking of you," but if she was just a friend it would be little more than a wisecrack, nothing that linked Yan Shouyi and Wu Yue romantically, and would not have any adverse affect. After writing the message, Shen Xue hesitated for a moment before sending it.

She began to regret it almost immediately. If they had been talking about Fei Mo's new book the whole time, then not only would her fears be groundless, but Shouyi would be livid when heard about it. And what if Wu Yue called after receiving the text message? Should she pick up or shouldn't she? That would be too much for her. What she hadn't expected was for Shouyi's phone to ping two minutes later, meaning that Wu Yue had sent back a text message instead of phoning. What she saw nearly made her head explode. There were no words, just a single photograph of Yan Shouyi and Wu Yue lying atop a bed, both stark naked.

Wu Yue would later tell Yan Shouyi that she'd sent the image for two reasons: first, as a threat, warning him that if he stood in her way of getting the job at "Straight Talk," he could see how easy it was to make the photo public; second, also a threat, but only that, since she had no plans to send it to anyone else—she wasn't shameless, after all—not for his sake, but for her own. Imagine her shock when it fell into Shen Xue's hands!

Shen Xue would later tell Xiao Su that when she saw the photo, she sat there dazed for more than an hour, her mind a complete blank. She didn't snap to until she heard Yan Shouyi's key in the door.

33

Yan Shouyi was running a fever, and felt hot one minute and cold the next, like his father, when he'd had a case of typhoid fever. Back when Shouyi and Yu Wenjuan had still been together, something like this had put him in the hospital, but this time it hit him when he was driving, and he nearly ran a red light. Bleary-eyed, he detected a line of bicycles passing in front of his windshield, abruptly clearing his head; he slammed on the brakes, barely missing an old man on his bicycle. The near miss scared both men stiff. Yan was sweating. When the light turned green, he just sat there as cars in front came his way and the driver behind him laid on his horn to get him moving. That snapped him out of his daze and he drove through the intersection.

Yan Shouyi opened the door and walked into the flat, where the first thing he saw was the shoe cupboard, now missing the phone he'd left on top that morning. His heart was in his throat as he assumed that Shen Xue had taken the phone and kept it with her all day. He could not have known that the phone had actually remained on the shoe cupboard until she'd picked it up when it rang a short while before. He was prepared to deal with the possibility that Wu Yue had phoned him sometime during the day, but Shen Xue had ruined his plans when she'd sent Wu Yue a text message and received an obscene photograph in return. In his mind, the only thing he had to worry about was a phone call from Wu Yue, never imagining that Yu Wenjuan would try calling him several times that day or that Black Brick would call him as soon as he left the house.

Once he'd collected himself, he changed out of his street shoes and walked into the living room, where Shen Xue was sitting on the sofa with no discernible expression as she lit matches, one after the other. A pile of burned-out matches littered the tea table beside her. She did not look up when he walked in; his cell phone was on the table next to the pile of matches.

Yan sat down beside Shen Xue, reached out, and picked up his phone. The photograph Wu Yue had sent was frozen on the screen, although the image of the two naked bodies was distorted, like two slabs of meat left out too long. An explosion went off in Yan's head; cold sweat oozed from virtually every pore in his body. As he thought back to the scene sometime later, he realized that his fever vanished at that moment. He did not have to be told that this was serious, very serious, and that the damage was surely irreparable. He was struck by how mean and vicious Wu Yue could be. She was someone who meant what she said—the land mine she'd laid had gone off, as she'd threatened. But at the moment, he had no interest in putting the blame on Wu Yue, who, in fact, had been tricked into doing what she'd done. He just looked at the photo and managed a bitter smile. Then he laid down the phone and waited for Shen Xue to say something. But she remained impassive and said nothing. A look out the window showed that the colors of sunset were fading fast and the darkness of night was settling in. Lights were coming on in distant high-rise buildings. Yan Shouyi's mind was a blank, a virtual repeat of what had happened during the taping earlier that day. But slowly a thought formed there that darkness in the city is not the same as in the countryside. In the city, the curtain of darkness settles from above and is welcomed by the lighting of streetlamps. But back in his hometown, the darkness rises from the fields and colors the sky like spreading ink that slowly merges with the canopy of heaven. As darkness engulfed the room, Yan Shouyi mustered the will to break the ice.

"How long have we been together, Xue?"

Her only response was to keep striking matches. He was forced to answer his own question.

"I just counted. We've known each other a year and three months and have lived together for ten months."

Shen Xue tossed a burned match onto the pile on the coffee

table. Yan Shouyi picked the phone up and took another look at the image.

"What you said this morning was right. There's no difference between Fei Mo and me. Wu Yue took this picture of us a few days ago when we were at the hotel. My situation is a lot worse than Fei Mo's, because Wu Yue is blackmailing me with these pictures."

Rather than respond, Shen Xue picked up another match and lit it.

"But she has no interest in me personally. She wants to be the host of 'Straight Talk.'"

A muscle in Shen Xue's face twitched, and still she said nothing. Yan Shouyi's phone rang. The sound not only broke the silence, but it grated on their ears, while the LED screen was nearly blinding. He looked down. The incoming call was from Yu Wenjuan. It was the first time she had called him in the year and more since their divorce, and his first thought was that something had happened to his son. He opened the phone, but before he could say a word, Yu Wenjuan started screaming at him. In the past, she'd never lost her temper, no matter how tense things got. Even when she decided to divorce him, she did so without a show of temper. But, apparently, all that had changed, and her angry outburst over the phone had him completely unsettled.

"All day!" she yelled. "Why haven't you answered your phone?"

He said the first thing that came into his mind: "Meeting, I was at a meeting. Is the baby sick?"

"No," she said, "the baby isn't sick, but your grandmother is. Black Brick called me first thing this morning. He said your phone was on, but you weren't answering. So she told him to call me. She must be in bad shape. You have to go see her, and right away."

Yan Shouyi had his doubts. "How could this happen so suddenly?"

"Black Brick said she's been ill for several days, but she didn't want you to know, not at first. But then, this morning she said she wanted to see you, you and the baby, and that doesn't sound good."

Yan Shouyi, thrown into a panic, said, "Don't do anything, I'm leaving right away."

He closed the phone, stood up, and said to Shen Xue:

"It's my grandmother, she's not doing well and she wants to see me. I have to go back to Shanxi right away."

Shen Xue just stared at the burning match in her hand and said nothing.

Having no time to deal with Shen Xue, Yan Shouyi left the flat, letting the door close loudly behind him. That was followed immediately by a howl from inside and the sounds of Shen Xue's wails.

34

Yan Shouyi would recall that there was a waning moon that night as he sped along the Beijing-Taiyuan Highway, reaching speeds of over a hundred miles an hour.

The Gansu woman he and Yu Wenjuan's brother had hired at the nanny market was sitting in the back seat, holding the baby in her arms. At Shijiazhuang the baby started to cry. The nanny told Yan that his son had to pee.

"Let him pee in the car," he said.

He stopped at the service station in Yangquan for gas. It took three minutes.

Yu Wenjuan had not come downstairs when he'd picked up the child on his way to the family home in Shanxi.

35

Yan Shouyi didn't pull into his Shanxi home until the following afternoon. The weather that day, he would later recall, could not have been more pleasant. The wall and arch over the gate they'd built the year before stood proudly in the bright sunlight.

His grandmother had passed away. Black Brick told him that she had been sick for a week. At first it hadn't seemed serious, an ordinary cold, which seemed she'd get over after a couple of days. But, given her lifelong obsession with cleanliness, she'd refused to relieve herself in her room at night, insisting on getting up and hobbling outside with her cane to the toilet. Her cold symptoms returned. Two nights before his return, she'd developed a breathing problem, which got worse as the night wore on. At first, she hadn't wanted Yan Shouyi to know, but early the following morning, she gasped to Black Brick:

"Tell White Stone to come home. And tell Yu Wenjuan I want to see the baby."

Granny's body lay on the brick bed where she'd slept and where she and Shouyi had sat and talked the previous summer the night before he returned to Beijing. She'd poked him in the chest with her cane that day. In the end Yan Shouyi had laid his head in his grandmother's lap and bawled like a baby. Granny's face wore a smile, no different than when she was asleep. When they saw Yan Shouyi walk in, Black Brick, his wife, and the others in the room burst into tears. But as he looked down at her, the thought that he ought to cry as well never occurred to him. Now that the baby was awake, the nanny carried him into his great grandmother's room, which he immediately filled with loud noises. Now that he'd seen Granny, Yan Shouyi picked up the baby and left the room, followed by Black Brick, who was drying his eyes. Shouyi looked out into the yard, where local men who had helped with the wall the year before were busy putting up a funeral tent. Lu Guoqing and Jiang Changgen showed up. When they saw Yan Shouyi, they did everything they could to avoid his eyes. When he was alone with Yan Shouyi and the baby in the living room, Black Brick carped at his cousin:

"I tried calling you all day. Why didn't you pick up? If you'd made it back even half a day earlier you could have spoken with Granny."

Black Brick started crying again; Yan Shouyi said nothing. After drying his eyes, Black Brick said:

"She told me things before she died."

Yan Shouyi looked at his cousin.

"She said there's half a crock of soybeans in the room inside. She picked them herself last autumn. We should make tofu for the mourners out of them."

Still, Yan Shouyi said nothing.

"She also said she wanted Lu Zhixin to preside over the funeral, since he has the loudest voice. Other people give him two packs of cigarettes, so we'll give him three."

Still nothing from Yan Shouyi.

"Granny said she doesn't want you to wail, said it's a waste of your voice, and you need that for your TV show."

Still nothing from Yan Shouyi.

"Granny said for you to send your son to school when he's seven, not six. You started when you were six, and the other kids all picked on you."

Still nothing from Yan Shouyi.

"She also asked about the friend you brought back with you last time, Mr. Fei. She said he's a good man."

Yan Shouyi, who still had nothing to say, discovered that the child in his arms suddenly seemed aware of what was going on around him, as he put his face up next to his father's. Until this trip he had only seen his son once—in the nursery right after he was born. After that, seeing the boy's picture had sparked no feelings in him; in fact, his only thought had been how burdensome the boy was. But now, fatherly feelings rose inside him, and when he looked down at the boy, he found that his son was looking up at him. He wasn't even a year old, and yet his eyes were tear-filled.

Over the days that followed, Yan Shouyi was like a headless

housefly, flitting aimlessly from place to place. He climbed the nearby mountain to the spot where his grandmother had carried him on her back all the way to Hongdong County to have his broken leg set. He went to the brick kiln where he and Fei Mo had gone together the year before. In the yard, beneath the date tree, he recalled how his grandmother had sat in her armchair in that very spot while work on the wall was underway and Shen Xue had brought over a basin of hot water, announcing in her fractured Shanxi dialect:

"Come wash up, the water's hot!'

They buried Granny seven days later. Before sealing her coffin, Lu Zhixin, who presided at the funeral, asked members of the Yan family:

"Does anyone want to say something?"

Everyone was weeping. No one spoke. Lu Zhixin turned to Yan Shouyi.

"Do you want to say something?"

He did not.

"The family has nothing to say. Seal the coffin!"

Once that was done, Lu shouted at the top of his lungs:

"Granny has nothing to say either. Start the procession!"

During those seven days, Yan Shouyi made only one phone call, to Shen Xue. Her phone had been turned off.

On the night of the funeral, Yan Shouyi climbed the hill behind the village with a flashlight, stopping at the spot where he and Zhang Xiaozhu had come with their cast-off miner's lamp to write words on the sky blackboard. Xiaozhu had written:

You're not stupid, Mom.

Shouyi had written:

Where are you, Mom?

The two lines of writing could linger on the black screen of the sky for up to five minutes.

The sky on this night was so black he couldn't see his fingers in front of his face. Now forty-three years old, Yan wrote with his flashlight:

Granny, I want to talk to you.

The words hung on the black screen for a full seven minutes.

Yan Shouyi broke down and wept. He now understood what a despicable person he was.

Chapter 3

Two Families: Yan and Zhu

1

In 1927, Yan Laoyou asked a fellow called Old Cui, a donkey trader, to take a message to Kou wai, some 2,000 li distant from Shanxi's Yan Family Village, for him.

Kou wai normally referred to Inner Mongolia, on the other side of the Great Wall, but in 1927 Shanxi it referred to the city of Zhangjia kou in Hebei Province. Yan Laoyou's eldest son, Yan Baihai, lived in Kou wai, where he specialized in gelding livestock.

Yan Laoyou was a farmhand for a rich landlord named Wan. Although he was only a tenant farmer, he loved to talk, a trait that made him appear to be someone with a large number of friends. In 1923, when his son, Yan Baihai—White Child—was only fourteen, his father apprenticed him to a carpenter named Old Song, an old friend of his who lived in Song Family Village. But friend or not, when his son was taken on, he still gave Old Song a gift of half a sheep. After the first year into his apprenticeship, Yan Baihai had learned how to make a wooden stool all by himself, but that summer he left the master carpenter and went off with a gelding master named Old Zhou. Now, Old Zhou was also a friend of Yan Laoyou, but he viewed carpentry as a proper way of making a livelihood, while gelding pigs and other farm animals was not the sort of work he felt comfortable talking about. He wanted to bring his son home to continue his apprenticeship with the carpenter Old Song.

"Let it go," Old Song urged. "The boy can't sit still."

But Yan Laoyou went and dragged his son home, where he bound him to a bench for five days, after which he called Old Song over. "Can't stand still?" he said, pointing to Yan Baihai. "See for yourself."

"Dad," Baihai said, surprising his father, "I don't have anything in common with the master. We've got nothing to talk about."

Yan Laoyou smacked his son across the face.

"Does that mean you've got plenty to talk about with a man who castrates pigs?"

"No, but I like the sound of squealing pigs."

He stretched out his neck and made the sound of a pig being castrated.

"*Jiiii–jiii–*"

With a sigh, Yan Laoyou rubbed his hands and said to Old Song: "He's a good-for-nothing little shit!"

Old Song tapped the bowl of his pipe against the doorjamb and stood up to leave. Yan Laoyou dragged out his second son, Heihai—Black Child—who was a year younger than his brother. Yan Laoyou turned to Old Song and said:

"Why not take this one with you? But I have to warn you, he's not too bright."

Old Song had not gotten angry when Baihai ran off with that other man, nor when Baihai made the sound of a pig being castrated. But his dander was up now.

"Are you saying it's OK to be a carpenter if you're not bright? You think all carpenters are slow-witted, is that it?"

With a withering glare at Yan Laoyou, he stormed out of the house.

The gelding master, Old Zhou, was a bold man. Once when he'd castrated all the pigs in the surrounding villages, other livestock as well, the wild thought occurred to him that he ought to go to Kou wai, where all of Shanxi's donkey's came from. He figured there had to be plenty of animals needing castration there. On the night before he was to leave for Kou wai with Master Zhou, Baihai assumed that his mother would cry up a storm and his father would tie him to the bench again. Neither happened. His mother sat under a lamp calculating the distance to Kou wai.

"Over two thousand li. At seventy li a day, it'll take you more than a month."

The distance, not her son, made her cry. Meanwhile, his father was standing in the doorway knocking the bowl of his pipe against the doorjamb.

"You don't know anybody in Kou wai," he said.

"I will after a couple of days," Baihai said.

"Then go ahead and end your days far away. From today on, I no longer have a son. If we meet again, it'll be as acquaintances."

So Yan Baihai went to Kou wai with his master and was gone three years with no word from or to home. He ought to have been eighteen by then. During the second year he was away, his father sent his younger brother, Heihai, to Wei Family Village to be apprenticed to a tofu maker named Wei. Heihai was not bright, no disputing that, but he was no dummy either. It customarily took three years to finish an apprenticeship in the tofu business, but after only a year and a half, he came home and opened his own tofu business. A boy not yet seventeen began walking mountain roads and traveling to neighboring villages with a supply of tofu on a carrying pole with two baskets.

"Tofu!—" he shouted.

"Yan Family Village tofu!—"

Throughout 1926 and 1927, years of ideal conditions in southeast Shanxi, with Yan Laoyou working as a farmhand for the Wan family and his son, Heihai, selling tofu, the family managed to save up fifty ounces of silver. So father and son tore down the three western rooms of the house and built new ones. All Yan Laoyou could say when he stood there looking at the new house and yard was:

"I'll be fucked!"

During the fall of that year, another of the Wan family's tenant farmers, a fellow named Ma, died of a lung disease. Old Ma had never been much of a talker. His favorite pastimes had been getting drunk and going into town during the slack winter season to watch cricket fights. Tired of being a spectator, he bought his own crickets and entered them in bouts. Having few if any friends, he began treating his crickets like family. He pawned a tattered old hat and went into town to bet on his crickets. He died without enough money to pay for a coffin, so his wife and children planned to roll him up in a grass mat and bury him that way. Yan Laoyou stepped in with two silver dollars, enough to buy a flimsy coffin for his fellow tenant farmer. Ma's wife didn't say anything, but Landlord Wan was moved enough to send for Yan Laoyou.

"You and Ma were friends, I take it."

"No," he replied. "He was impossible to get along with. We had nothing in common."

"And still you paid for his coffin?"

"The fox grieves when the rabbit dies. We worked side by side for over a decade, and were friends without being friendly."

Landlord Wan rubbed the back of his head and nodded. Then he summoned his steward and told him to pay for Old Ma's funeral with five silver dollars. Four tables were set up for a banquet on the day of the funeral, with Landlord Wan himself coming to offer the messages of condolence. Old Ma, who'd been a loner most of his life, was the beneficiary of posthumous honors. That night, following the funeral ceremony, Old Ma's wife, whose face was pitted with smallpox scars, came to see Yan Laoyou.

"Old Yan," she said, I didn't truly realize I was a widow until they put the coffin in the ground."

Since she mentioned the coffin, he replied:

"I don't want to hear anything about money. Nor the landlord either. We were his friends."

"Then as a friend, I'd like you to promise me one more thing."

"What is it?"

"That you'll take our daughter, who's sixteen, as your daughter-in-law."

Yan Laoyou was speechless.

"My face is pitted," Old Ma's widow said. "Hers isn't."

Yan Laoyou's wife laughed after Old Ma's widow left.

"You've bought yourself a daughter-in-law for two yuan. A good deal, I'd say."

Yan Laoyou made as if to spit in his wife's face.

"You think she's just sending over her daughter? She's sending her whole family!"

He shook his head.

"Old Ma never had a thought in his head, and so I expected the same of his wife. I was wrong."

He looked over at his new house.

"All because of those new rooms," he said.

It was the tenth month, two months from the Lunar New Year, and what Old Ma's widow had in mind was to have the nuptials take place before the end of the year. The problem for Yan Laoyou wasn't the idea of nuptials—he was fine with that—but for whom? In terms of age, it ought to have been Yan Baihai, but he was off in Kou wai; where the good of the family was concerned, his brother, Yan Heihai, was the logical choice, since half of the money for the western rooms had come from the sale of tofu. He was already growing restless. At the first crowing of a rooster, around the fifth watch of the night, Yan Laoyou got up to go to the toilet, and was frightened by a rising and falling figure in the moonlit yard. When he got closer, he saw that it was his son Heihai, practicing his ceremonial wedding bows. Out in the mill shed, the family donkey was quietly turning the mill to grind soybeans into slurry for tofu. His father had been leaning toward him as the prospective groom until he saw what he was up to. With an angry kick, he growled:

"You little bastard, what matures first, the big grain—barley—or the little grain—wheat?"

So the decision was made: Baihai was to be married. But he was in Kou wai, some 2,000 li away. How would the word get to him? As luck would have it, a donkey trader passed through the village the very next day. The trader, a Hunanese named Old Cui, was on his way to Kou wai with his apprentice. Since it was late in the day when he arrived in Yan Family Village, he decided to stop over, and spent the night in Landlord Wan's livestock shed, where Yan Laoyou found him. He brought along a square of tofu, two leeks, and half a jug of fermented sweet potato spirits. Trader Cui's apprentice set up a pot on a pile of bricks in the shed, lit a fire under it, and tossed in two handfuls of rice he took out of his sack. Trader Cui lay down on a grass mat he'd covered with his bedding, put his hands behind his head, and rested as he watched the livestock eating out of the feed trough. When he turned his head, Yan Laoyou saw that he was jug-eared. The fellow feeding the livestock, a mute called Old Wu, was annoyed by the way Yan Laoyou was always talking, so when he saw Yan walk in, he threw down his mixing stick and glared at Yan before walking out of the shed. That didn't bother Yan a bit. But Trader Cui was taken aback by Yan's entry into the shed with food. He stopped in mid-bite, sat up, and took a good long look at his visitor.

"Who are you?"

"I'm someone who likes making friends."

Trader Cui's ears flapped as he shook his head and laughed. He pointed to his apprentice, who was cooking the rice.

"He's Xiao Liu."

Xiao Liu, a squat young man with a round head, smiled. He had a slow, but kindly, look about him. Yan handed him the tofu and leeks, picked up a couple of little bowls, and sat down beside Trader Cui to share the spirits he'd brought. After three friendly toasts, Yan said:

"I hear you're heading to Kou wai to trade in donkeys."

Old Cui nodded.

"I have a little favor to ask of my elder brother."

Old Cui stopped him. "Before we get into that, what sign of the zodiac do you belong to?"

"The dragon."

"You're dragon, I'm chicken, so you're the elder brother."

Yan Laoyou laughed.

"Well then, I have a favor to ask of my younger brother."

"Leave it to me. Want me to bring back a pair of donkeys?"

Yan Laoyou shook his head.

"No donkeys. I'd just like you to deliver a message."

"What sort of message?"

"My no-account elder son lives in Kou wai, where he gelds livestock for a living. If you see him there, I'd like you to tell him to come home right away. He's eighteen, time for him to start a family."

Old Cui laughed.

"So that's it. Leave it to me."

Xiao Liu broke into the conversation:

"Kou wai is a big place. How are we supposed to find him?"

"You'll have to look for him," Yan said to Trader Cui. "It's urgent and important."

Before Xiao Liu could say another word, Old Cui stopped him with his hand.

"If I don't find him right off," he said to Yan, "I'll just look for someone with a Shanxi accent. Finding one person from Shanxi is the same as finding everyone from Shanxi. Leave it to me."

Yan Laoyou raised his bowl to Trader Cui.

"As soon as I saw you, I knew you were a man of the world. You've seen and done a lot more than I have. The boy's name is Yan Baihai. He has a large mole under his left eye."

"When's he supposed to come home?"

"Before the end of the year. His intended bride is waiting for him."

Old Cui emptied his bowl.

"Don't you worry. I'll take care of everything."

Yan Laoyou emptied his bowl.

"Any time you pass through Yan Family Village, you're family."

Yan and Old Cui got mightily drunk that night.

2

Trader Cui's home was in Hunan's Jiyuan Prefecture. His grandfather had been a farmer, his father a salt peddler. He was the first donkey trader in the family. To raise capital, he had two partners, one named Jiang, the other Xing. Only Old Cui went on the road with the animals. His trips from Hunan to Kou wai took more than two months; the trips back, with animals, more than three. That added up to two round trips a year. Xiao Liu, who was Jiang's nephew, had been Old Cui's apprentice for two years. Before going on the road, Old Cui had been a man who liked to talk and was quick to laugh, but he had hardly any family life, since he spent so much time away from home. One year, not long before New Year's, his wife ran off with a peddler. His partners, Jiang and Xing, found a new wife for him, one quite a bit younger than her predecessor, but from then on, Old Cui was sociable only when he was with others; the rest of the time he brooded over whatever was bothering him. His partner Xing said to him:

"Why don't you take a couple of years off and let me go on the road for a change?"

"No, I'll do it. I'm used to it. I actually like it better than staying home with nothing to do."

The year he passed through Yan Family Village he was forty-one. A man mellows when he reaches the age of forty. But Xiao Liu, a mere seventeen, had little patience. Out on the road together,

Old Cui liked to stop to rest in the late afternoon. Sometimes, Xiao Liu pressed him to go a little farther.

"The sun's still up," he'd say.

So they'd keep traveling till nightfall, too far from the next village and the last inn, by then cold and hungry, with no place to bed down.

"Are you rushing to your father's funeral or something?" he'd rail at Xiao Liu. "You had to keep going, didn't you?"

Xiao Liu would just smile. "Traveling at night's easier."

They took leave of Yan Family Village early the next morning, Old Cui carrying a bag over his shoulder, Xiao Liu burdened with a carrying pole for the bedding and millet. Yan Laoyou saw them a few miles down the road. As they crossed a mountain ridge, they looked out onto the city of Changzhi.

"Go on home now," Old Cui said to Old Yan.

In the most elegant language he could manage, Yan said:

"Ahead lie tall mountains and a long journey. Be well, my brother."

He handed a large hunk of tofu to Xiao Liu before reminding Trader Cui:

"That favor for your new nephew, please don't forget."

"Don't you worry. He'll be back home before the end of the year."

Back then villagers were not in the habit of shaking hands, so they said their good-byes the traditional way, with clasped hands in front of their chests. Yan Laoyou did not turn and head back to Yan Family Village until Trader Cui and Xiao Liu had walked down the mountain and were little more than two specks in the distance.

Old Cui and his apprentice made their way to Kou wai, stopping when they were tired, and managing eighty or ninety li a day. In ten days they reached Yangquan Prefecture, and there Old Cui felt the first rumblings in his stomach as diarrhea hit him. There was no way to tell if the cause lay in Xiao Liu's cooking or in a cold Old Cui had picked up along the way or maybe the climate. They checked in to a local inn, where Old Cui raised hell with Xiao Liu:

"How the hell are you going to learn a trade when you can't even keep clean enough when you're cooking?"

Xiao Liu stuck out his neck and defended himself:

"I washed the millet five times in the river."

Then he added:

"We ate the same stuff, so how come my stomach's OK?"

Old Cui was irate.

"So what if the last meal was clean? Back in Hongdong there was a rat in the porridge!"

With a pout, Xiao Liu chose not to respond. Old Cui assumed that the runs would stop after his innards were cleaned out. That night, to his horror, his bowels acted up eight times, and each time he barely made it to the latrine before the foul, mostly liquid, discharge evacuated noisily. He was weak as a kitten and lightheaded the next morning. Forced to extend his stay in Yangquan, he confined himself to bed in the inn to regain his strength, while Xiao Liu went to a local pharmacy to buy herbal medicine, which he heated in a borrowed medicinal pot for his master. The medicine effectively brought an end to the diarrhea, but produced the side effect of a pain in the pit of Old Cui's stomach, requiring a new herbal concoction. That in turn led to symptoms of malaria—burning with fever one moment and freezing the next. More medicine. For Old Cui, who had enjoyed perfect health for years, the onset of one illness after another forced him to remain in Yangquan for the better part of a month and cost him five silver dollars for medicine and his room at the inn. By itself, a bit of ill health was of no major concern, since the illnesses would all run their course, after which he and Xiao Liu could be back on the road. But disaster struck before that happened. One night, a gang of bandits armed with butcher knives scaled the inn's walls and cleaned out all the guests. The bandits all wore masks and spoke with a Yuci accent. Old Cui's bag contained all his capital for buying donkeys in Kou wai—two hundred silver dollars—so, alternating fever and chills be damned, he shouted for Xiao Liu and put up a struggle with one of the bandits, who clubbed him in the head. When he came to, his money wasn't all that was missing— the bandits had taken Xiao Liu with them. The owner of the inn, who was shivering with fear, reported the robbery to the police the next day, but by then the bandits had vanished without a trace, and all anyone had to go on was what sounded like a Taiyuan accent.

Two hundred silver dollars, enough to buy thirty-four donkeys, all gone. Trader Cui was sweating profusely, but no more fever or chills. The money he'd lost hadn't been his alone. How was he going to deal with his partners, Jiang and Xing? And that's if it were only the money. He'd also lost his apprentice, and Xiao Liu's family would surely demand his return. How in the world was he going to do that? When he and the innkeeper returned from the local yamen, the owner analyzed the situation for him. Xiao Liu might look honest, but his eyes were in constant motion, a sign of shrewdness. He'd been running around town the past few days, with no one to watch him, since Old Cui was sick in bed, and who's to say he hadn't hooked up with bandits to rob his master of money only he'd known about? That made sense to Old Cui, but it was only conjecture. On the other hand, the innkeeper looked like someone who could have been in league with the bandits, and that made a good case for keeping one's stays at an inn short. But without solid evidence, it was just a useless theory, worthy neither of talk nor of thought. The day before he'd had two hundred silver dollars; now he was penniless. Knowing no one in town, Old Cui was reduced to walking the streets in a daze. Before long his steps had taken him out of town and up to the bank of the Fen River, roaring along at the foot of a mountain, where he realized he had no home to go back to and no country to rely on; worse yet, his first wife, a woman he'd been able to talk to, had run off with a peddler. So he undid the sash around his waist, tied it to the crooked limb of a scholar tree, which he tugged to see how strong it was, then thought about it for a minute before kicking the boulder out from under his feet and swinging by his neck.

When Old Cui came to, he noticed the smell of liquor. As he opened his eyes, his head seemed to swell. He looked around. He was in some sort of distillery, where a bunch of half-naked men were pounding grain for fermentation. He was lying on a pile of it, hot and steamy. An elderly, overweight man with a round, smiling face was watching him through slitted eyes. Seeing that he was conscious, he brought his face up close to Old Cui and asked:

"Where are you from?"

Old Cui's mouth felt dry and brittle; his voice was too far gone to say a word. The fat man had one of his helpers bring a bowl of water, which Old Cui drank greedily. Finally, he was able to speak.

"Henan."

"What drove you to do that?"

The young helper spoke up before he could answer:

"You're lucky the boss was in his cart along the riverbank. If he'd happened by a minute or two later, you'd be having this conversation with Yama, the King of Hell."

Old Cui poured out his tale of woe: from arriving in Yangquan on his way to buy donkeys to resell, to falling ill, to being set upon by bandits, with the loss of all his money and his apprentice. He was in tears by the time he finished. The moon-faced proprietor responded with consoling words.

"Heaven never seals off all the roads. There's more money to be earned."

"But how am I supposed to trade in donkeys if I'm penniless? And I've lost my apprentice. There's no way I can go home now."

The proprietor gazed into Old Cui's eyes.

"You look like an honest man," he said. "You can stay here for the time being. We'll talk about what comes later over the next few days."

Old Cui took another look around. "But I'm a donkey trader. I don't know the first thing about distilling liquor."

"There are people who will not learn, but nothing that cannot be learned."

"But I have nothing to offer, and the way I feel right now, I'm not in the mood to learn anything."

The moon-faced man nodded thoughtfully.

"What besides trading in donkeys have you done in your life?"

"Before I traded in donkeys," Old Cui said, "I was an assistant cook in a restaurant in town."

"All right, then, you can cook for the men who work in my distillery."

So Trader Cui worked as a cook for the man who ran the distillery, a fellow named Zhu. At first, until he got over his depression, the meals he served were either too salty or too bland, the steamed bread made with either too little yeast or too much. The dissatisfied workers spoke to Boss Zhu, but he brushed off their complaints. Then, after a couple of months, as the loss of his money and his apprentice bothered him less, he was able to concentrate on what he was doing and began serving tasteful food. Even more important, he sensed that he'd become a different person. He no longer missed home, no longer thought about his wife, and could hardly believe that he had once made all those trips to distant Kou wai to trade in donkeys. Thoughts of his past seemed more like tales he'd read in a book. On the road he'd dined on the wind and slept in the rain; but in the distillery, no wind blew and no rain fell. In his mind he'd been a cook at the distillery for about as long as he could recall. At year's end, the workers said that Cui from Henan had put on weight, a comment that drew a bashful smile from him.

The following spring, on the second day of the second month, when the dragon raised its head, there appeared in Yangchuan a Shanxi opera troupe, a favorite form of entertainment of Boss Zhu's, who invited the performers to bed down in the grain storage room. After nightfall, when the day's work was done, Old Cui, Boss Zhu, and the workers enjoyed a night of opera at the local racetrack. That despite the fact that, as a Henanese, Old Cui hardly understood a word of the Shanxi opera. The only times he laughed were when he looked over at Boss Zhu, sitting in his armchair, his round face split into a broad smile. After each performance, Boss Zhu had him prepare a noodle soup with plenty of vinegar and sliced ginger for the entertainers, and he stood behind them, wiping his hands on his apron and watching them eat, their faces still painted for the stage. In a matter of days, Old Cui became friendly with one of the troupe members, a scabbie-headed drummer from Heze, Shandong called Old Hu. Old Cui's new friend had once traded in tea, not successfully, it turned out, and he'd turned up jobless in Shanxi ten years before. Since he'd participated in village festivities as a youngster, he'd signed on with the opera troupe as a drummer. His life story wasn't all that different from Old Cui's.

Winds managed to find their way through cracks in the grain storage room, turning the nights uncomfortably cold, so Old Cui invited Old Hu to share a space with him behind the kitchen, where lingering heat from the stove kept the room warm enough for them to lie there and talk through the night, until the first rooster sounded the coming of day. Their conversations hardly strayed beyond talk of family and the experiences they'd encountered on the road. Some time before daybreak, Old Hu said:

"Let's get some sleep."

"Just what I was thinking."

They both fell asleep.

The opera troupe performed in Yangquan for the better part of a month. Then it was time to move on to the next town, Xinzhou.

Old Cui saw the troupe all the way to the river, where Old Hu, his drum strapped to his back, said:

"This is far enough."

Then, in the style of an opera singer:

"Though we travel a thousand li, in the end we must part."

That did it, Old Cui broke down.

"My good brother, I'd love to be a drummer and stay with you."

"Drumming can't hold a candle to cooking. You don't know where your next meal is coming from."

"Where will you go after Xizhou, good brother?"

"Wherever the troupe leader says. After we make it through this tour, it looks like we might be off to Kou wai."

The mention of Kou wai abruptly reminded Old Cui of his promise to deliver a message for Yan Laoyou when he'd passed through Yan Family Village as a donkey trader. Yan had shared a jug of liquor with him that night, and they'd struck up an immediate friendship. He described the incident to his new friend and asked Old Hu if he would look up Yan Baihai when he got to Kou wai and urge him to return home.

"I'm not sure if a delay of two years counts as bad faith where a favor for a friend is concerned, but since I cannot go, please do this for me."

"Don't you worry," Old Hu said, "your business is my business."

"His name is Yan Baihai, he castrates animals for a living, he has a large mole under his left eye, and he speaks with a southern Shanxi accent. Now don't forget."

3

Forty-eight-year-old Old Hu the drummer was born in the year of the tiger. As a boy he'd suffered from scabies, which left scars on his head. Over his nearly half century on earth he'd done a bit of everything: porter, herder, candy maker, and tea vendor, the pursuit of which had sent him to many places. But for the past ten years he'd been a drummer in the opera troupe, and had no desire to do anything else, not at his age. The troupe leader, an uncommunicative man with chiseled features named Old Bao, who was six years older than Old Hu, moped around most of the time, and when he did open his mouth to speak, hardly anything but criticisms ever emerged. He'd been openly critical of every member of the troupe at one time or another, but not Old Hu, at least not often. That was because he was an old man. In Old Bao's view, longevity not only referred to the length of time someone had been with the troupe—a long time for Old Hu—in other words, seniority, but also to age. In the late 1980s in China, a man in his fifties was considered old. Old Hu played the drum for opera performances day in and day out, but he never took a fancy to what was sung up on stage. As a transplant from Shandong, he could not abide the way Shanxi singers drew out the words—*yaaa . . . yiiii*—though he liked the spoken parts; in that, he and Old Cui were of one mind. Actually, Old Hu didn't like all the spoken parts; in fact, only one line pleased him every time he heard it. When the actor who played the old man parts was angry at how another character dealt with a dilemma, he would shake his head, wave his arms, and announce in a faltering voice:

"Slowly, slow—ly—"

After leaving Yangquan the troupe went to Yuci Prefecture, and from there to the much larger venue of Taiyuan Prefecture, where they stayed twenty-five days. Their next stop was Wutai County, where they met a woman named Xin Chunyan, who sang female roles in Shanxi opera. Troupe Leader Bao had met Xin on a previous occasion, but this time she asked if she could join up, since she could not get along with the owner of the troupe she'd been singing with. Now Old Bao had never enjoyed the luxury of having a star in his low-budget traveling troupe. But here was the renowned Xin Chunyan, wanting to join up, and for the first time in history, Old Bao actually smiled. The addition of Xin Chunyan changed the troupe. Every member took one step up the social ladder, thanks to her, and the venue, barely forty percent filled yesterday, was now standing room only. Operas they'd never performed before became part of their repertoire. But for Hu the drummer, Xin Chunyan did not constitute an improvement; about all he could say was that her voice was shriller than the other women's. A fellow called Old Li, who played the clappers, set him straight, telling him that shrillness was a cherished quality in Shanxi opera. She could reach heights the other women could not, and while other women in the troupe could hold a note for as long as it takes for a match to burn out, she could hold it long enough for someone to finish off a pipeful of tobacco. As soon as Xin Chunyan was added to the troupe, plans to move on were scrubbed. They stayed in Wutai for a full month, and no one would deny the possibility that they could remain there permanently with no decrease in ticket sales. They performed *Dream of the Red Chamber, Romance of the Western Chamber, Rouge Tears, Tears of Yang Guifei*, and *The Butterfly Lovers*. They even put on *Legend of the White Snake*. None of that pleased Old Hu. Up till now they'd specialized in operas in which there were old men roles, and only they included the line "Slowly, slow—ly—" Now, thanks to the addition of Xin Chunyan, women's roles moved to the forefront. His displeasure, of course, counted for nothing, and had no effect on audience enjoyment.

Spring came and went, and the troupe finally left Wutai; the departure could not have come too soon for Old Hu. The next stop was Fanzhi County, where a minor disaster struck while they were performing *Yearning for the World*. When the principal character, Chang'e, desires to descend to the world of mortals, the Queen Mother sends down celestial troops to stop her. During the interlude that occurs at that point, the powerful Queen Mother's troops perform acrobatics on the stage, giving the Chang'e actor a chance to rest. Old Hu, suffering a full bladder, asked Old Li, the clapper musician, to take over the drums during the interlude while he went out to relieve himself. Fanzhi County was not wealthy enough to have its own opera house, so they'd set up a stage in an open field and ringed it with curtains. Tickets were sold at the entrance.

Old Hu parted the curtains and went out into the field under a full moon. He was sweating heavily and shivering as gusts of summer wind hit him, but he shrugged it off and kept walking until he reached a clump of bushes, where he unbuttoned his pants and relieved himself. He'd just finished when he heard a rustling sound in nearby bushes. With no particular purpose in mind, he went over to see what was going on. He spotted a pile of colorful costume clothing in the moonlight and recognized it as belonging to the character played by Xin Chunyan—Chang'e.

Old Hu was married back when he was peddling tea, but he hadn't so much as touched another woman in the decade following her death. In a momentary lapse of judgment, as streams of heat suddenly coursed through his body, he instinctively went up to her. His view was blocked by the bushes, but he heard the distinctive hiss of a woman urinating; when Xin Chunyan was finished, she hitched up her pants and found herself face to face with Old Hu, throwing a fright into him. If that had been the end of it, as fellow members of the troupe, they could have brushed it off and everything would have been back to normal. In the two months or more that she had been with the troupe, she hadn't uttered a word to Old Hu. But as luck would have it, the cymbal player, a fellow named Du, had also taken advantage of the interlude to come out to relieve himself, and when he saw Old Hu and Xin Chunyan standing there face to face, he assumed the worst and screamed. Suddenly embarrassed, Xin Chuyan slapped Old Hu across the face and ran back to the protection of lights in the stage area.

They finished the performance that night, but when it was over, every member of the troupe—those who played female roles, those who played male roles, and all the musicians—knew that Old Hu had stolen a look at Xin Chunyan while she was relieving herself. After finishing their post-performance noodle soup, they bedded down for the night behind the stage, all but the troupe leader, who told Old Hu to come out front, where he just glared gloomily at him. Old Hu's face went from flushed to blanched under Old Bao's withering glare.

"I didn't see a thing," he protested.

Old Bao still said nothing.

"Then maybe I should leave."

Old Bao sucked in his breath, not knowing what to do.

"Watching her pee, was it worth it?"

Later that night, Old Hu packed up his things and left the opera troupe in the fading moonlight. He hadn't walked far before turning around and seeing a single lantern hanging over the stage. He wept at the sight.

Old Hu left Fanzhi County and returned to Wutai, where, for the second time in his life, he took up work as a porter, carrying coal and kindling, rice and a variety of greens, whatever he was told to carry, up and down the mountain. But he was no longer a young man, and it took him four hours to make a trip the younger porters managed in only two. They would put down their loads and engage in a round of lighthearted banter while he sat wearily off to the side and tried to catch his breath. It took a month, but he finally got used to the grind. The one thing he didn't do was talk, not to anyone. What was he supposed to say?

One day, as he was carrying a load of rice up the mountain, he encountered a so-called doctor who removed corns and calluses. The fellow had spread a white cloth with the drawing of an oversized human foot atop a boulder by the footpath. On another white cloth, which he'd spread out on the ground, he displayed some dried and dark meaty objects that looked like beans. The thought that he might have foot problems would never have occurred to Old Hu if he hadn't encountered this so-called doctor. But he had, and all of a sudden his feet hurt. So he removed his sandals and took a look. Both feet were like a breeding ground for corns and calluses, the result of two months of carrying loads up and down the mountain. So he rested his carrying pole against a rock, sat down across from the doctor, and stretched out both feet. He flinched each time the doctor removed a corn; the final count was thirty-two. The removal charge was ten cash apiece, altogether three-twenty, and when he handed over the money, he saw that the doctor had a sixth finger on one hand. While he was working, his head had been bent over Old Hu's feet. But he looked up at Old Hu as he took the money, and when he spoke, Old Hu could not have been happier—the man, with his delicate features, was from Shandong. For two months Old Hu had hardly spoken a word, but now he smiled and asked the man:

"Where in Shandong are you from?"

Hearing a familiar accent, the doctor returned the smile.

"Tai'an."

"I'm from Heze myself. What's brought you all the way out here?"

"Shanxi people walk everywhere, and that means plenty of corns and calluses."

That made Old Hu laugh.

"Where do you go from here?"

"I'm thinking of heading to Kou wai, where there are lots of herdsmen and plenty of corns and calluses."

A light went on in Old Hu's head. The distillery cook, Old Cui from Henan, had asked him at the beginning of the year, when the troupe was in Yangquan, to deliver a message for him in Kou wai. He and Old Cui had bedded down behind the kitchen and talked half the night. Since then, he'd been on the road, had run into trouble, and had drifted back to Wutai. He told the corn and callus doctor about his promise and asked him to deliver a message to the son of a friend of a friend, a youngster named Yan Baihai, when he was in Kou wai.

"I wouldn't ask just anybody," he said, feeling a bit uneasy about the request, "but since we're both from Shandong..."

He saw that the corn and callus doctor was thinking it over, and didn't seem happy. So Old Hu took out a silver dollar, his bonus from the opera troupe, which he'd carried with him all this time, and placed it on the white cloth.

"We've just met, and I shouldn't be asking you to do this."

Then, in the style of opera lyrics, he added:

"The request of a friend is weightier than Mt. Tai."

That, of course, referred to Tai'an, the doctor's hometown. With an embarrassed look at the money on the cloth, the doctor replied:

"That's too much money to spend for asking someone to deliver a simple message."

But he didn't pick the money up and hand it back to Old Hu. He just looked down at it thoughtfully, and Old Hu could tell that he was not an unselfish person. But as far as Old Hu was concerned, people like that were reliable.

"The boy's name is Yan Baihai. He gelds livestock for a living and speaks with a southern Shanxi accent. He's got a large mole under his left eye. If you see him, tell him to return home right away."

The doctor looked up.

"What's happened to make him return home with such urgency?"

That stumped Old Hu. He smacked his own forehead. It had been months since Old Cui had asked the favor, and he didn't know how to answer the doctor. But he clapped his hands and said:

"Whatever it is, they need him at home."

"Besides," he added, "why is not important. He just has to go home."

Suddenly he was reminded of something else.

"Here we are chatting away," he said, "and I don't even know your name. I don't know what to call you."

"That's easy," the man said, "my name is Luo. You can call me Young Luo."

4

Young Luo had practiced his trade for twenty of his thirty-two years, following in the footsteps of his father. Throughout the first half of the twentieth century, the primary mode of transportation for most people in China was walking, so corn and callus specialists never had to worry where their next meal was coming from. That was especially true in the Tai'an district, the home of Mt. Tai, where it became a profession. With so many practitioners concentrated in one place, Young Luo's father took his eleven-year-old son with him to find a better place to ply his trade.

Young Luo was forced to go out on his own when his father developed a debilitating respiratory illness that kept him confined to home. Young Luo fathered five children, a large family that relied upon his income alone. His father's volatile temper—the smallest thing could set him off—and miserly nature had caused his disease. Having suffered under the domineering influence of his temperamental father for years, Young Luo had grown timid and fearful, afraid of doing the wrong thing when faced with a tough choice. This trait was exacerbated by the presence of a sixth finger on his right hand—the surgical hand. Removing corns and calluses never bothered him; interacting with people did. As soon as the procedure was completed, both hands retreated into the shelter of his wide sleeves.

Young Luo accepted Old Hu's silver dollar and memorized the message he was to deliver to Yan Baihai, but since he was in no hurry to head up to Kou wai, he stuck around Wutai County another two weeks removing corns. After Wutai he went to Hunyuan County, and from there to Datong Prefecture. After Datong, he went to Yanggao County. He spent a month in each county, two months in each prefecture. Six months later he left Shanxi Province. His brief encounter with Old Hu in Wutai had occurred during the harvest season; when he left Shanxi snow had begun to fall. His first stop after leaving Shanxi was at the Great Wall, where the winds were especially ferocious. He spent the next two weeks in Huaian County, removing corns on the street, the spill-off from his runny nose falling onto his surgical hand the whole time. He arrived in Zhangjiakou just before the Lunar New Year, where he spent the next two weeks removing corns and forgetting all about the message he had promised to deliver. When he was totaling up his earnings at year's end, he noticed that the nose of Yuan Shikai on one of his silver dollars had been rubbed off, and that sparked a memory. It was the coin his fellow Shandong traveler, Old Hu, had given him when he was removing corns in Wutai County. At the time, the missing nose of Yuan Shikai on the silver dollar had made him laugh. But that much money for delivering a simple message struck him as excessive, and he'd decided to give it back to Old Hu the next day. He'd set up shop beside the mountain path the porters took, but Old Hu never showed up. Six months later, as he wondered how the fellow with the scars on his head, whom he'd met just that once, was getting along, he recalled that he'd been asked to deliver a message to Yan Baihai, a young man with a Shanxi accent and a large mole under his left eye, who made his living castrating livestock, telling him that something had happened at home, requiring his immediate presence. That reminder made Young Luo uneasy—he'd been fine until the coin jogged his memory—and the very next day, as he set up shop, he began keeping an eye out for people with a Shanxi accent, anyone with a large mole under his left eye, and those with gelding tools hanging from their belts. It was not a fruitless task, since he did encounter people with a Shanxi accent, men with large moles under their left eyes, and tradesmen with gelding tools hanging from their belts. But not all three together, so no Yan Baihai. He asked around, with the same result. He'd have been better off if he'd simply abandoned the search, but by repeatedly trying and failing, he was tormented by the thought that he'd let a good man down by taking his money and failing to do as he'd promised.

On this particular day, after gathering up his tools, he returned to the inn where he was staying and sat on the brick bed deep in thought. The innkeeper, an old man with a bent back, came in with a basin of water for him to wash his feet and, when he saw the pensive look on Young Luo's face, said:

"Looks like business was bad today."

With his hands hidden in his sleeves, Young Luo shook his head.

"Then you must be homesick after all this time on the road," the innkeeper said.

Young Luo shook his head again.

"What is it, then?"

Out it came, the whole story, and that was why he was feeling dejected. The old innkeeper laughed.

"How in the world do you expect to be lucky enough to simply bump in to this person?"

"I know that's true," Young Luo said. "But a promise is a promise."

"If that's how you feel, whether you manage to find the person or not, you've done the best you could and have no reason to be ashamed."

This time Young Luo nodded, for the old innkeeper made sense. So he washed his feet in the hot water, lay back, and went to sleep. Over the next couple of months, he kept an eye out for Yan Baihai, as before, and with the same result. By then he realized that delivering a message to someone wasn't as easy as it sounded. Traveling to India to fetch Buddhist scriptures had been hard, no denying that, but delivering a simple message could be just as hard. Slowly but surely, his conscience stopped troubling him.

Winter gave way to spring, and as Young Luo eked out a living removing corns from people's feet, he watched donkey carts and camels pass up and down the streets of Kou wai. On the day of the Dragon Boat Festival, he suddenly felt a tinge of homesickness. He'd been away from home more than a year this time, and could not help wondering how his wife and children were getting by. And what about his father, who suffered from a respiratory illness? Over the course of the year he'd managed to save up thirty-two silver dollars, ten cash at a time, more than he ought to be carrying around with him. He made up his mind to leave Kou wai the next day and head back to Shandong, where the Dragon Boat Festival was celebrated by eating noodles, not the traditional glutinous dumplings. You can scrimp the rest of the year, but not during one of the holidays. As evening approached, Young Luo decided to celebrate by having a bowl of noodles at a restaurant instead of cooking a meal in his room at the inn. And so he went looking for a place to eat, passing one restaurant after another—they were either too expensive or too shabby—until he found one in Xiguan where the prices were reasonable. He walked in. A nice bowl of noodles was all he'd been thinking about before walking into the restaurant. But once he was inside he had second thoughts. Every itinerant peddler, it seemed, had had the same thought, and the place was packed with people, all speaking their local dialects and all sitting at tables enjoying their holiday noodles. Young Luo turned to leave, but then he figured, I'm already here, and if I go back to the inn I might wish I'd stayed. So he sat down and ordered a large bowl of lamb noodles in a spicy soup. As he waited patiently for his order to come, he sprawled across the table and let his thoughts roam back home, where he'd talk to his father about taking his eldest son with him the next time he went on the road to ply his trade. The boy was eleven, and while it was a good time for him to learn a trade, the main reason Young Luo wanted his son with him was so he wouldn't have to be alone all the time. They'd work together during the day and talk about things in their room at night; on holidays they'd go out together for a special meal. The way things were now, the only conversations he had were with people whose feet he was working on, never his own family. And so he passed the time in thought, until his noodles were brought to his table. He looked up and discovered that he was not alone, that some other customers had taken seats at his table. Undisturbed by the new faces, he lowered his head to concentrate on his noodles, which had taken a long time to emerge from the kitchen, but were everything he had looked forward to: spicy soup, plenty of greens, sliced onions and ginger, with half a dozen slices of fatty lamb floating on the top. Worth whatever he paid for it. Putting all thoughts aside, he dug in, slurping up his noodles until there was an angry outburst from across the table.

"Damn it, waiter, where the hell are my noodles!"

Young Luo's head shot up in alarm. A young man—one of the three sitting across from him—had run out of patience, which would not have bothered Young Luo if the man hadn't underscored his displeasure by banging his fist on the table, oblivious of Young Luo, whose bowl jumped into the air and landed hard. Even that would not have bothered him if some of the hot soup hadn't splashed him in the face. It burned like crazy. Not normally given to angry flare-ups, Young Luo could not let this pass. Without even wiping his oily face, he pointed at his face and complained to the man:

"You can scream for your noodles any way you want, but what's the big idea of doing this?"

One of the other customers, an older man, clasped his hands in front of his chest to defuse a volatile situation.

"You sound like you're from Shandong," he said. "We owe Second Brother an apology. The boy's got an explosive temper, and sometimes forgets himself."

The apology had its effect on Young Luo, who was pleased to

note that the old man was familiar with Shandong etiquette: he'd called him "Second Brother" instead of "Eldest Brother," since the latter referred to the feckless Wu Dalang, while "Second Brother" referred to Dalang's brother, the heroic Wu Song. Happy to let the incident pass, he wiped his face and returned to his noodles, only to be surprised that the offending young man wasn't buying what his companion was selling.

"So what if he's from Shandong," he said as he elbowed the older man. "We've been here as long as he has, and he's got his noodles, but we haven't. That's why I need to pound the table!"

He raised his fist, and Young Luo quickly leaned back in his chair. The fellow was a real hothead, and the only way a slight man like Young Luo could deal with someone like that was to get out of the way. He picked up his bowl and looked around for another place to sit. He stole another glance at the young man as he stood up to leave.

"You got a problem?" the man reacted with a glare.

Young Luo shook his head and walked off. But he'd only taken a couple of steps when a light went on. He turned to look again. The man spoke with a Shanxi accent, had a long face with a large mole under his left eye, and had gelding tools hanging from his belt. Young Luo sucked in his breath and dropped his bowl down on the table with a loud thump, sending drops of soup into the face of the young man, who assumed that was an invitation to fight. He jumped to his feet, grabbed his stool, and was about to fling it across the table when Young Luo shouted:

"Yan Baihai!"

The young man froze, stool held high, as drops of soup on his face fell to the floor. He was slow to react.

"How do you know my name?" he said at last.

Young Luo pounded the table. "I've been looking for you all year."

He sat down. He now had the attention of all three men. But

he was so excited he was practically incoherent, not sure how to begin. So he started with what had happened when he was removing corns in Wutai, where he'd met up with Old Hu, and how Old Hu had made a promise to someone else, and so on. In a nutshell, several people had been involved in delivering a message to Yan Baihai that something had happened at home, and that his family wanted him to return home at once. Young Luo's story turned the hothead into a blockhead. His nerves suddenly taut, he demanded of Young Luo:

"What happened at home? Tell me!"

Young Luo's head drooped as he racked his brains to recall what it was, but failed. And that wasn't all he could not recall. He couldn't say if Old Hu had forgotten to tell him what it was back in Wutai, or if it had migrated out of his brain over the year he'd been searching. He'd have been a fool to admit that, so he said:

"Old Hu neglected to tell me whatever it was when he asked me to deliver the message."

"Something really big?"

With a clap of his hands, Young Luo said:

"Would they ask someone to tell you to return home immediately if it wasn't?"

"Did my dad die?"

"Not sure," Young Luo said after a brief pause.

Imagine his surprise when Yan Baihai began to wail in front of all those diners.

"Dad—" he shouted, grief-stricken.

"You told me not to travel to Kou wai, but I wouldn't listen. And now you're dead!"

He elbowed the old man beside him.

"It's all your fault, you tricked me into coming with you. Give me back my father!"

He picked up his stool and swung it at the old man, who scurried to safety under the table.

5

Over the next three weeks, day and night, Yan Baihai made his way from Kou wai to Yan Family Village, a trip that would normally take well over a month, racing along at some points and plodding along at others. His feet were blistered by the time he got there. Nothing could have stopped him on his way home, and he collapsed the moment he reached the gate of his home, not from fatigue, but from the mistaken thought that his father was dead. He walked through the gate, awash in tears, only to see his father watching a young man with an ax and a plane making a stool in the yard. For a moment, neither recognized the other. His father's hair had turned gray, while Yan Baihai had grown into a man with a prominent beard, after going without shaving while he was on the road. The youngster building a bench was the family's third son, Yan Qinghai, who had been apprenticed to Old Song the carpenter. There were changes in the house as well.

Seeing the anxiety in his eldest son's eyes, Yan Laoyou took his bedroll from him and proceeded to explain that he had sent a message to Kou wai for him to come home right away for one reason only: it was time to start a family of his own. When Old Ma, with whom Yan Laoyou had served Landlord Wan as tenant farmers, died, he'd paid for the man's coffin, in thanks for which his widow had promised their daughter to the Yan family. After hearing his father out, Yan Baihai shed his worries; hearing that his family thought it was time for him to get married struck an emotional chord in him and sent a surge of heat coursing through his body.

"Old Ma's daughter, you say. Where is she?"

The rest of Baihai's family came out to welcome him home. His father pointed to a round-faced young woman among them. She held one child in her arms and was well on her way toward having another. The family had waited and waited for Baihai to return home, until finally, Yan Laoyou had approved a marriage between his second son, Heihai, and Old Ma's daughter.

"Think about it," his father said apologetically, "it's been more than two years since I sent the message and nearly five since you left home."

Seeing that there was nothing he could do to change the situation, Baihai said:

"Well, then, I'll hang around for three days or so, then head back to Kou wai."

"Hold on," his father said. "I've got an idea."

That idea, as it turned out, concerned Baihai's young brother, Qinghai, who was seventeen that year, and would soon be married. The prospective bride was the daughter of Old Zhu, who turned the millstone for the wealthy Wen family. Strictly speaking, the girl was not a maiden. Although only sixteen, she was already considered a widow. But that too was not quite accurate. The year before, she had been married to the son of Old Yang, a vinegar distiller in Yang Family Village. The boy was only fourteen, but since early marriages were common at the time, the match seemed appropriate, even though they were both still children. The Yang boy hated the look of the girl's normal sized feet—even as late as the 1920s and 1930s, bound feet remained an ideal among some Chinese—so at night, he was in the habit of cutting the girl's feet with shards of broken glass (glass had only recently been introduced into southern Shanxi), leaving bloody gashes that turned into scars. When she returned to visit her parents, they noticed that she walked with a limp, something she hadn't done before she was married. Only after repeated questioning did the girl break down and tearfully relate what had happened. Her father, Old Zhu was a feckless man whose only talent was turning a millstone for the wealthy, but her uncle, who hunted rabbits in cotton fields in the fall, had a fiery temper. When he saw what had been done to his niece, he and a dozen or so of his friends, armed with shotguns, went to Yang Family Village, where they smashed ten or fifteen vats of vinegar, after which they demanded a letter from the Yang family officially annulling the marriage. The girl never went back to the home of her one-time husband. Then one day, Yan Laoyou and his good friend Old Zhu met on their way to market, and the millstone turner told him what had happened to his daughter.

"The girl is a gentle soul. The only thing wrong with her is her unbound feet."

Knowing exactly what his friend was getting at, Laoyou went home to talk to his wife, who was a little hesitant.

"I saw the girl in the marketplace a few years back. She didn't talk to anyone and there was no shine to her hair. I wonder if she might be simple-minded."

Then she said:

"And those big feet of hers. They're not like potatoes that you can pare down with a knife."

And finally:

"And she's a widow. Like a bedpan, she's been used before."

Yan Laoyou nearly spat in his wife's face.

"So what if she doesn't talk to people! What the hell good does talking do, anyway? I've been talking all my life, and I'm still a common laborer!

"And what's so bad about big feet? That just means she'll be able to work. You and your bound feet—you can't even carry a bedpan from one place to another."

"And then there's that bit about being a widow. A woman who's been married knows things. She knows what to say and when to say it, not like you, who never met an idiotic comment she didn't utter!"

Yan Laoyou had the final say in the matter. He sent a matchmaker to Old Zhu's house to arrange a match with his daughter and his third son, Yan Qinghai. But now that Baihai had returned home, he had a change of heart. Qinghai was removed from the picture. But Baihai was not pleased to learn that the girl had been married before, while Qinghai wept against the door when he heard that the girl who was to be his wife was going to marry his brother. For that he received a well-placed kick from his father.

"You little bastard, what matures first, the big grain—barley— or the little grain—wheat?"

On the sixth day of the seventh lunar month in 1929 Yan Baihai and the daughter of Old Zhu from Zhu Family Village were married.

Old Zhu sold his lambskin jacket to give his daughter a gold ring for a dowry.

The following year, the girl's father had a stroke while he was turning the millstone, came down with typhoid fever, and died.

Thirty years later, the girl became Yan Shouyi's granny. Forty years after that, Shouyi's granny died, and he lost his chance to talk to her ever again.

About the Author

Liu Zhenyun, born in 1958, has earned a reputation over the past two decades as one of the most serious and dedicated practitioners of realist fiction of his generation. After publishing several popular and highly praised novels and shorter fiction in his twenties (at a time when Chinese writers still enjoyed a vast readership), he became a virtual recluse for eight years to write a four-volume, million-word novel that was the literary event of its time. While acknowledging that the project was, to some degree, a bit of an indulgence and can hardly boast of a large readership, at least in its entirety, the work gave him ample opportunity to hone his craft and to become more observant of the tricks people use to survive innumerable difficulties. The results, both in style and in content, are immediately obvious in *Cell Phone*.

About the Translator

Howard Goldblatt is Research Professor at the University of Notre Dame, where he directs the Center for Asian Studies. He is well known as a literary translator of Chinese fiction. In 1999, his translation of *Notes of a Desolate Man* (with Sylvia Li-chun Lin), by Taiwanese novelist Chu T'ien-wen, was chosen translation of the year by the American Literary Translators Association. Recent translations include *Wolf Totem* by Jiang Rong, winner of the 2008 Man Asian Prize, *Life and Death Are Wearing Me Out* by Mo Yan, recipient of the 2009 Newman Prize, and Su Tong's *Boat of Redemption*, winner of the 2010 Man Asian Prize. He has received two translation grants from the National Endowment for the Arts and, in 2009, a Guggenheim Fellowship.